Jake and Josie's Discovery

A Search for Identity

You are God's beloved treasure.
June (JB) Price

JB Price

Copyright © 2015 JB Price.

Cover design by Navigation Advertising, Murfreesboro, TN
Art Director and Photography by Christian Hidalgo
Graphic Design by James Neal

All rights reserved. No part of this book may be used or reproduced by any means, graphic, electronic, or mechanical, including photocopying, recording, taping or by any information storage retrieval system without the written permission of the publisher except in the case of brief quotations embodied in critical articles and reviews.

Scripture taken from the Holy Bible, NEW INTERNATIONAL VERSION®. Copyright © 1973, 1978, 1984 by Biblica, Inc. All rights reserved worldwide. Used by permission. NEW INTERNATIONAL VERSION® and NIV® are registered trademarks of Biblica, Inc. Use of either trademark for the offering of goods or services requires the prior written consent of Biblica US, Inc.

The author chooses to capitalize all references to God.

WestBow Press books may be ordered through booksellers or by contacting:

WestBow Press
A Division of Thomas Nelson & Zondervan
1663 Liberty Drive
Bloomington, IN 47403
www.westbowpress.com
1 (866) 928-1240

Because of the dynamic nature of the Internet, any web addresses or links contained in this book may have changed since publication and may no longer be valid. The views expressed in this work are solely those of the author and do not necessarily reflect the views of the publisher, and the publisher hereby disclaims any responsibility for them.

ISBN: 978-1-4908-7527-9 (sc)
ISBN: 978-1-4908-7528-6 (hc)
ISBN: 978-1-4908-7526-2 (e)

Library of Congress Control Number: 2015905138

Print information available on the last page.

WestBow Press rev. date: 04/24/2015

**A Sequel to
Callie's Treasures**

Virginia
1976

The Lord is close to the brokenhearted and saves those who are crushed in spirit.
Psalm 34:18

Dedication

This book is dedicated to all who have experienced the silent pain and secret shame of sexual abuse. Wherever you are in your journey, may Jake's and Josie's stories remind you there is healing and there is freedom.

PROLOGUE

It was the second day of May, 1976. Twenty-one-year-old Josie Roberts stood in front of the full-length mirror gazing at her body. That and her face had turned the head of many a male since her early teens. But today it was the unseen that had her attention. She slowly spread her hands over her now empty and sore womb. Yesterday she had followed through with the abortion her dad had financed and her brother and Nicolas had encouraged. Though she agreed it was the only sane choice, she couldn't stop thinking about the life that could have been ... and whose it was.

When she had first realized she was pregnant, she thought it might give her a chance with David. Even though there was a fifty-fifty chance it wasn't his, there was a fifty-fifty it was. Mr. Holy Joe would have taken the baby even if it wasn't his, but wanted nothing to do with her.

The other possibility was her old friend, Nicolas. He, on the other hand, wanted nothing to do with a baby ... even if it was his, but he was definitely interested in her. He offered no rebuke the night she showed up confessing she had been with David earlier.

She reached for the phone and relayed the news. "No more baby, Nick."

"I knew you were a smart girl, Josie. How long to heal?" His voice was upbeat.

"They recommended four weeks."

"Take care of yourself. Hey, did I tell you that I've accepted a job with the accounting firm of Houser and Vaughn in Richmond? I'm moving next week. Why don't you join me for the summer? It would give us a chance to see how compatible we are with a twenty-four seven relationship. What do you think?"

She considered this ruggedly attractive, tall, blue-eyed, Italian boy-turned-man who had been in her life since high school. It wasn't just the physical attraction that kept drawing her back to him. He was fun to be around … until the urge to make another man yield to her charms hit.

Regardless of what others thought, her lifestyle wasn't as much about sex as it was control. She was addicted to the power she had over eager males. Nicolas didn't like that part of her life, but he had never turned her away when she knocked on his door.

Would a long term relationship with him curb her compulsion? She'd never know if she didn't try. "Give me a few days to think about it and run it by my folks. I'll get back with you."

"Sure, Babe. Maybe a summer job at the firm will open up. I'll check with you later."

True to his word, Nick stayed in touch.

ONE

With her dad and her brother, Jake's approval and in spite of her mom's tears, Josie moved in with Nicolas the first of June. A month later, her personal belongings were packed in her car.

She was in the middle of a *Dear John* letter when she heard Nicolas' vehicle pull into the driveway. She had hoped to avoid this scene. His recent acknowledgment that he liked the way things were working out hinted of his response.

She wanted to stay, but knew she couldn't.

Nicolas barreled through the door. "Mind telling me what you are doing, Josie?"

With a twinge of sadness, she handed him the unfinished letter.

He set his briefcase on the chair by the door and began reading.

> Dear Nick,
>
> I'm leaving before you get home because you will ask questions I can't answer. I find myself incapable of putting my thoughts or feelings into words anymore. This melancholy is only part of the problem.
>
> I talked to Mom yesterday, and she suggested I come home for the rest of the summer. Maybe that will help.
>
> You are not the problem ... I am. I don't know if this is good-bye or just a break. Something has come up. Please don't be angry. I do care for you.
>
> Maybe sometime in the future ...

Josie didn't look up.

Nicolas wadded up the confusing message and threw it in the waste can. "What has come up? Another man caught your eye?"

Placing a hand under her chin, he lifted her bowed head. "I was beginning to think you might be ready to settle for one man who cares about you, instead of chasing dozens who only want your body."

She had always found his eyes fascinating. The blue was almost transparent, like looking into two matching pools of shimmering water. Other than David, Nicolas was the only guy she had ever cared about. "Nick, I don't know if it's hormones or something else, but I feel emotionally unstable right now. That's not fair to you."

His face took on a hurt expression as he eased into the chair opposite her. "Have you heard me complaining?"

He reached for her hand. "Does your obsession with David play into this? I can't figure out if you care for that religious fanatic or if his rejection just made you more determined."

Josie was doodling on the writing tablet. "I've wondered the same thing. Even now thoughts of him confuse me."

He took the pen out of her hand. "Well, you confuse me. I've been your fallback guy since you were a junior in high school. You know why? Because I care for you."

She glanced at him. "You say that, but until the abortion, you never indicated you wanted more than a bedroom relationship."

Disbelief was written all over his face as he leaned forward. "Are you kidding me? You've been in and out of men's lives so fast I get dizzy trying to keep up. Do you know you are the only girl I've ever been with?"

"Are you serious? Why?"

"Lots of reasons, but mainly because I keep hoping that one day you'll decide to stay. But the opposite happens. You come and go, and sometimes you leave behind unpleasant gifts. Josie, I've been treated for an STD, not once, but twice."

"Yeah, I should have told you. Are you okay?"

"So far." He grabbed her shoulders. "Are you? Your lifestyle is dangerous in more ways than one. In addition to that, your reputation would make a priest blush."

She tried to shrug off that painful truth, but its barb found another vulnerable spot and hung on with the multitude of other derogatory remarks hurled her way over the years. "You make me sound ... like a slut."

She looked at him in desperation. "What if I actually wanted to settle down? With you?"

He shot out of his chair. "If that's what you want, why in the name of heaven are you leaving? What do you think these past weeks have been about? I want you in my life."

He gathered her loosely within his arms. "We've never talked about it, so I guess you need to know that I'm not ready for marriage or kids right now."

Josie stiffened as she processed that statement. He released her to grab a beer.

Staring out the window at nothing in particular, she confessed, "I think I'm pregnant again."

His head jerked her way. "Pregnant? Again?" After littering the air with thoughts best left unsaid, he moved close. "I thought you took birth control pills faithfully."

She reached for a tissue. "I do, but I didn't know that certain antibiotics can render the pill useless. Remember when I had that infection?"

"Antibiotics?"

"Yeah, I'm told a number of surprise babies could be given that name."

Her eyes sought his. "My period was due two weeks ago and the only other time I've been this late was the first time I was pregnant."

That information defused his anger. "In that case, I guess it's no more your fault than mine."

With a look of relief and a sly grin, he pulled her into an intimate embrace. "This has all been your hormones talking. Let's get you unpacked, line up an abortion and get on with living. I think we have the potential for something good, Josie."

She slipped out of his arms and reached for her purse. "I can't rush into another abortion, Nick. Not this time."

He reached for a hand. "Please don't go. We can talk it out."

Josie zeroed in on those shimmering pools of blue. "But you won't change your mind about a baby, will you?"

His answer left no wiggle room. "No."

Rare tears escaped. "I'm going to miss you, Nick."

"Josie, if you walk out on me this time, don't come knocking on my door again. I'm weary of trying to rescue you. I'm going to broaden my horizons and look for someone who will appreciate a guy who just wants to have a steady girl he doesn't have to share with every appealing stud who comes along."

With a sigh of surrender he stepped aside.

"I'm sorry, Nick." She walked out of his apartment … and possibly his life.

Sad and perplexed, Josie Roberts headed home.

Two

Charlottesville, like the rest of the nation, was buzzing with evidence of bicentennial fever. Old Glory was flying far and wide making red, white and blue rival the colors of summer. The city and university had big plans, but Josie's festive mood was buried beneath whatever had taken over her mind and emotions ... and possibly her body. Maybe being with her family would help.

Their stately home at 4284 Rugby Heights had never looked so inviting. Patriotic Dad had joined the frenzy. There was a new flag pole in the middle of the circular drive flower bed that displayed flowers planted in the shape of the USA. No wonder Jake's nickname for him was *The Duke*. His size alone would qualify him, but sometimes they questioned if John Wayne and William's gene pools shared any common ancestors.

A mob was milling around the lawn of the mini-castle next door. Evidently someone had bought the Parker place. Ten thousand square feet of living space and a ten acre professionally landscaped lawn made it the premier estate of Rugby Heights. Judging from the size of the crowd, an entire clan had moved in.

Josie parked close to the front door for easier unloading. As she exited her car a member of the throng called her name and began jogging her way. Josie watched her mom open and close the gate that allowed access between the two properties.

She smiled as a memory surfaced. Mr. Parker had the opening cut in his wrought-iron barrier and a gate installed after Jake broke his arm scaling the fence to sneak into his neighbor's swimming pool. He must have been five or six at the time.

Virginia Roberts was an attractive forty-five-year-old woman who spent half her life taking care of her family and the other half doing volunteer work. She was one of those submissive, devoted wives. It worked well for her folks, but Josie had other ideas.

After exchanging a warm greeting with her mom, Josie turned to check out the busy swarm next door. It reminded her of an active ant hill.

"Would you like to meet some of our new neighbors now or later?" Virginia quietly studied her daughter as she often did.

Josie tried to count the bodies, but there was too much movement. "Some? You mean there's more?"

Virginia chuckled as she turned to view the sight from Josie's viewpoint. "Ten people now call that place home. Their oldest son is out on his own."

Socializing was the last thing on Josie's agenda. "Another time, Mom. I'd like to unpack first." The possibility of one child was unraveling her. But nine? That thought made her shudder, inside and out.

Virginia returned her focus to Josie. "Sure. Let's get you settled in." Each loaded their arms with belongings. "I'm pleased that you'll be here for a few weeks before you head back to school. It'll be like old times with all four of us together again."

Lugging her personal effects up the stairs alerted Josie that her load was heavier than she realized. She stopped to catch her breath. "The four of us? Jake is coming?"

Virginia paused beside her daughter. "Have you and Jake not talked this summer?"

Josie heaved her cargo into the sitting room of her suite and plopped on a chair. "Not a word. What's Romeo been up to?"

Virginia eased onto the love seat. "Jake moved back home last week. I think the boy has found his Juliet."

Josie raised her eyebrows. "Our Jake? No way!"

"Miracles do still happen, you know."

"Yes, and seeing is believing in my book," Josie said, as they trekked back downstairs for another load.

Their actions had attracted three of the neighbors. A charming lady who could not possibly be the mother of nine children led the trio. She was accompanied by a younger clone and a lovely, possibly Korean girl. "Hey, Virginia, can we give you two a hand?"

"That would be great!" Virginia waited until they were closer. "Thelma, this is our daughter, Josie. She's going to be with us the rest of the summer. Josie, this is Thelma, Madison and Maria Diamond. They moved in about the time you moved out."

Mrs. Diamond was the vivacious, friendly sort. She extended her hand towards Josie and chatted about being neighbors and getting to know each other. "Our girls have been hoping to meet you. Both are enrolled at the University of Virginia this fall." The girls were polite and friendly, but not as outgoing as their mom.

Add helpful and considerate to the lady's traits. Mama Diamond pulled a box out of the car. "Grab something, girls. Let's help Josie get her belongings to her room." All three Diamond females grabbed luggage and boxes and headed inside the house. "Which way, Virginia?"

"The suite on the right at the top of the stairs, Thelma. Just put it all in the sitting area." And the threesome disappeared.

"Gee whiz, you two have become friends fast." Josie studied her usually reserved mom for a second.

"You're going to love them, Josie. They have definitely livened up the block. Your dad and Henry are already weekly golfing buddies. Thelma and I have coffee together at least one morning a week. If you ask me, I'd say they are a godsend."

Josie cocked her head and eyeballed her mom. Before she could log the observation, the do-good-unto-others neighbors reappeared. "Anything else to tote in?"

"No, thanks, ladies. We can get the rest," Virginia answered.

"Okay, see you Saturday." Turning to Josie, Thelma added, "Nice to meet you. The invitation includes you too."

"Thank you." Josie watched the trio rejoin the ant hill activities.

The Roberts women managed to get the remaining bits and pieces in one load. "What do you think of Madison, Josie?"

"Hmm. I'm sure the male population finds her attractive. She may have the most fascinating green eyes I've ever seen, and her enchanting smile hints of intriguing secrets. Why do you ask?"

"Your brother." Virginia set the last load of belongings on the floor. "William and I thought Jake would lose interest and move on like he always does, but not this time. He's mesmerized to the point that he acts like a school boy with his first crush."

Doubt caused Josie's rounded eyebrows to peak. "Honestly, Mom. That sounds more like your wishful thinking than my twenty-two-year-old brother. Besides, she's not his type."

Virginia's knowing smile reinforced her words. "Your qualms will be erased tonight."

Josie was dumbfounded. "So you think the love bug finally bit, huh?"

"Oh my, yes! It's better entertainment than watching the *Love Boat*."

As she ripped the tape off the first box, Josie wondered if she should relay her own news. Before she could decide, Virginia terminated that possibility. "I need to run to town before your dad gets home. Unpack and we'll talk later."

"Sure, Mom. Thanks for your help." She began emptying her first box and wondered how her parents were going to respond to this pregnancy.

Her thoughts drifted back to Nick. He was not ready for a baby. She wasn't sure she was, but she was determined to consider the options this time. In spite of everything, she felt a touch of compassion for the life forming inside her.

Weary from the emotions of the day and all the questions about the future, she yielded to her body's plea for a nap. Curling up with her favorite old teddy bear while listening to Casey Kasem and the top forty on her favorite radio station was the perfect formula for an afternoon nap.

Three hours later, she woke to a familiar voice. "Hey, Sleeping Beauty. You're going to miss dinner if you don't wake up."

As she forced her eyes open, she saw her tall, athletic brother leaning against the door jam. With the height and build of their dad, thick, sun-streaked, sandy brown hair and sapphire eyes that matched her own, he'd never had trouble finding a girl. In fact, he had a reputation of loving them and leaving them.

Wiping the sleep from her eyes, she remembered her mom's surprising update on the man. "Hey, what's going on with you? I thought you had a job in Virginia Beach this summer."

He stepped inside the room and sat on the foot of her bed. "I had a change of mind. What brought you back? I hoped you and the Italian finally had something going."

"Promise you won't fuss at me and I'll tell you." She offered him her pinkie.

He linked his with hers. "Promise."

Hugging the bear a little tighter and lifting her eyes with a hint of embarrassment, she shared about her current pregnancy and Nick's reaction.

"Antibiotics, huh? I still don't see the problem."

Josie dangled her legs over the side of the bed. "The first abortion happened too fast, Jake. I was upset with David and felt pressure from you, Dad and Nicolas. I caved in without giving it much thought. There have been moments when I've wondered if I did the right thing."

Jake pulled back in disbelief. "You aren't going religious on me, are you?"

She scoffed. "Me? You know better than that. But we are talking about potential life here. What if I want this baby?"

He stood. "Ah, come on, Sis. Get real. You can't quit school to have a baby." He halted at the door. "You haven't told Mom and Dad, have you?"

She shook her head. "What if they get upset?"

"They may, but you still need to tell them … and promise it won't happen again."

She moved off the bed and slipped into her shoes. "I just need some time to think about it. Okay?"

He winked. "You're smart, Kiddo. Come on. Mom and Dad are waiting."

Sure enough, the folks were sitting at the table conversing while politely waiting for their offspring to join them. Josie hugged her dad.

"You and Nicolas having problems?" he asked.

All eyes focused on her. "Leaving was my decision, not Nick's."

William put his napkin in his lap and reached for the meat platter. "I'm sorry to hear that. I thought it might work with Henderson out of the picture."

"It's more complicated than that, Dad."

He held the platter in mid-air. "Speaking from a man's perspective, Josie, I suspect that Nick's been in love with you since high school and was hoping you had the wanderlust out of your system."

"In love with me? I know he cares, but love? That word hasn't surfaced between us."

William uttered a few curse words. "Maybe that's because you spent the last three years making a fool of yourself chasing Henderson ... and a dozen others. A man has his pride, Josie."

Virginia cast a pleading glance at her husband. "Be nice, William. This is the first time our family has been together in weeks. Don't provoke."

Glimpsing his wife's face brought a change to his. "Sorry, Jo. Didn't mean to preach."

He redirected the conversation. "How about you, Jake? Have you given anymore thought to staying with your old man in the insurance business instead of jumping into the legal frying pan this fall?"

Jake had been the only one enjoying the meal. He swallowed the bite in his mouth and glanced at William. "I'm pretty sure I'll be back on campus come September. It's an itch I have to scratch, Dad."

Josie tapped Jake's foot under the table. "Hey, Lover Boy, I hear you and one of the new neighbor girls are experiencing some fireworks. Any truth in that gossip?"

Jake winked at his mom and grinned. "Don't I wish? Right now I'd settle for a few sparks."

"This is a first! Jake Roberts settling for sparks? What's the problem?"

Jake's face took on a reflective appearance and his words softened. "She's unlike anyone I've ever met. I'm pretty sure she's attracted to me, but she resists all my attempts to get to know her better. I keep asking myself why."

Josie stopped eating. "And your answer is ...?"

His bewildered look was uncharacteristic. "I honestly don't know. Get this. We are playing chess tonight ... at her house ... in the game room … probably with her dad in attendance. Can you believe that? I've begun to wonder if she has cast some kind of spell on me."

Josie glanced between her parents. "Who is this stranger at our table?"

That question lured her parents into the conversation. While William and Josie were merciless in their harassment, Virginia was calmly defending and encouraging her son. "Maybe it's time for Jake to find a good girl, settle down and start a family."

"Well, I wouldn't go that far, Mom, but those two need to lighten up. My self-esteem has hit an all-time low the last four weeks."

His mom patted his hand.

Observing the sweet moment between mother and son stirred something in Josie.

"What's their story? Who are they and what are they doing here?"

William responded. "Henry is an accountant turned businessman. He bought out the Burkhardt and Boyd accounting conglomerate in the state. He also owns one in Kentucky. Thelma sold an interior design enterprise back home. Evidently they have plenty of resources."

He stroked his chin and smiled at his wife. "Their second interest is obvious. They are majorly into their family. They have nine children."

Josie played with her food as thoughts of the life within her womb surfaced. "I always thought the Parker house was too big for one family. The Diamonds have proved me wrong."

She buttered her roll. "Back to Madison, Jake. I'm still wrestling with your unexplainable attraction."

"You? What about me?"

Her smitten brother got lost in his private thoughts again. "Attraction? She scores a ten in that department." He took a deep breath. "I can't decide if it's that or simply that she fills any space she enters with a warmth that makes me glad she is a girl and I'm not."

Jake looked at his interrogator. "Remember how I used to make fun of you for your crazy crush on David? I apologize. Sometimes, there's no explanation for the inclinations of the heart. I'm in big trouble if she has a boyfriend back in Kentucky."

Remembering her own ill-fated attraction for David, she asked. "You don't think they are hung up on religion, do you?"

William spoke up. "They are people of faith, but I've not found them to be aggressive or confrontational about it. Henry is a respected businessman who is fun to be around. Besides, he is the most challenging golfing buddy I've ever had."

"I find them to be wonderful neighbors, and Thelma is becoming one of my best friends," Virginia was quick to add.

"You three have aroused my interest."

Just before seven o'clock, Jake excused himself to join Madison and family. Josie decided this was not the night to share her news and headed back to her room to finish unpacking and do a bit of serious thinking.

THREE

Dennis answered the door with three-year-old Melinda riding on his back. "Come on in, Jake. Dad's in the game room. Madison is helping with the snacks."

He lowered his voice. "Warning. The lady is competitive. Don't play the nice guy and let her win."

"Madison, competitive?" He cataloged that interesting revelation. "Don't worry. I always play to win, but right now I need a guide or I'll get lost in this maze and miss the game."

Dennis snickered and took the lead. The three-year-old rider was eyeing Jake. When he winked, she closed both eyes trying to imitate his behavior. *Cute kid.*

"Do you enjoy being part of a large family, Dennis?"

"I can't think of anyone I'd want to give up, so I guess I like it fine."

"Neat way to put it. Hey, I meant to tell you earlier. I've moved home for the rest of the summer, so I'll be available for your weekend volleyball tournaments." Jake was relatively sure his motive was not a secret.

"Awesome! We've added a weekly swim meet on Sunday afternoons. Are you interested? If so, are you fair, good or great?"

"Probably on the high end of good. Put my name in the pot."

"You got it. And I'll make sure you and Madison get to tag team." Oh, yeah. Things were looking up. "How good is she in the water?"

"She's a better swimmer than chess player, and only Dad beats her in chess."

Jake pushed his fingers through his short-cropped hair. "I've not seen that side of her yet."

Dennis whispered. "Underneath that mild-mannered exterior is a female Clark Kent."

Both were laughing as they entered the game room.

It looked like half the neighborhood had dropped in. Jake chatted as he made his way to the chess table.

Henry looked up from his newspaper. "Good evening, Jake. Madison will join you shortly."

The host politely laid aside the *Charlottesville Daily Progress* and removed his reading glasses. "Your dad tells me that you've moved back home for the rest of the summer and are working with him. I think he is hoping the arrangement becomes permanent."

"Yeah, he mentioned that fact. He has a few weeks to convince me."

Madison entered the room with a pyramid of popcorn balls on a large tray that reminded him of a snow saucer. Maria followed with two gallons of homemade lemonade and a stack of cups. The minute the refreshments landed on the food bar, the corners emptied.

From the moment Madison entered, Jake drank in her presence like a thirsty man who had found an oasis in the desert. He couldn't stop imagining what kissing her would be like.

Mr. Diamond cleared his throat. "Excuse me, Jake. Am I detecting more than a slight interest in one of my girls?"

Embarrassed to be caught staring, he faced his host. Thankfully, the corners of his mouth were upturned.

"Yes, Sir, though I'm at a loss to explain it." With perplexity evident in his voice and eyes, he sought an answer from the one who knew her best. "Does that make any sense to you?"

Mr. Diamond's smile enlarged. "Oh, I understand. Matters of the heart are hard to explain most of the time. I want to remind you that she is one of my princesses."

Uneasy with the direction of this conversation, Jake found his eyes returning to the subject of the conversation. "I can understand why, Sir."

The man didn't bat an eye. "I'm asking for your word as a gentleman that you will treat her as such."

Pooling all of his will power, Jake shifted his focus on Mr. Diamond. "I'll do my best, Sir."

"As long as your best doesn't fall short, we'll get along fine. Anything less and we'll be getting better acquainted."

Henry wasn't as tall as Jake but he wasn't a wimp. That in itself generated respect, but it was the look in his eyes that convinced Jake it would be wise to agree. Besides, the man lived next door.

Jake nodded. Henry smiled and reached for his glasses and newspaper as Madison moved in their direction.

Jake's pulse reacted to her approach like a Geiger counter to radiation. Was the woman magnetized? There was no doubt she was messing with his left brain functions.

"You ready to be humbled, Jake?"

He grinned playfully. "Your dad took care of that. Not sure you can come close."

Mr. Diamond chuckled good-naturedly. "Glad we understand each other, Son. Enjoy the evening ... and the company."

In his other life—the one before Madison—Jake would have inwardly mocked such guidelines for pursuing his daughter. No parent had ever done that before, but he had never been interested in anyone like *Green Eyes* before.

Even though Madison and Jake talked and played and played and talked, it was evident winning the game was her top priority. To his delight, she was a challenging opponent. After three enjoyable, but intense hours of calculated moves, he was finally able to call, "checkmate." Both took a deep breath.

"I'm impressed, Jake. Don't be surprised if Dad challenges you."

Jake pulled out his Groucho Marx voice. "I don't know, Sweetheart. He's not nearly as easy on the eyes." He wiggled his eyebrows, mimicked the eye movements and flicked his pretend cigar.

She giggled. "Not bad."

Staying in character, he continued. "Do you think we could go for a walk, Gorgeous?"

"Let me see how Dad feels about older men." As she and her dad talked, the king of the Diamond clan glanced at Jake and smiled.

"Dad said Groucho is a married man, so he's off limits, but he encouraged me to see if the neighbor's son might be interested."

"Oh, he's interested." He reached for her hand as they strolled into the balmy, July night.

"Listen," Jake suggested as they stood hand-in-hand beneath the stars as a choir of hundreds, if not thousands, of chirping crickets serenaded all who ventured out.

"Do you know that if you count the number of chirps a cricket makes in fifteen seconds and add thirty-seven, you'll have a rough idea of the temperature?"

"Did you make that up?"

"Nope. And do you know that only male crickets chirp? Those handsome creatures are hoping some good-looking female will respond."

Jake began imitating a cricket.

"Jake Roberts, you are a man of many talents."

"Alas, a fair damsel has answered. Would you mind accompanying your new cricket friend to the arbor swing?" Jake responded in the voice of Walt Disney's famous little cricket.

Madison put her hand over her heart. "Well, now, Mr. Jiminy, how did you know that is one of my favorite getaway spots?"

Jake moved closer. "Does this mean you have frequented this spot with other cricket friends?"

"No, just a good book or my guitar."

"Ah. A lover of the arts."

He settled in the middle of the swing and rested his arms on the top slat ... both directions.

She glanced at her choices. "You don't play fair."

She twirled around, walked seven feet and flipped a switch. Not only had Henry installed hundreds of tiny, twinkling lights throughout the arbor, he had added a new garden bench across from the swing.

His heart stopped. If she knew what he was thinking, she would turn those fairy lights off. Her magical spell was taking over his mind and body again.

She smiled knowingly. "Think I'll sit on the bench."

It wasn't working out as he had hoped, but he was so caught up in the vision sitting seven feet away that he didn't respond.

She interrupted his fantasy. "Now that you've graduated, what's next for you, Jake?"

"I'm enrolled in the school of law at the University of Virginia, although I'm not sure that's what I want to do the rest of my life."

He deserted the swing and joined her on the bench. "What about you?"

She scooted closer to the edge. "I'll be finishing up my nursing degree at UV. Maria and I have been hoping Josie will show us around. I didn't realize that you'd be on campus too."

"You're looking at the best tour guide in town. I could take you tomorrow."

A slight smile preceded her response. "A cricket by night and a guide by day. I'm impressed."

"Anything to spend time with you, *My Fair Lady*," he offered with a close impersonation of Professor Higgins.

"Jake, do you work at the imitations or do they come naturally?"

"A little of both, Eliza, a little of both."

"I find that fascinating."

"Hmm, does that mean you are pleased, Fair One?"

"And amazed, Professor." Her Eliza impersonation was woefully lacking. They both laughed.

She rose and faced him. "Jake, it's been a fun night. Thanks for the chess match and the free entertainment."

As she turned to leave, he reached for the closest hand. "Please don't go, Madison."

She hesitated and he reached for her other hand. "There's so much I want to know about you. Couldn't we go out Saturday night?"

"Our family has invited your family for dinner. I had hoped you were coming."

He was close enough to get another whiff of that tantalizing fragrance she wore. "Do you think we could manage an hour or two alone after the meal? We've known each other over four weeks and I don't even know how old you are.

"I want to know your favorite color, food and place to eat. Your favorite car, movie, song. I want to know what makes you laugh and cry. What are your hopes and dreams? I want to know *you*, Madison Diamond."

She moved back to the swing and gazed into the star-studded heavens as hundreds of arbor lights reflected on her face. "I may not get them in order, but here goes. Twenty-one ... the color of your eyes ... dark chocolate ... Doug's Seafood Shack ... Chevy Malibu ... *Fiddler on the Roof* ... *When I Fall in Love* ... *ah-ha* moments ... Ethan and others trapped in addictions ... to make a difference in someone's life ... to love and be loved."

He approached the swing. "What about my eyes, Madison?"

There was a hitch in her voice. "They are my favorite color."

He sat close. "To love and be loved is your dream?"

She nodded and put some distance between them.

"Madison, is it conceivable that you like me ... just a little?"

Her eyes locked with his. "Yes," she offered softly.

That look mingled with that three-lettered word released a surge of desire throughout his body. He had to employ all the restraints in his arsenal to keep from pulling her into his arms and finding out what those lips tasted like. "Have you guessed that I like you ... more than a little?"

Her mesmerizing smile and those dazzling green eyes did nothing to calm the intensifying longings inside him.

"Yes ... and so have several others in the family."

It was a good thing she moved off the swing. He had reached his limit. Then with a more serious look and tone, she wiped him out. "They've also figured out that I feel the same way about you ... but we all know the timing is off."

He felt a bolt of lightning penetrate his heart and electricity spread through his body. *Could there be a God in Heaven?* He lunged to his feet.

"The timing is off? What in the blue blazes are you talking about? We are both of age."

He began circling her while massaging his neck and trying to rein in his emotions. This woman was driving him crazy.

He took several deep breaths and approached her again with a calmer voice. "Madison, if you are experiencing anything close to what

I am, how can it not be the right time? Is there an old flame back in Kentucky?"

She moved into his space, placed her hand on his chest and branded his heart. "No past hindrances or boyfriends. Hopefully just a temporary hurdle."

He covered her hand with his and brought it to his lips. "Madison, we can work through it." He had never wanted anyone as much in his life.

"There's a possibility that we can't, Jake."

"I refuse to believe that."

Intuitive green eyes were penetrating his façade. "Do you trust me?"

What a strange question. He released her hand and stared into the night sky. "Trust you? I'm not sure I've ever trusted anyone except Mom, but yes, I think I do trust you."

He was fighting a strong urge to embrace her. "Madison, you are the girl I didn't believe existed."

He lost that battle and gently pushed through the invisible boundary she tried to keep in place ... and hugged her.

The feel of her soft body next to his unleashed passion he had never experienced before. "Madison, why are you fighting this?"

"Give me two days, Jake. Let's tour the campus tomorrow and have dinner with our families Saturday. Then we'll talk. Okay?"

Right now she could have asked for the moon and he would have made a fool of himself trying to bring it down. He breathed in the fragrance of Madison. "On one condition."

He lifted her face to his. "Don't send me away still wondering what it would be like to kiss you."

Slowly she tiptoed as he leaned down and lightly brushed his lips with hers.

Jake wasn't even sure he was breathing until she began to pull away. Instinctively, he pulled her closer and caressed her lips with the longing her kiss had kindled. Never had he felt so alive.

Much too soon, she began to gently push against his chest. With what was left of his self-control, he eased away.

"Oh, wow! My imagination wasn't even close." Euphoria had a name ... Madison.

"Walk me back to the house," she requested as she flipped off the lights and offered her hand. He laced his fingers with hers to keep his feet on the ground.

As they neared the rear entrance, she stopped and faced him. "See you in the morning, Jake."

"Thank you for tonight, Princess." He brought her hand to his lips before releasing it and watched her walk back into her world and out of his ... temporarily.

He moseyed home slowly and thoughtfully. Hurdle removal coming up.

Four

Jake's mood matched the songbirds outside his window the next morning. He was humming and whistling as he knocked on Josie's door. She, on the other hand, would not be accompanying the birds or her brother in song today.

"Morning, Sis. I'm taking Madison and Maria on a tour of the campus today. Want to join us?"

She placed a hand over her stomach. "No thanks. I'm a little queasy."

His brow wrinkled as her problem registered. "Maybe it's time to do something."

"Maybe. How was last night?" She moved towards a chair.

"Amazing!" His face lit up as memories emerged. "And we're going to talk about *us* tomorrow night after dinner."

He turned to leave, but hesitated. "Guess what, Sis. She likes me as much as I like her." He made the sign of the cross and clasp his hands. "If I were a praying person, I'd be talking to the man upstairs today."

He puckered his lips and mimicked the birds as he sauntered out of her room. Five minutes later he dashed by her door. "Wish me luck today, Sis. And tell Mom your news while I'm gone."

Jake couldn't remember when he had been this exhilarated. After last night's breakthrough he was confident they would soon be much more than friends and neighbors.

Henry was the morning greeter. "Good Morning, Jake. Appreciate your showing my number one and two princesses around campus today."

"My pleasure, Sir."

The back entrance emptied into a massive space that reminded Jake of a classy hotel lobby. Thelma had created multiple eye-catching seating arrangements, yet brought them together to construct a fashionable gathering place.

"Have a seat, Jake," Henry suggested as he chose a Paxton leather wing chair close by.

"Madison says you are a formidable chess player. You wouldn't be interested in trying your skills on a more seasoned competitor, would you?"

"It was probably just luck, Sir."

Henry's face took on a bold and challenging expression. "There's only one way to find out."

When the gauntlet is thrown down, a man is forced to respond. "Sure, Mr. Diamond. Just let me know when it's convenient for you."

"How about tonight?"

Jiminy Cricket, the man was eager. Confident Madison would be present, Jake agreed. "Sure."

He heard Madison and Maria before he saw them, but couldn't make out the conversation. Finally the girl of his dreams stepped into the lobby and he was awash in liquid sunshine. While his eyes feasted on her beauty, his heart was deluged with desire.

"Morning, Jake," she said with a shy smile. "Maria had something else planned for this morning, so it will be just the two of us."

He endeavored to temper his excitement with a shade of regret. "Too bad she's going to miss an excursion led by one of the university's best guides."

Madison's eyes twinkled as she jingled her keys. "Your car or mine?"

"My parking permit is still valid."

"We'll be back before the evening meal, Dad," Madison announced as they headed for the exit.

A day alone with Madison. He grabbed her hand. "Glad you wore decent walking shoes. We have some hills to navigate."

With an endearing look of dependence, she confessed. "I'm warning you ahead of time. I'm directionally challenged. If I get lost, you may not find me until school starts this fall."

He opened the car door and pushed her wind-blown hair off her face. "Fret now, Fair Maiden, I'm not about to lose you ... now that I've found you."

Jake and Josie's Discovery

When she blushed and lowered her head, he caught another glimpse of eye lashes that would rival a baby giraffe's. As he bounded around the car and dropped into the driver's spot, he began singing the old love song of the 30s that Art Garfunkel put back on the hit parade last year, *I Only Have Eyes for You*. She began to softly harmonize.

"Well now, Kenny and Dolly may have some serious competition," Jake teased.

"Think we should go on tour?"

"Sweetheart, I'll go anywhere you suggest."

"How about the next symphony?"

"It's a date." Jake smiled.

Once on campus, Madison's fascination with American history surfaced. A place he had taken for granted all his life was a living museum to her.

"Jake, how mindboggling to be in this place two hundred years after the founding of our nation! When I close my eyes, I can almost see and hear those who made all this possible."

When he explained about the *Academical Village*, the original university founded by Thomas Jefferson, she was speechless. She meandered in a circle, taking in every building as he explained that *the Pavilions* were still inhabited by faculty and *the Lawn* rooms filled with fourth year students who had excelled in academics and service.

After touring the Rotunda and reviewing its history, they rested on the lawn surrounded by this preserved and treasured piece of early American history. When she learned that Queen Elizabeth and Prince Philip would be visiting the Rotunda next week, she shook her head. "Ironic, isn't it? The nation we had to fight to gain our independence is now sending their queen to help us celebrate our victory."

The guide was as fascinated with the lady as she was the university.

"Jake, I fell in love with the rugged beauty of Virginia the day we arrived. Now I find I'm just as enthralled by its history. What an exciting place to be!"

He put his arm around her shoulders. "Honey, I happen to think *you* are beautiful and exciting."

She shooed him away. "This is supposed to be an educational tour, Sir."

Jake bowed. "Touché, Madam, but are you not acquiring new knowledge of this historic campus? And are we not discovering more about each other?"

"Point well taken, Sir."

Without hesitation, he resumed the protested show of affection. "I can't decide whether to take you to the Corner or the Historic Downtown Mall, so I think we'll tour both and stop for a taste of history along the way."

They concluded the day by checking out the hospital and buildings related to the nursing program.

"You really are an outstanding tour guide, Jake. It's been an educational and fun day."

"Glimpsing this place through your eyes has been inspiring, Madison. We'll take in the homes of Presidents Jefferson, Madison and Monroe before the snows come."

She glanced at him with uncertainty in her eyes. "If it works out for us, Jake."

"Oh, it's going to work out. No more games for us, Madison. We're going to see where this relationship could go if given a chance."

She shared a hopeful look and squeezed his hand but didn't comment.

Their ride home was reflective and uneventful except for Jake's frustration with the inebriated driver in front of them. When Jake pulled into the driveway, Madison faced her tour guide. "Today was special, Jake."

There was much unsaid in her eyes and he waited. But she quickly scooted out of the car and leaned in. "See you tomorrow."

And she was gone before he could answer. He watched her race to the gate and beyond. Remembering his chess match with Henry tonight, he gave himself a pat on the back. *Sooner than that, Sweetheart.*

Thelma and Henry were in the kitchen when Madison walked in. "How did it go, Hon?"

She shared an abridged account of their day, including the history of the school. "I can't put Jake off any longer."

Thelma put her arm around Henry and leaned close. "Remember, Madison, I was a Josie when your father and I met. God wasn't on my radar. It was the attraction between us that the Lord used to open my heart to a different kind of love. None of us would be here if not for his belief that God was reaching out to me through him."

She moved beside Madison. "You are exposing your heart to a man you may have to walk away from if he refuses God's overtures. But on the other hand, you could end up with a love like your father and I share. It will depend on Jake's response to both you and our Father."

Henry cleared his throat. "By the way, Madison, Jake is coming over for a game of chess tonight. I don't think he'll play his best game with you in the room, and I'm eager to see how good he really is."

"Got your message, Dad, but promise to take it easy on him."

"No mercy on the chess board, Daughter. I'm playing to win."

Madison flashed an understanding smile. "I mean in the conversation."

"I promise. By the way, you need to talk with Donald. He has heard some scuttlebutt about Jake's reputation around town and he's concerned about the two of you becoming more than neighbors. He may be younger, Madison, but he's taken on the role of big brother for all his sisters and woe to the young man who gets out of line."

"Thanks for the warning. Wouldn't want those two tangling."

Sweet and painful memories of Ethan flashed into her head. Donald took on the big brother role when Ethan forfeited it. She went to her room praying and hurting for her oldest brother.

Five

Mr. Diamond didn't just win the game. He humiliated Jake. Thunderation! Madison never showed up. How was he supposed to defend his king when his queen was missing?

His opponent wore an indefinable smile all evening. When the game was over, he explained Madison's absence. "It seems my plans to ensure a great match actually sabotaged it."

"You asked Madison not to come?" Jake left relieved, but frustrated. *Wish he'd told me that up front. I'd have thrashed him just to get even.*

That was last night. This evening would be different. Jake was walking with his mom and dad across the lawns to join the Diamonds for the evening meal. Josie had disappeared early afternoon.

As each guest was directed to a chair at the massive table, Jake found himself seated across from his favorite Diamond. Henry cleared his throat and explained their habit of having each person share something for which they are thankful.

One by one the family spoke up. By the time it got to Jake, he was ready. "Our new neighbors."

Daniel good-naturedly challenged him. "Come on, Jake. We all know which one of us you're referring to."

Madison blushed and averted his glance while Mr. Diamond caught Daniel's eye. "He's our guest, Son."

"Gee whillikers, Dad. Do you want me to apologize for telling the truth?" The kid looked perplexed.

Henry smiled. "No, Son, I want you to learn when to speak and when to be silent."

"Oh, okay." He turned to Jake. "Sorry my timing was off, Jake."

Jake glanced at Madison, then Daniel. "You're right, Buddy. I'm thankful that Madison is part of your family."

Three-year-old Melinda spoke up. "What about me, Jake?"

He flashed a big smile at the little one sitting in a booster seat beside her mom. "And I'm thankful for Melinda."

She fluttered her eyelids ... trying hard to wink at Jake. Everyone chuckled.

"Looks like you have competition, Madison," Daniel added.

When Henry ended the time of reflection with a simple prayer, platters and large bowls of food were soon passed around and the soft sound of conversations filled the air as food satisfied the stomachs. After the meal, the children were excused except those on clean-up detail.

The men were enjoying their dessert when Jake moved behind Madison's chair and announced they were going for a ride.

"Have fun."

"Be careful."

"Don't be out too late."

Jake whispered to Madison. "If we wait long enough the fourth one will have some words of advice."

"If you pass a grocery store, Jake, would you pick up a gallon of milk?"

Jake smiled knowingly and waited for what was coming.

"Virginia, shopping is the last thing on that boy's mind. I'll go get you a gallon of milk."

Madison and Jake were holding in their giggles.

"Scratch that one, Jake. I can handle it."

Jake clasped Madison's hand. "Thanks, Dad."

As they headed out the door, Donald drove in and quickly exited his vehicle. His grease smudged face and matching clothing left no doubt about his career path.

"Hey, I thought the party was inside. Where are you two going?" He removed his glasses and approached them with fire in his eyes.

Madison regretted not following through on her dad's suggestion. She released Jake's hand and stepped in front of him "We're going for a ride."

Donald forced his body between Madison and Jake. He was a couple inches shorter than Jake's six feet five inches, but wore about thirty extra pounds of solid muscle. Looking directly into the possible predator's eyes, Donald delivered his warning.

"Just want you to know that I'm known for taking action first and asking questions later. I know it's not a good trait, but so far it's kept my sisters safe. I've heard of your reputation, Jake. This one better not be on your score sheet."

Another Diamond guardian? Jake threw his hands in the air. "Look, Donald, your sister is doing fine protecting herself, but if you are aching for a fight, I'm your man."

Madison stared at the Neanderthals and squeezed between them. "Will you two stop?"

She faced Donald first. "I appreciate your concern for my well-being, but I assure you that I can take care of myself in this case. We'll talk tonight when I get home."

Then she turned to Jake. "Don't let his age fool you. What he lacks in years, he makes up for in experience. He was the captain of the runner-up high school wrestling team in the state of Kentucky last year. I'd advise you to avoid all physical challenges if possible."

Seemingly pleased that Jake now understood the playing field, Donald stepped beside Madison and extended a hand of reconciliation. Jake looked at Madison and slowly clasped the offering of peace ... only to suffer the pain of an agitated wrestler's grip.

"Glad we had this conversation, Jake."

Walking backwards, he addressed Madison. "I'll be waiting up for you, Sis."

Jake massaged and shook his hand while watching Mr. Sumo walk into the house. Madison's efforts to hide her amusement failed. Little bursts of laughter kept escaping.

Jake glared at her. "First your dad and now your own WWA champion. Henry's Diamonds are well guarded."

"That makes a girl feel valued, Jake."

The short ride was filled with small talk ... and anticipation.

Jake pulled into a driveway about a mile from their place. As he turned off the engine, he reached for her hand and sniffed her wrist. "Hmm. Unfair advantage."

"A new fragrance from Dior." She pulled her hand from his and looked at the house whose driveway they now blocked. "Won't these folks mind us parking here?"

"Oh, the Harringtons go on vacation every 4th of July week, and we watch the place for them. Thought it would be an ideal place to talk privately."

She nodded and continued to survey their surroundings.

Reaching for her chin, he gently turned her face towards his. "Hey, it's talking time."

Reflected light framed her face. "Can we begin by agreeing to be honest?"

Honest? That statement made him more nervous than he already was. "Uh ... I think I can handle that stipulation."

Already lost in her alluring green eyes, he enclosed her closest hand in his. "I'll start. Are you experiencing an unusual chemistry between us?"

A suppressed grin escaped. "Yes, from the first day."

Heat began to rise inside him. "Then why in the name of heaven are you resisting it so?"

"Do you think this is just a physical attraction, Jake? Or is there more?"

"It's definitely physical, but for me, that's just the beginning. I think I may be falling in love. I want to be with you all the time. I think about you when I'm not. The thought of you with another guy torments me. When I see another girl I think I might be interested in, images and thoughts of you take over."

His eyes spoke of his desires. "I want us to be more than friends, Madison. And tonight wouldn't be too soon for me."

"Tell me about the other girls in your life."

That request made him uneasy. "I've been dating since I was fifteen, but I've never had a steady girl."

"Were you sexually involved with any of those girls?"

The woman was dissecting him. "I've sown some wild oats, if that's what you are asking. But you could persuade me to quit sowing elsewhere."

Was that moisture forming in her eyes? "What about you, Madison?"

As that question left his mouth, he knew he would hate every male she had ever been with. He wanted her to be different ... and almost before those thoughts could pass, he knew she was. He didn't wait for her to respond. "You've never been with a man, have you?"

She shook her head while the moisture that had gathered began to trickle down her cheeks. "No, Jake, that's a gift I'm saving for my husband."

Saving for her husband? Shock ran through his body like a powerful, slow-moving electrical current. That translates into no sex until marriage. Vexation colored his expression as understanding dawned.

"You are what?" He dropped her hand as though she had developed a case of leprosy.

"I'm afraid to ask. Are you one of those *in-the-beginning-God* believers?"

A smile of amusement emerged. "Well, I've never heard it explained like that, but yes, I guess that's what I am."

Jake began cracking his knuckles ... one at a time. "You've never been with a man and no matter how much you like me or—heaven help us—even love me, you don't intend to make love unless I put a wedding band on your finger, do you?"

He wanted to hand her the car keys and run the mile back home ... and along the way he'd tell her God what he thought of Him.

She had the audacity to smile at him. "I'm glad we understand each other, Jake."

A force of fury flowed through his body to the extent that he had to resist the urge to do major damage to his vehicle. With a curt tone, he challenged her. "Understand each other? Oh, there's zero understanding on my part, Snow White, in spite of the fact that I had to live and play basketball with David Henderson my entire college life. He drove Josie berserk for three of those years. It will be a cold day in you-know-where before I let you do that to me."

He exited his car and stormed up and down the driveway. He had been blindsided. As he glared at her through the windshield, all he could think about was Josie and David. *What is it about these God fanatics that attract us so?*

All of a sudden getting her out of his life became his top priority. Step one ... get her out of his car. His heart was staging a major protest, but his mind was vetoing all objections.

She wants honesty? Okay! He crawled back in the car. "So this is the hurdle between us? If I remember correctly, you *hoped* it was only temporary. I've got a news flash for you, Miss Saving It. This is not a hurdle. It's an immovable mountain that I refuse to climb."

An array of emotions flashed across her face before acceptance settled in. "I was afraid that might be your answer." She wiped the few tears that were escaping and addressed him with acceptance and compassion. "Since I may never have this chance again, may I ask what *you* believe?"

He was livid and being kind was a stretch. "I don't believe the Bible is true, so that eliminates God. It's that simple."

As she held his gaze, the continuing tears began to drench the fire in him. "I'm interested in how you reached your conclusions, Jake. Have you ever read the book you say you don't believe? Have you ever checked out its history? I've heard you mention God in your conversations. If you don't believe He is real, why curse or address Him? Have you ever wondered if you could be wrong? Have you never felt the need or urge to cry out to a higher power?"

After uttering a few choice curse words under his breath, he responded. "No, I've never once read the Bible or checked out its history. I don't know why I use His name sometimes. And no, I'm not crazy enough to seek help from a deity I do not believe exists. That would be insanity."

Her tear flow increased. "You think so? Well, this *insane* person is convinced that God is eager for you to know that He is real. But He is a gentleman and waits for an invitation."

He smirked. Why did the most attractive and desirable woman he'd ever met have to be a religious zealot? "If you and David are any indication, your God is a party crasher. He has shown up in my life without an invitation."

There was that smile again. "You may not have invited Him, but someone has. Having a godly roommate who happened to also be a teammate those four years has God's fingerprints all over it. Now a clan of believers has moved next door. Someone has been bombarding heaven on your behalf. Now there's two."

"Well, you and that unknown someone are wasting your time." The compassion in her eyes was defusing his anger.

"I do not understand you, Madison, and I don't understand me when I'm with you." He had the greatest urge to kiss away those droplets that were washing away his resistance.

He suddenly realized that if he didn't get away from her, he was going to be pulled into her fanatical world.

His body wanted her more than any woman he'd ever known. His heart was convinced she was the love of his life. His brain was fighting both to prove that she was untouchable and dangerous. Jake knew one of them was messed up and he was pointing his finger at her.

His hesitation evidently gave her the courage to share.

"The day we met I felt like I had found a missing part of me. I fought the attraction when I learned of our differences of belief. My heart ignored every reason I raised.

"Dad reminded me that love is not just something that happens, but it also involves a deliberate choice. I couldn't help falling in love with you, Jake, but I can choose not to act on that love."

"You love me?"

"Scary, isn't it?"

"Scary? That's a mild word for what is happening. Lady, you are not only messing with my head, you are breaking my heart and tormenting my body.

"First, you want me to talk to someone I don't believe is real. Then you, the girl of my dreams, tell me that you are falling in love with me, but I can't have you. Why? Because I don't believe in your irrational concept of God."

He began massaging the muscles in his neck.

She reached for his hand. "Jake, God doesn't ask you to have blind, irrational faith. After all, if He is the Creator and God of the universe,

He's fully capable of meeting you where you are in a way that you'll know it's Him.

"And this heart tug you are experiencing isn't just about me, but also Him. Through me, He is calling to you. We both love you and want to be in relationship with you."

He enclosed her hand in his. "Madison, I've never wanted anyone or anything more, but I have no interest in your God."

"He is not put off by your honesty, unbelief or disinterest, Jake. He wants to prove He's real and cares for you. And He will if you'll quit being so pig-headed and admit that you might be wrong."

She leaned close. "Jake, if He's real, you need to know. If He's not, what have you lost?"

Her lips were too tempting. Her breath too close. He took her face in his hands and kissed her with the passion he was experiencing. She responded and he was on the doorstep of heaven until she pushed him away.

She took a deep breath and scooted closer to the door. "Jake, I'd be lying if I said I didn't want you right now, but I can't go there."

"Yeah, I know. It's that God of yours and His guidelines for sex outside of marriage."

He inserted the keys in the ignition. "I have to get you and your God home. You two could drive a man insane."

With that he started the car and drove as fast as he could. Getting her out of his car and sight was going to be easy. He'd have to find a way to get her out of his heart or he'd end up believing in her *in the beginning* God.

Neither said a word on the short ride. She was out of the car before he could round the vehicle. "Living next door may complicate our situation for a while, Jake. I hope we can still be cordial neighbors."

She offered her hand and when he didn't respond, she wiped her tears and turned for home. Jake watched as his hopes for a different life slowly moved out of his reach. His heart was screaming for intervention. He caught up with her at the gate.

"I love you, Madison Diamond, and you say you love me; and yet, you are willing to walk away because I don't believe in your God."

"I believe you are the one who called it off, Jake, because of my unwillingness to engage in sex before marriage."

She moved to the other side of the gate and waited for his response.

"If God does exists, He wouldn't be interested in the likes of me. I've broken too many of His *thou shall nots*."

With that he hurried away determined to eradicate her from his life.

Six

It was late and the younger generation was asleep, or at least in their rooms, when Madison entered the house. She heard her folks in the sitting room connected to their bedroom suite watching the late night news. After pouring a glass of milk and grabbing a couple of homemade cookies, she joined them.

"Looks like you've had a tough evening," Henry said as he turned off the television.

Dropping to the floor Indian style, Madison replayed the events of the evening, including Jake's Christian roomie and teammate. "That piece of information convinced me someone is praying for him, but he's going to fight this for all it's worth."

"You know ... I'm betting Virginia is a silent believer. She gets so excited when I share anything of a spiritual nature. Guess it's time to ask," Thelma announced.

The three Diamonds talked a while longer before calling it a night.

As Madison was putting her glass in the dishwasher, Donald walked in. "How did it go?"

She joined him at the breakfast nook. "You can relax. Looks like it's over before it got started."

Donald leaned back. "Sis, he and Josie have bad reputations. I'm relieved."

After they chatted a while, he smiled and scooted off the bench. "Think I'll head to the men's dormitory."

She watched as he sauntered out of the room and wondered how Jake was doing. He hadn't denied being with women, but he never mentioned how many. She had a feeling he was a bona fide womanizer. *Why this one, Lord?*

The man she was wondering about had lingered outdoors a while processing the turn of events. By the time he walked into the house, there was enough emotional steam radiating from him to power a small engine.

Josie was filling the dishwasher when he stormed into the kitchen and headed for the refrigerator. "What is wrong with you? I thought you'd be singing *How Sweet It Is*."

Jake pinched the bridge of his nose. "You wouldn't believe it if I told you." He snatched a beer. "I suddenly have great compassion for you."

He popped the lid, took a swig and headed for the closest bar stool. His nerves were rattled and his body was screaming.

Josie joined him. "What do you mean by that remark?"

"Your three-year crush on Henderson that I brushed off."

"You know David loves Callie more than anyone else on this earth and he'll wait for her till one of them dies if necessary ... even if he has to be celibate the rest of his life. I'm only jealous there's not a man who loves me like that."

"What if I told you that Madison and David have a lot in common?"

He watched her questioning expression turn to shock. "I'm not kidding." He downed the can of Bud and returned to the refrig for two more.

She took the third beer out of his hand. "Before your thinking gets too fuzzy, I want to know what happened."

As he relayed the events and conversation of the evening, her eyes filled with tears. "Jake, what is going on with us? At least she loves you and there's not another man in her life. David always loved Callie."

She waited for him to look at her. "Exactly how much do you care for the girl next door?"

He began pacing the floor and massaging his neck. "More than anyone I've ever known. I've used girls to satisfy my masculine desires for years and God knows I want her that way, but it's more. I can't get her off my mind and she owns my heart. Is that love? I think so."

He emptied the second can and dropped onto a bar stool. "What did you do with my other beer?"

She handed it to him. "Jake, do you think David and Madison could be right?"

"No way, but then my reasoning powers evaporate when I'm in her presence. I've got to stay as far away as possible or I'll start believing that stuff."

He popped the lid on his next can of therapy and headed for the stairs.

"Not yet." Josie said, as she snatched the beer from his hand the second time. "We need to talk this out."

He didn't argue and walked with her into the sunroom. Jake gazed at the lights in the valley below and wondered if anyone else out there was trapped by a forbidden love. All his hopes for a different life plummeted. It was back to life as usual and that was depressing after getting a glimpse and feel of the real thing.

After much discussion, the Roberts siblings accepted the fact that folks hung up on religion could never be part of their lives.

"Goodnight, Sis."

He ambled out of the room and headed for the stairs. Josie lingered. Taking in the night and lights … and thinking about David and Madison … and the life within her womb … and the one she had already ended.

SEVEN

Although it was Sunday, the 4th of July, most bicentennial celebrations were scheduled for Monday. The atmosphere at the Roberts' household was far from jubilant. Josie woke with vomiting added to her nausea and knew she could not keep her pregnancy hidden much longer.

Jake gave up trying to sleep and volunteered to help his dad mow the lawn. Wouldn't you know the jewels next door were exiting their mansion at that moment ... probably heading to church ... all ten of them in their larger-than-life van.

Jake looked at his dad. "Looks more like a team bus than a family vehicle."

William smiled and waved. So many waving arms appeared out the windows that it reminded Jake of a motorized centipede. He suppressed the smile that tried to escape. His logical mind instructed him to turn away. His turncoat heart overruled. As commanded, his eyes located their target.

She was smiling and waving. He halfheartedly returned her wave while trying to back out of sight. Next thing he knew his large frame was awkwardly flying through the air and colliding with the ground. He had tripped ... backwards ... over the push mower.

William's amused smile didn't help. "Anything besides your pride hurt, Son?"

"I'm fine, Dad." His effort to stand proved him wrong. By this time his moving audience was in direct line with his prone body. *Why is there not a house between our driveways?*

"Need a nurse, Jake?" Henry shouted, as he stopped the church bus.

Still on the ground and trying to save what little dignity he had left, Jake assured Henry that he was okay. He motioned his dad to his side and whispered. "I believe I do need some help, but please wait until they leave."

The neighbors' chariot pulled out of their driveway only to reveal that one of its passengers had been left behind. Without a word, Florence Nightingale opened the gate that separated them and walked back into Jake Roberts' life. Forget his ankle. His heart was under attack—and loving it.

"Where is your injury, Jake?" Florence asked.

He pointed to his left ankle. She suggested William take Jake's left side and stationed herself on his right. Together they managed to get him on his feet. He put his arm around his dad's shoulders and tried to walk ... minus her help. Painful mistake. He tried hopping on his one good leg. That prideful miscalculation caused him to connect with the ground ... again.

When his dad managed to get him up the second time, the nurse lifted his right arm over her shoulders and positioned her left arm around his waist. At that moment, ankle pain became his secondary problem. Warmth spread through his body and his heart shut down his brain.

His dad was making matters worse. "Are you feeling faint, Jake? You look pale and a little green."

If looks could inflict pain, William would not be enjoying Jake's fiasco quite as much.

Unaware of the nuances of communication passing between father and son, the nurse concentrated on her mission ... caring for the wounded.

"The pain may be making him queasy, Mr. Roberts. Let's get him in the house."

Both of the robust men stared at the unsuspecting source of that suggestion. William was close to losing it. Jake was speechless. As ordered, they proceeded into the house.

Every time Jake tried to put weight on that ankle, it protested, but the sweet thing snuggled against his right side made the misery bearable. Seemed like a justifiable reason to hold on tightly.

His dad? Jake turned loose of him as soon as possible.

After Jake was situated in a comfortable chair, Virginia walked in on the drama. William grabbed her hand and quickly pulled her into the kitchen to prepare the ice pack. Jake could hear the echoes of his dad's explanation punctuated with repeated rumbles of laughter.

Unaware of Jake's trepidation regarding her nearness, Nurse Extraordinaire began a careful medical examination of his ankle while naming all the bones and ligaments involved. Looking up with informative, yet innocent eyes, she asked, "Do you know that over twenty thousand people sprain an ankle every day, Jake?"

He could only shake his head. Those were not the facts on his mind at the moment. Her silky, sleeveless dress that highlighted her mature figure was taking his mind other places. He kept trying to remember all the reasons he walked out of her life last night, but every time her fingers pressed a spot or probed another part of his ankle or foot, he suffered severe memory loss.

By the time she had convinced his folks that he needed to go to the ER to be checked for broken bones, he couldn't think of one good reason why he had been so hasty in his decision.

Virginia pulled the car as close as possible to the front entrance. With help from his two human crutches, Jake dropped onto the passenger's seat. It wasn't until he was separated from the woman's touches that any hint of last night's upsetting conversation surfaced.

With more than medical concern, Madison touched his arm. "Jake, I'm sorry you've been hurt."

Bam! Now he remembered. Miss Touch-Me-Not was speaking of more than his ankle. "Don't worry about it, Neighbor. I'm a quick healer."

The brain was back in charge. He could not allow this woman back in his life ... no matter how much his heart protested.

As his dad started the car, Jake added sarcastically, "I'm sorry you missed church on my account."

If there really was a God, He'd know that was a lie. Jake had enjoyed every painful moment of her attention and was livid as he recalled why it had to end. What a waste!

The drive to the hospital solidified his resolve. He could not and would not compete with her God and His guidelines. There were plenty of girls who didn't live in the dark ages.

The ER doctor confirmed what Madison had suspected. No broken bones, just a bad sprain. Nothing that crutches, ice, something for pain, elevation, rest and an ace bandage wouldn't cure in time.

His heart? That was a different story. He hadn't figured out all the details on that yet.

Eight

July 5 was hot and humid. Sweat was exiting every pore of Jake's body as he and his crutches were getting acquainted. He was disgusted with himself, but at least he had an excuse to stay away from the Diamond festivities today. He dropped in a chair on the patio and turned toward the noise next door. Madison and a few others were already in the pool. Nice place to cool off.

His head and heart started battling again. He had to be decisive. "Dad, I'm staying home today. Need to rest this leg."

William smiled while watching Madison dive into the pool. "Bet a pretty nurse would make it feel better."

Jake was nervously drumming his fingers on the arm of his chair, but his eyes were glued on the object of the conversation. "You might as well know, Dad. It's over between us."

"Over?" William studied Jake whose eyes were glued on Madison. "You don't sound convincing or convinced, Son."

Dragging his eyes away from the activity next door, he faced his dad. "Yeah ... well, I'm working on that problem."

Virginia exited the house with an antique, white-enamel, red-rimmed dishpan filled with cut up watermelon. "William, will you step inside the kitchen and bring the blue speckled enamel-ware Dutch oven of cantaloupe and blueberries?

"Don't wait too long, Jake. You don't want to miss all this yummy food and summer fun."

"You and Dad go on, Mom. I'm going to nurse this bum leg today." He watched them stroll across the lawns to the ever-growing gathering at the neighborhood country club.

Instead of feeling sorry for himself, Jake hauled his injured ankle and aching heart into the house and called Denise. They made plans to meet at her place tomorrow evening. There! That should take care of the five feet eight inches of desirable female next door.

William returned shortly with a tray of food for Jake. "Okay, Son! What has happened between you and Madison? The vibes you two are giving off could start a landslide."

"Dad, I told you ... it is over. We've decided to settle for being neighbors. Besides, I have a date with Denise tomorrow night."

"Hmm." William leaned forward. "I've got news for you. Your heart is not in agreement."

William looked across the way and spotted Madison. "You would give up a treasure like that for a girl who has slept with half the men in this county? I thought you had finally come to your senses."

"Dad, Madison is twenty-one years old and has never been with a man. And get this. She intends to save herself for her husband. Does this remind you of anyone we have known the last four years? She freaked me out with talk of God last night." He reached for a grilled chicken leg.

William settled back in his chair and scanned the surrounding landscape. A couple of noisy mockingbirds were sounding off in a nearby tree. Bluebirds were flying in and out of the boxes he had installed around the perimeter of the property. Goldfinches were feeding at the birdfeeder hanging from a nearby tree. Four or five hummingbirds were flitting between the red nectar feeder and the blooms on the hibiscus bushes. Various species of butterflies were fluttering among the colorful array of flowers throughout the landscape.

"God and religion are topics we haven't discussed in this family. I had enough of that growing up."

Jake watched as a beautiful Monarch butterfly landed on his propped, injured ankle.

William continued, "Henry is the first man who calls himself a Christian that I can actually talk to about my background without being judged. He said the God I grew up with was a God of religion and works, not a God of faith and relationship.

With his eyes glued to the insect resting on his foot, Jake questioned his dad. "I thought your silence indicated a lack of belief, Dad."

Jake's visitor had caught William's attention. "It's not that I don't believe, Jake. I simply rejected the God presented to me by my dad. The Diamonds' faith doesn't make them mean and condemning. They are kind and gracious people."

A couple of playful rabbits drew their attention away from the newly metamorphosed butterfly.

Jake reached for the Coke on his tray. "They are an unusual family, aren't they?"

"Yes, and that takes us back to the original topic of this conversation. Something rare is happening between you and Madison. Why are you throwing it away?"

"Dad, I can't abstain from sex until we marry and she's not going there. I have to walk away. God or no God. It's over."

William stood and challenged his son. "I faced that same decision when I met your mom. She was worth the wait, Jake. Girls like Madison are hard to find and you can bet your last dollar that some smart guy is going to figure that out quickly. Probably some young intern at the hospital.

"Is your temporary pleasure worth more to you than a lifetime of what you and Madison could potentially share? Don't take the short look, Son."

William left Jake with much to chew on. *Dad waited for Mom?* Could he wait for Madison? Thoughts of her with another man left him feeling like someone was twisting a knife in his gut.

Denise and a few other girls would help him forget, wouldn't they? Temporary pleasure?

While he was dealing with his excuses for not going next door, morning sickness extended to the noon hour for Josie.

"Hey, Mom. Where are you?"

"Mom and Dad have gone next door for the big hoorah. I begged off because of my ankle. What's your excuse?"

"Hugging the toilet. You wouldn't believe how keeping it clean matters all of a sudden."

"I could do without the details, Sis."

"And I thought boys liked the gross side of life." She shook her head and walked into the kitchen.

Nine

Nausea hit Josie with the force of a storm the second morning in a row. It was ten o'clock before all systems were quiet.

She stuck her head in the laundry room. "Morning, Mom."

"Good morning, Josie. I left you an omelet in the oven. Thelma has invited us to join the Diamond women for a brunch at eleven. Don't overeat."

"Both sound great. I could eat a bear." She managed to keep her breakfast down and by the time the brunch came, she was ready for more. That, plus getting to know the female who was rocking Jake's world, made the invitation appealing.

She hadn't been in the old Parker place in years. From the moment she stepped inside, she felt a connection with the lady who had accomplished astounding wonders. The furnishings, artifacts, arrangements, colors and textures created such a welcoming ambiance that Josie felt at home even though it was a massive place.

Interacting with Thelma and her five Ms was thought provoking. Having a sister would have been nice. She was particularly drawn to Maria and Melinda. *What if they had been aborted?*

The little one was delightful. "Miss Josie, do you like the grapes? I helped clean them." She displayed both hands for examination. "I washed my hands first ... in case you are wondering."

Josie reached for those pint-sized hands and turned them over as though checking meticulously. "These clean hands explain the delicious grapes, Melinda." The kid beamed and scooted the tray closer. A warm fuzzy sensation stirred in Josie's womb.

About half way through the meal, the life growing inside began to cause a digestive disturbance. Josie asked directions to the nearest bathroom and excused herself. After puking her insides out for the umpteenth time today, she knew it was decision time. She was rinsing her mouth out with water when she heard a soft tap on the door. "Are you okay, Josie?" She recognized Thelma's voice.

After opening the door and assuring her hostess that all was well, Josie stepped into the hall. The discerning neighbor placed a hand on her arm. "How far along are you, Sweetie?" Josie's stunned expression must have prompted further explanation. "Honey, I've been pregnant sixty-three months of my life. I know the symptoms."

Stammering a bit at first, Josie confessed. "I'm still in the first weeks. Please don't say anything. I've not decided what I'm going to do yet. I had an abortion in May and here I am pregnant again. The father wants me to abort. I'm at least thinking it through this time."

The lady was not judging her. "Other options are available."

"Oh, I know, but I don't think I could take care of a baby and finish school. Besides, what man wants a woman with a baby?"

"Henry did. I was sixteen when my first child was born. The father was eight years older and wanted nothing to do with me or our son.

"I made up my mind that I would prove I was more than a body to satisfy some self-centered man's pleasure. An education became the means to that end. My mom practically raised Ethan while I finished high school and college."

The honest woman paused. "Josie, I had been sexually abused as a child and was sexually active by the time I turned fourteen."

Josie knew her face was betraying her shock. "Sexually abused? A baby? When did Henry enter the picture?"

Thelma looped her arm through Josie's and laughed. "Actually I met Henry my senior year of college. There was chemistry between us from the beginning, but Henry was a big God fan. Me? I trusted no one except myself. That posed a problem for him, but that's another story."

Thelma stopped their progress. "Henry Diamond is the best thing that ever happened to me. He introduced me to a different kind of love. That and his patience won my heart, and we married the summer after I graduated from the University of Kentucky with a degree in design."

The perfect family wasn't perfect after all. "Where is Ethan, now?"

Tears welled up in Thelma's eyes. "Our Ethan is in prison, Josie."

Jake and Josie's Discovery

Josie knew her face was flashing her astonishment, but she couldn't help it. Not only did the perfect mom have a baby out of wedlock, the perfect family had a son in prison.

Obviously money wasn't the only thing in abundance in this household. They also had a stash of secrets. She thought of a dozen questions but dared not ask them. "I d-don't know what to say, Mrs. Diamond."

"I understand." She stepped into the adjoining room for a tissue. "Maybe knowing about Ethan will help you understand why we place such a high value on our children. I know my past has been forgiven, Josie, but I still see the impact it had on him."

Thelma nodded toward the kitchen area. "I think you should tell your parents. You need all the support you can get right now."

She waited until Josie's attention was directed at her again. "And if adoption becomes one of your options, Henry and I would consider it a blessing to adopt your baby."

Add surprises to that horde of secrets and money. And what was it with these people and kids? With a stunned look on her face, Josie answered honestly. "Adoption never entered my mind."

"Henry and I have learned that babies are God's most precious gifts and that adoption can be a beautiful answer to a difficult situation. Think about it. That's all I ask." She put her arm around Josie's shoulders as they walked back to the kitchen. The rest of the time was a blur. Her own secrets had been stirred.

As soon as she could, Josie hurried home. Jake was hobbling out of the kitchen when she bopped in. "Man, am I glad you're home! We have to talk. The sooner, the better. Someplace private."

"That must have been some get together! Is the sunroom private enough or are you going to make your crippled brother haul his injured body to the balcony?"

"Upstairs, Bro. This will be worth the effort. I'll grab the drinks."

Jake hesitated. "You're not trying to play matchmaker between Madison and me, are you? Because that's over. Kaput! I'm taking Denise out tonight."

"No, it's not that." She punched his arm. "Denise? I can't let you do something that stupid."

TEN

The balcony was located on the back of the house and offered a grand view of the valley. To the satisfaction of Jake's curious nature, it also offered a better view of the activities next door. As he stood by the railing, he caught a glimpse of Madison and Maria at the pool. Before he made it to his chair, an unfamiliar vehicle pulled into the driveway. Two unknown males exited.

By that time, Josie had joined him. "What or whom are you checking out, Sherlock?"

He pointed with his right crutch. "Who are they?"

She placed a hand over her heart. "The tall, sandy-headed fellow with a body like Atlas? Or the dark, handsome one that reminds me of a young Elvis?"

Jake moved closer to the railing. "I don't remember seeing either one of them before."

Josie twirled around. "Hmm. Atlas seems interested in your ex."

Jake grunted and positioned his chair with his back to the neighbors.

"I believe that unfamiliar sensation rolling through your gut is called jealousy, Jake, and turning your back on the soap opera being played out next door won't help. Your imagination will only make it worse. I need your attention for this conversation."

He compromised and scooted his chair to face the front rail.

"Oh, that's cool. You'll end up with whiplash trying to keep up with them and me. Just pull your chair by me so we can both watch the show and still talk. I have some tasty tidbits to share with you about that picture perfect family."

Reluctantly, he scooted his chair next to hers and plopped down. Just as he laid his crutches on the floor, Madison did a high spring off the board and nailed a perfect entry into the water. Atlas and Elvis stepped out of the beach house in their swim trunks and proceeded to do flawless replications.

Josie poked his ribs. "I'd give them a nine or nine point five. Wouldn't you?"

Jake looked at her with a less than happy face. "Are you referring to the dives or the divers?"

She giggled. "Both actually. Yes siree! They are fine looking specimens."

"You are not helping matters, Josie."

She punched him. "Hey, Thelma unloaded some shocking family secrets today. I know the truth about their missing child."

Jake was finding it difficult to keep up with the activity next door and listen to Josie. "Are they playing *Marco Polo*?"

Adjusting her sunglasses, Josie checked out the pool action. "Looks like it from here."

She punched his arm ... harder this time. "Hey, maybe we need to go inside so you can follow this one-sided conversation."

He jerked his head towards her. "No, no ... I'm listening. You said their secret child is missing."

His eyes were back on the rejected object of his affections and Atlas, who was much too friendly. He moaned. He had been wrong. It wasn't one knife twisting in his gut. There were at least a dozen. He reached for his crutches.

Josie jumped in front of him. "This is not working. You already have one bum leg and jumping off this balcony to attack Atlas is not going to improve your health or change what is happening next door. I was wrong. Either turn your back to them or we have to put a wall between you and your beloved ex."

Reluctantly he scooted his chair around and turned his back on the entertainment. Jealous? Yeah, he now knew exactly what that green-eyed monster was capable of. His stomach, mind and heart were all under attack.

"Back to my tale. His name is Ethan and he is not Henry's biological child. He was born out of wedlock and is currently in prison."

"Prison? Madison has a brother in prison?"

"Yeah, and that's not all. Thelma offered to adopt my baby."

His eyebrows shot up so high they formed a peak in the middle. "Adopt your baby? You told her you were pregnant?"

"Nope. She guessed it when I ran out of the kitchen and started hugging her toilet. Seven times nine equals sixty-three, Jake. That's a lot of months to be pregnant."

Jake was rubbing his hand through his messy hair. "Can you believe they would want another child? Like nine is not enough?"

He looked into eyes that were replicas of his. "Surely you're not considering adoption, Sis. You'd have to carry that baby for eight more months. What would the folks say? What would you do about school? I don't see that as an option."

"Until she mentioned it neither did I, although being around Maria and Melinda puts abortion and adoption in a different light. What if their mothers had aborted, Jake?" She looked at the dark-skinned beauty next door. "Thelma has given me something to think about. I'm pretty sure I don't want to keep it, so I have to decide between adoption and abortion."

She brought her focus back to Jake. "When do you think life begins?"

"I've never given it much thought, but like you, being around Maria and Melinda has prompted some questions. I don't linger on them long."

He looked at his pregnant sister. "Josie, do you ever think of David or Nicolas?"

Fingering the hem of her top, she glanced at her brother. "Some. I have accepted the fact that Callie will always own David's heart, and I think Nick's just tired of my inability to settle down."

Memories of David and Callie surfaced for Jake. "Yeah, the man sure is hung up on that girl."

"Jake, if Madison is offering you the kind of love David has for Callie, why are you running away?"

He leaned back and chewed on that question. "As crazy as I am about Madison, I'm not waiting until marriage for any girl. I can't."

Josie Roberts was scrutinizing her brother so intently it made him nervous.

"Don't look at me like that. Neither could you. We have more in common than Dad's blue eyes. We are two peas from the same pod."

A sadness came over Josie's face and entered her words. "I know why I'm addicted to sex, Jake, but why are you?"

That statement detonated inside him. He jerked upright in his chair. "What do you mean addicted to sex? Just because I like it, doesn't mean I'm addicted. Explain yourself."

Addicted was a word he had hated all his life. He had an occasional beer or glass of wine, but had avoided drugs like they were the plague. Some of his buddies had ended up addicts of one or both and wrecked their lives. Horse feathers. He didn't even smoke. Addicted to sex? He'd never heard of such a thing.

A restlessness settled over Josie. "Some things have happened in my life, Jake, that I've never told a soul. I had hoped Mom or Dad ... or even you would guess. No one ever did."

Jake went pale. "Sis, what are you talking about?"

With tears beginning to pool in her eyes, Josie traveled back to a time and place and unlocked memories no one should have to remember. She placed her feet on her chair and hugged her legs with her chin tucked as close to her body as possible. Her eyes took on a faraway look. Tears trailed down her cheeks as soft moans began to escape.

Her voice was unsteady. "Do you remember ... the night of your senior prom?"

He nodded and tried to swallow the knot that was shutting off his air passage.

"Remember Felix? He had only been in our school for two months. I think his family moved here from New York. He was cute and funny, so when he asked me to the prom, I agreed."

"Why don't I remember that fact or him?" Jake was reaching for his crutches. "And?"

"After a few dances, we sampled the punch." She couldn't make eye contact. "I had no idea that he had laced mine with a drug."

Jake's face had become a portrait of rage. "I've heard guys brag about such events." He began pounding his thighs with his fists and promising to do horrible things to Felix.

Josie was struggling to separate her emotions from the incident. "I lost hours of memory. My next recollection occurred in a motel room.

I was naked and three naked men were stationed in chairs around the bed. One was my date. The other two … I had never seen before."

Jake felt like an out-of-control train. Adrenaline overload took over his body. He managed to pull himself out of the chair. He leaned on his crutches and spoke with a raised voice. "I'm going to hurt him, Josie. I swear I'm going to find all of them and inflict some major hurt. Better yet. I think I'll castrate them." He was limping around the deck like a caged, angry animal and dirtying the air with his thoughts.

When he noticed the shape Josie was in, he laid his crutches to the side and dropped to his knees in front of her. "Are you going to be okay, Sis?"

She nodded while allowing more memories to surface. "Images of that night are like … the flashes of a camera. A flash of recall … and then darkness. When I finally woke with enough willpower over my body and mind to react, it was morning. At first I thought the men were sleeping, but gradually realized they had passed out. As quietly and quickly as possible, I crawled out of bed, dressed and escaped."

She shuddered and took a couple of deep breaths as Jake began rubbing her arms. "I don't know why I didn't think to call the police. They could have caught them. But Jake, I was filled with so much shame and fear that I couldn't bring myself to even tell Mom and Dad. Deep down, I wanted them to guess. Especially Dad."

She remained in the fetal position with her head bowed … still weeping … reliving a nightmare so horrible she had been afraid to share it.

"Josie, I was so lost in my own selfish indulgences that night that you couldn't have found me if your life had depended on it. That fact makes me loathe myself right this minute."

She shook her head. "My thoughts weren't clear enough to think about you, Jake. Home was the only sane thought I had." Tears that had been held in for years were now escaping.

"Dad had a few choice words about my being out all night. He accused me of being a tramp. I couldn't bring myself to tell him the truth. I wasn't sure he would believe me."

Emotions stuffed down for years were begging for release, but she had become an expert at denying them exit. "Looking back it makes no sense. A physical examination would have proven I had been drugged and raped. Maybe I was still under the influence of the drug because that thought didn't register."

Slowly her countenance changed. "That night also introduced me to an STD. It didn't take long to decide that no man would ever do that to me again. I'm not sure this makes much sense, but my addiction to men isn't so much about sex as the power my body gives me over them. I control them instead of them controlling me. Crazy, isn't it?"

Shame began to cloud her face. "I was already sexually active, thanks to Uncle George, but after that night, I became even more aggressive."

In spite of his ankle Jake managed to get up using one crutch. He yanked her off her chair, grabbed her shoulders and shook her body. "What in the blue blazes does Uncle George have to do with you and sex? I thought we were talking about the rape and Felix." Jake was close to losing control. "Explain!"

She pointed to his chair. "Sit down, Jake."

He slammed his body back into his chair. "Explain George."

"Remember the weeks we spent each summer in Ohio with Grandma and Grandpa Roberts?"

"Yeah, I remember." Jake was looking for a waste can. He felt like everything inside him was going to make an exit.

Josie began twisting her hair around her fingers. "Uncle George started visiting my room when I turned seven. At first he said we were playing games. I remember the first game involved exploring the difference between boys and girls. He had several different games that we played, and I hated them and him the first summer. I begged Grandma to sleep with me, but she told me I was a big girl. My child mind assumed she and Grandpa knew. After that I quit resisting. How was a seven year old supposed to know what should and should not happen when a trusted person does such things?"

She sat back down and closed her eyes. "A couple of years later, Uncle George said that lots of boys and men would love me because he had taught me how to please them."

Her eyes widened as understanding dawned. "David exposed that lie, didn't he? He loves Callie more than his own life and they've never engaged in sex. They are saving it for marriage, like it's a special gift they give each other."

Madison's words from the night before echoed inside Jake's head.

Was she right? Was he wrong? His sister had been the victim of sexual abuse since she was seven years old and no one knew it. David had tried to tell both of them by his life and words that they were screwed up sexually, but they mocked him.

Josie knew that she had housed dark secrets. Jake had been ignorant.

"How could I have been so dense all these years?" He was now upright and hugging his crutches. "Uncle George came to my bedroom during those times as well, Josie. He told me he was teaching me the pleasures of being a man. He started with magazines. Other activities were added through the years. He made it seem like an education, not abuse. He was my cool, teenage uncle. I believed him."

Josie sprang out of her chair and shouted in his face. "Don't you see? We are both addicted to sex."

Jake stared at Josie as the repulsively foul revelation registered. He was dazed. Josie was numb. Both had been victims of abuse, which resulted in sexual addictions, twisted thinking and messed-up relationships.

Josie moved to the railing. "Why did Dad or Mom never figure anything out? Why didn't we tell them? Or at least each other?"

Jake hobbled in her direction. "It never dawned on me that it was abuse, Josie."

That truth was already working its way into his thought processes with lightning speed. Listening to Josie's stories and admitting his own had set off a mental domino effect inside his head. His previously held mindset was caving in by the second as scenes and memories of his past began crashing one on top of the other. Was it possible that what he had always considered normal and natural was neither?

He hated Felix and his feelings for Uncle George had switched from cool dude to malicious abuser the last hour. And in the midst of it all, a seed of self-loathing had been planted inside him.

"Go see if Mom and Dad are back yet. If so, ask them to meet us in the sunroom. Better grab some glasses of water and a box of tissues. I have a date to cancel first." As she neared the door, he asked, "What was Felix's last name?"

"I think it started with an *A*. Check your yearbook and see if his photo was included."

Eleven

By the time Jake made it to the sunroom, Josie and their folks were settled. Jake decided to share the abuses in the order they occurred. For a fleeting moment, he almost petitioned a power outside himself for help, but quickly shook off that foolish impulse.

"Mom and Dad, Josie and I have had an eye-opening conversation that we need to share with you."

He was counting on the fact that the two of them were already mentally and emotionally drained to help him maintain a reasonable level of control.

As unemotionally as he could, Jake shared about his summer experiences with Uncle George. A chameleon couldn't have changed colors as fast as William's expressions. Anger dominated. By the time Jake finished, William was swearing like a seasoned sailor, clearing tables in one swipe, slamming his fists in walls and vowing revenge.

William turned to Jake with blood-streaked hands and tears pooling in his eyes. "Son, if I didn't know you, I'd swear you were lying. I cannot believe that my own brother did this to my child. George, a pedophile? It's preposterous! I don't know how to process this information."

Jake watched as his dad struggled to regain control. "When did it start and how long did it last?"

"It started when I was eight or nine and it ended when George moved away."

William was wandering aimlessly around the room at this point. "Lord, help us! What do we do now? I want to turn him in to the police. I want to beat him senseless."

He stopped in front of his wife who had not uttered a word, though the sounds of her pain were audible. "This explains some questions we've had about Jake's sexual behavior, Virginia."

He turned to Jake. "Why didn't you come to me?"

"Dad, my kid brain accepted what he told me. After all, he was your baby brother and my super, cool uncle. Why would he lie to me? I believed him."

With a trembling voice, Virginia addressed Jake. "Can you forgive us? I can't imagine a child's reaction to such behavior and I grieve as your mother for the loss of your innocence at the hands of a trusted relative. At what point did you realize it was abuse?"

He looked at Josie and felt the color flee from his face as a fresh ache developed in his heart for her own stories yet to be told. "Not until today, Mom. Josie helped me see it for what it was."

Panic took over William's face. "One of you needs to explain that statement."

"Sis, can you talk?"

She shook her head.

Jake watched his parents collapse emotionally as he related George's abuse of their daughter.

Virginia jumped up and began beating his chest with her fists. "You are lying, Jake. Tell me you're lying."

Jake grabbed her wrists and pulled her into his arms. "I'm sorry, Mom."

She pulled away and knelt in front of Josie. "Tell me he's lying, Josie. Tell me!"

By this time Josie was rocking her fetal-positioned body back and forth with her head down and eyes closed. She did not respond.

William reached for his wife and pulled her into his arms. They hugged and wept as though the events explained had just happened. Their sobs and groans touched Josie's heart. She uncurled her body and wedged herself between them.

The sounds of pain emitted by that trio hinted of the inferno below. "Josie, why didn't you tell us?"

"S-s-shame and fear, Mom."

Jake and Josie's Discovery

Virginia lifted her head and sought her husband's eyes. "Why were we so blind, William? What kind of parents send their children into such a place? Why didn't your parents notice? How old was George at this time?"

William thought for a minute. "He would have been around fifteen or sixteen when it started." He took a deep breath. "He was and may still be a pedophile. He has to be confronted."

They moved to the sofa with Josie between them as the shock and rawness of the tragedy began to sink in, William voiced the need to find help.

Jake wasn't sure either parent could handle the rest of Josie's story. "Folks, there's more."

Virginia began to tremble. "More? God, help us!"

Josie was trying to calm her mom.

"Josie, why don't you and Mom go to your suite for a while?" Jake suggested.

When the females departed, Jake shared the facts he knew about Josie's gang date rape. Anything left intact in the room from William's previous explosions was demolished during this last fit of rage. Jake couldn't restrain him.

"Dad, I know this is hard, but you have to be strong for Mom and Josie." And with those words, Jake's own tears pushed through his walls of restraint.

When William saw the tears streaming down Jake's cheeks, he pulled him into his arms. Jake had been a little boy the last time that had happened.

As William pulled away and began to pick up the debris that littered the place, Jake used a crutch to scoot a wastebasket into the center of the room. "Dad, are you upset with us? Were we wrong to tell you?"

"A thousand times no, Jake. I'm thankful you finally felt you could. I'm outraged that anyone would do such things, but I'm also furious that no adult, especially your mother and me, picked up on it. I grieve over the fact that we, as your parents, didn't prepare and instruct you to come to us immediately if anything like that should happen."

When the wastebasket was full, William slumped in the closest chair. "Would you mind going next door and asking Henry and Thelma to come over if at all possible?"

Madison hadn't been far from Jake's thoughts all day. How could he face her? "Are you sure this is what we need to do, Dad?"

"Yes, Son. I'm sure. Your mother needs them. Do you know they have a son in prison?"

"Actually, that news played a part in bringing all this to the surface."

William rose and put a hand on Jake's shoulder. "Go see if they can come."

Jake's expression must have revealed his objections.

"Their visitors today were for their children, so I don't think it will pose a problem."

That statement reminded Jake of Atlas and Elvis. He grabbed his crutches and began the trip next door while wishing he could have a do-over of his last conversation with Madison.

The crowd around the pool had thinned out. Only the younger ones were swimming. Jake targeted one of the boys. "Hey, Daniel, are your folks home?"

The swimmer climbed out of the pool and grabbed a towel. "Yeah, they are in the house. Madison isn't. She and Maria went somewhere with Jonathan and Grayson."

Checking out Jake's crutches and bum ankle, he added, "Guess it'll be a while before you can help me with my basketball moves or join our tournaments."

"Yeah, it will be a while. Dad was wondering if your folks could come to our place for an hour or so."

Daniel nodded. "Probably. There's enough of us to watch Melinda. I'll tell them." And he disappeared.

A few minutes later, Henry exited the rear patio door and greeted Jake with his strong handshake and friendly smile. "What's that dad of yours up to this time, Jake? The last time he called me over, he had rewired a lamp and the thing blew a fuse when he turned it on."

"It's a little more serious than an electrical problem this time. We've had a tough afternoon. Will Mrs. Diamond be able to come at some point?"

"Yeah, she'll be along soon."

Jake was leaning on both crutches. "You go on. Dad's in the sunroom—what's left of it."

"Oh, okay."

Henry went to the sunroom entrance and stopped in his tracks as the condition of the room and the man slumped in a chair with his head in his bloody hands came into view. He entered without knocking. "What has happened, William?"

A broken man lifted his head. "Henry, we need help, and I didn't know where else to turn."

"That's what friends are for. Feel like taking a walk?"

Without answering, William moved out the door, and Henry followed.

Neither said a word as they walked the perimeter of the two properties. As they neared William's home, he clasped his hands behind his back and stilled. "Other than death, Henry, what would be the worst thing that could happen to one of your children?"

Henry reflected on that disturbing question. "Kidnapping, I think."

A surprised look revealed that wasn't the expected answer. "I think I agree with you. Dealing with the unknown would be the hardest of all."

Henry studied his hurting friend. "You know about Ethan's addiction and imprisonment." He played with the change in his pockets as he contemplated the man's question. "Tell me what you're dealing with."

"Both of my children have been sexually abused, Henry."

The neighbor was visibly shaken. "Oh, William, I am so sorry."

With tears and outbursts of anger, William divulged the stories of his own brother's experimentation and abuse of both of his children and Josie's rape.

Henry hugged his friend briefly as tears began to drip off his cheeks. "Thelma has walked this path, William. She is the one who can help your children."

"Thelma? I see no signs. How did she overcome the fallout?"

"God's love and the counsel of folks who cared."

"I'm not glad she was abused, but I am glad she will understand."

"How is Virginia?"

"Devastated. She knows about George, but not the rape. I'd like for you and Thelma to be present when Jake tells her the rest."

"I'll go get her. You check on your women and we'll meet back at your place in fifteen minutes. How does that sound?"

"Thanks, Friend."

Henry shared the heartbreaking stories and relayed William's request to Thelma.

"My story is different, Henry, but the pain and shame I recognize. Let's go."

Together they walked the path that was beginning to materialize between the two houses. "We need to put down some foot stones or this worn down grass will soon become dirt and mud."

William met them at the door. "Come in. They are in the family room."

Thelma made her way to Virginia and Josie. The trio shared hugs and tears and grief.

When everyone was seated, William focused on his wife. "Virginia ... Honey, are you ready?"

She grabbed Josie's hand and nodded.

William signaled Jake.

As Jake shared Josie's other story, Virginia lost it. William moved between his girls, extended an arm around both and drew them close.

Josie laid her head on her daddy's shoulder as years of unspoken cries for help and suppressed groans of enduring shameful and repeated abuse finally found a safe outlet.

Virginia, on the other hand, was reliving the event as a woman who understood the wickedness and depravity her daughter had endured.

As Jake witnessed the damage self-seeking men had inflicted on his sister and the repercussions it was having on his mom and dad, that seed of self-loathing developed a strong tap root.

William managed to speak. "Jake and Josie ... can you forgive us for not figuring out what George was doing and sending you back summer after summer to endure more?"

He broke. "Josie ... I really messed up the morning after the prom. Can you forgive me?" Josie wiped his tears and nodded.

"I can't turn back the calendar, but I can and will see that you get the help you need. Henry tells me that God can redeem the hardest, darkest places in our lives. That must be true, because Thelma understands your pain ... first hand, yet I see no evidence of it in her life. Makes me wish I knew their God."

Virginia was still unable to speak, but she enclosed as much of her daughter and husband in her arms as possible.

When things settled some, Henry gathered everyone in a circle and prayed a short and simple prayer for help.

As the prayer ended, Thelma turned to the young people. "It's important that both of you know your past doesn't have to define your present or predict your future. There is hope and there is help. It's not easy, but it is possible."

Thelma briefly shared the story of her own abuse. By the time the conversation ended, Jake and Josie were encouraged. When Thelma rejoined the others, the siblings headed outside.

TWELVE

Jake and Josie backed their cars out of the garage and collected the equipment and materials needed for cleaning them.

"As hard as it was, Josie, aren't you glad the secrets are out?"

"Yeah. Thelma's story gave me the courage to get honest."

Jake washed and rinsed the roof while Josie kept applying elbow grease to the bug splatters and oil residue on the bumper and grille. "Sorry I can't do more, Sis. This bum ankle is a royal pain."

Josie stopped. "Amidst all the hype, you never told me how it happened."

"Let's just say I made a fool of myself over a certain girl."

"In that case, I'm sorry I missed the show. Speaking of Madison, how does all of this affect your thoughts about her?"

He glanced toward the house next door. Images of Madison with Atlas were wreaking havoc on his heart.

"Until today I thought I was a normal, red-blooded, American male and she was the weirdo. And that's sad, because I now know that I'm the messed-up one. I can't imagine her having anything to do with me when she finds out." He rinsed the part she had washed.

"I think you ought to give her a chance to decide for herself." And with the first real smile he had seen since the secrets had been unearthed, she whispered, "And that opportunity is approaching as we speak."

Three-year-old Melinda was racing across the lawns with Madison close behind. The younger Diamond wrapped her arms around Jake's legs. "Throw me, Jake. Throw me."

Bending as low as he could, he hugged her. "Sweetheart, I'm afraid to throw you today. I'm not steady on my feet. Will a hug do?"

She smiled and returned his hug.

"Smiles and hugs like that will make my leg heal faster, Melinda. Thank you." He kissed the top of her head.

She tugged on the hem of his shorts. "If Maddie smiled and hugged you, would your leg get all better?"

Though his words were addressed to Melinda, his eyes focused on Madison. "Melinda, I think a smile and hug from your big sister would do wonders for my leg."

He watched as Madison's expression fluctuated between guarded and surprised. Melinda reached for Madison's hand and led her to Jake.

Putting her thumbs under her chin and her pointers pulling up the corners of her mouth, she demonstrated a smile. "Now you do like this."

She held the pose until Madison complied. "Good." She pushed her sister closer to Jake. "Now give him a hug and his leg will get all better."

Sensing Madison's reluctance, Jake disregarded the audience of her little sister and his bigger one and bridged the gap between them. "I don't know if my leg will heal any faster, but I'm confident my heart would." Leaning on his crutches, he put one arm around her.

Madison smiled shyly and gave him a quick hug.

He leaned on his crutches and put his other arm around her. "We need to talk," he whispered.

Melinda started clapping and jumping up and down. "You'll get all better faster now, Jake. I know you will."

As Madison stepped away, Jake grabbed her hand. "You are a good nurse, Miss Melinda. Thank you." He squeezed the hand that was trembling in his.

Madison freed her hand and picked up Melinda. "I was looking for Mom and Dad when this one spotted you and ran away without asking."

Jake's eyes sought hers. "Your folks are with ours. Don't be upset with Melinda."

"We'd better get home." And they were gone as quickly as they had appeared.

Jake helped Josie finish washing the cars, but offered no further conversation.

Josie broke the silence. "I envy you, Jake." She was cleaning the windows. "I don't think she'll run out on you ... even when she hears the truth. I wonder if I'll ever find someone to love me like that."

He grabbed both crutches. "No time like the present to find out. I'm going to call her. Wish me luck."

Molly answered the phone. "It's for you, Madison. Sounds like Jake."

Madison agreed to meet him at the arbor in thirty minutes. Jake was already seated on the far left side of the swing when she arrived. She motioned for him to scoot to the other end. He questioned but she insisted. She settled in his previous spot and patted the swing. "Put your leg on the swing."

He looked at the swing and her lap. She knew well where his foot would be resting. He hesitated. "Come on, Jake. You need to elevate that ankle."

He looked at her and slowly lifted his leg until it rested on the swing with his foot nestled in her lap. She patted his bandage. "You have to take care of this injury if you expect it to heal."

"There hasn't been time for that today."

"What's going on?" Even through the bandage her touch stirred his heart and warmth flowed through his body.

"Saturday I foolishly walked out of your life, Madison, and today I'm afraid you'll walk out of mine."

She gently massaged his foot without hurting his ankle. "Try me, Jake."

"Josie's luncheon with you and the other Diamond women unearthed years of family secrets."

He related the events of the day in the same sequence they were brought to light. Thankfully he had stuffed his pockets with tissues anticipating her tears. She was a mess and he had only shared about Josie's rape.

"Oh, Jake! The rape had to be devastating, but living with a secret like that for four years is unimaginable to me."

Her tears never let up. "How is she? How are your folks?"

"Hopefully Josie can now get the help she needs. It's been a nightmare for Mom and Dad. It's still impacting me. But there's more to the story, Madison." And with that he shared about George's abuse of both of them.

The girl was not doing well. He wanted to hold her in his arms, but doubted that would ever happen again after what she had just learned about his disgusting past. She looked at him and tried to speak, but couldn't.

She gently lifted his foot, scooted off the swing and walked away without saying a word. Her back was to him and all he could hear were her sniffles. After ten minutes or more she slowly turned and closed the gap between them.

"Would you mind lowering your leg for a few minutes, Jake?"

When he responded she sat down, lifted his left arm and scooted close enough to wrap her arms around him. As he encircled her in his arms, they wept together for his and Josie's losses ... and theirs. His grief was weighty. Her comfort gave him hope.

As a calmness began to settle over them, Madison spoke up. "Jake, what happened to you and Josie is tragic. The years of silence without help and the resulting lifestyles that followed not only add to the pain, but make change more challenging.

"Mom is living proof it doesn't have to control your life or ruin your future. With God nothing is impossible. He sees your heart and hears your spoken and unspoken cries for help. He's willing to be there for you."

She knelt in front of him. "And so am I ... as long as you are willing to be open to Him and quit your womanizing."

"You mean that?"

"I do. God's love is the catalyst for change, Jake, and it seems my assignment is to love you like He loves me until you learn that fact for yourself."

He marveled at this unconventional girl and her God. "Why would God want you to love someone like me, Madison?"

"Because He is crazy about you, Jake."

He fingered the braid that was hanging down her back. "Until you, all my relationships were superficial and only involved physical gratification. That's all I've known and I'm scared. I haven't the foggiest idea how to change."

"Jake, what if God is the change agent you need and with the change comes a new identity?"

"Sounds like a fairy tale, Madison."

She scooted to the other end of the swing so she could see his face. "It's better than that, Jake. It can become your reality."

"If I thought that was possible, I'd sign up today. I'm open, Madison, but I just don't get this God stuff."

"That's okay, Jake. You've admitted your need. Will you promise to be open to the possibility that God is real and cares about you and your needs?"

"I promise."

She reached for both his hands. "That's all I can ask."

"I love you, Madison Diamond."

"And I love you, but until your life matches your changed mindset, we can only be friends."

"Does that mean you'll be dating other men?"

"Now why would I date someone else if I'm in love with you?"

Jealously reared its head. "Well, you did today."

A look of surprise manifested. "Oh … you're referring to Grayson and Jonathan. Grayson is interested in Maria. She's not sure about him yet, so she keeps me close when he comes around."

"That explains the one. Who is the other one interested in?"

"I gave him no encouragement, Jake."

"Glad to hear that. I'd appreciate it if you kept a little more distance between you and him next time. And if you don't mind, avoid the pool when he's around and I'd prefer you don't go to the movies with him again."

She chuckled and hugged him. "As I recall, you had walked out of my life at the time. I didn't think you'd care. Do I detect a smidgeon of jealousy?"

"Nope. There's nothing small about it. It's super-sized."

She hooted. "I was struggling with the thought of you dating someone else too. Will you do something for me?"

"What? Go to church? Talk to a preacher? Confess to some priest? That's blackmail, you know."

"No, actually, I was going to ask you to read the gospel of John a couple of times and tell me what you think."

"Sorry to disappoint you, but I don't own a Bible. The only one I've ever seen in our house is on Mom's night stand."

"Don't go away." And with that order, she sprinted across the lawn and dashed into her house. In a few minutes she was back with a small pink book. "This is a New Testament with Psalms and Proverbs that Mom and Dad gave me when I graduated from high school."

She opened it to the gospel of John. "Jake, when you can't sleep at night or when the torment or guilt gets more than you can stand or temptation drives you to distraction, reach for this with an open heart and mind. Give God a chance. Okay?"

He reached for the book … and her. "Come here." He pulled her onto the swing. "For you … I promise that any night I can't sleep … whatever the reason … that I'll read out of this pink, girly book of yours. If God is real and if Jesus is who you say He is, I need to know."

Her countenance was glowing as she leaned close and lightly kissed his cheek. "I can't wait until you find out how much God loves you."

Holding her in a loose embrace, he whispered. "If God loves me enough to send you as His messenger, then I'm going to like Him."

"Yes, you are. His is the love you have been searching for. His is the intimacy you have craved. You've been trying to satisfy spiritual needs with physical pleasures and that is the breeding ground for addictions.

"Forgiveness for your past, healing of wounds inflicted by others and freedom from the fallout are all possible, Jake." She pointed to the pink book. "It's all in there."

He grasped her wrist as she began to move away. "Maddie, your love gives me hope."

Pulling her hand free, she placed both of hers on his chest. "That's not just my love, Jake. I'm the conduit from Him to you. God wants to make a direct connection, so you can get the full benefit. Read His book."

He whispered in her ear. "For you. For us. I promise."

She helped him off the swing. "Today, we're doing something different. I'm walking you home."

They talked as they sauntered toward his house. When she turned to leave, Jake used his crutch to block her way. "I thought you were the problem in our relationship until today. Right now I loathe myself and have no idea why you are even giving me a chance."

"Jake, this *in the beginning God* specializes in new beginnings. He's got one tailored for you." She tiptoed and kissed him on the cheek and followed the footpath back home.

He watched until she disappeared.

A new beginning? Is it possible?

Thirteen

Jake was aware of a stirring inside. Was it his shame? His love for Madison? Or was it more? He flopped in the nearest chair in the family room, dropped his crutches to the floor and ran his fingers over the cover of Madison's pink book. Engraved on the leather cover were the words, *Loved and Treasured*. On the inside cover was a note from her mom and dad confirming that statement.

As he flipped through the pages, a verse that Madison had underlined caught his eye. *The thief comes only to steal and kill and destroy; I have come that they may have life, and have it to the full. I am the good shepherd. The good shepherd lays down his life for the sheep.*

As he closed the book, he turned his eyes and heart heavenward. *I'm familiar with the stealing and destroying ways. I need to know about the full-life stuff.* He lingered a while ... listening and pondering. All was quiet.

He lugged his body up the stairs and crashed on his bed. The next sound he heard was his mom's voice alerting him and Josie that breakfast and a family conference would occur in thirty minutes. After showering and shaving, he lumbered down the stairs.

Josie caught up with him on the landing. "How did you sleep?"

"I passed out the first half of the night and wrestled with demons the second half. How about you?"

"Add Junior's digestive disturbances and we could be soul mates."

After eating and talking about all that had transpired, William looked at Josie. "Now, is there anything else your mom and I need to know?"

"I take it you are referring to the fact that I'm pregnant again?"

"How far along are you?" There was only compassion in Virginia's tone and words.

"I haven't had a period since my first abortion. That's not a good sign and already the nausea and vomiting have started."

William patted her hand. "Is this why you left Nick?"

She nodded. "He wants nothing to do with the baby, and I'm determined not to rush into another abortion. I've already ruled out keeping it. That left me with an abortion until Thelma offered to adopt the baby."

"They would take another one?" William questioned audibly.

Jake didn't want her pushed into anything this time. "She has a couple of months before school starts to decide."

The men agreed the decision was hers. Virginia offered no advice though she kept wiping stray tears.

Moving to the next subject of discussion, William announced that a Dr. Metcalf had been recommended as a counselor, and appointments had been made for both of them.

"I've hired a private investigator to located Felix and George. He will report regularly on his findings," he added.

He turned his attention to Virginia. "Your mom has convinced me that we need a complete renovation of the sunroom, and the expert designer next door has graciously agreed to help. Josie, I'd like for you to help your mother with this project rather than go back to your usual summer job at the office."

"Dad, sometimes you surprise me. I'd like that."

And she did. As the project progressed, Josie peppered Thelma with thoughts and questions involving interior design every step of the way.

Nobody tried to persuade Josie one way or the other about the life inside. Thelma did alert her that the father's consent was needed if she opted for adoption. With that in mind she dialed Nick's number. His oldest sister answered.

"Would you have Nick call me when it's convenient, Bella?"

"He's right here, Josie."

Nick was kind, but cool. She asked how he felt about adoption and would he be willing to sign away his parental rights.

"Josie, if that is your decision, I will. But why would you go to all that trouble so someone else could have a baby?"

"I know it sounds crazy, Nick, but getting to know the two adopted girls next door makes me wonder if abortion is fair to the life inside me."

She heard his sigh. "I'll call if you need to sign."

"Take care, Josie."

The next sound she heard was a dial tone.

The days and weeks passed and Josie wasn't any closer to a decision than the first day she knew for sure she was pregnant. No doctor had been contacted. The Diamonds' offer to adopt was tempting, but carrying a baby would interfere with her schooling and shut down her love life—unless there was a stray, young Henry in her future.

Exposing the truth had not eliminated the addiction. The old urges were strong, and she was struggling with Dr. Metcalf. Jake was struggling with his addiction but not the good doctor. They were driving home after a double session.

"Doc is on target, Josie. Every session he deals with some aspect that helps me understand what happened and how it has impacted my life and will continue to do so unless I deal with it honestly."

"Yeah, I was shocked that, like me, many people have been abused by more than one person. It's as if we wear invisible targets that predators can detect."

Jake added, "The session that flipped a major switch for me was the one dealing with the magnitude of abuse. Not only were our bodies violated, Josie, but also our minds, emotions and wills. Unlike some crimes—and I struggled with that label at first—it is a crime against the whole person."

Josie was chewing on a hangnail. "I know. I've never had any trouble identifying the rapists as criminals, but until talking with Dr. Metcalf, I struggled with attaching that word to Uncle George. Learning that we tend to excuse or minimize the behavior if the abuser is a relative or trusted friend helped me see him in a whole new light."

Jake braked as a squirrel scampered across the highway. "What about the sense of shame involved even though we were innocent at the time? You've lived with it for years, Sis, but when that freight train pulling fourteen years of shame and guilt hit me a few weeks ago, I was crushed into a million pieces and I don't know how to put *Humpty Dumpty* back together again. I can't imagine what it's like for you."

"It's all so crazy, Jake. When Granny ignored my cries for help and George kept coming, I took on the blame for what he was doing. I hear Doc's words that I was an innocent child, but somehow the continual abuse convinced me otherwise. Since then I've taken on the identity of my abuse. Innocence is only a word to me. I have no concept of its meaning."

Jake turned on the windshield wipers as a light rain began to blur his vision. "You know what I've been wondering? At what point did our innocence end, and we became responsible for our choices and actions?"

"I don't know the answer to that question, but I do know that the sexual drive was aroused and now I can't control it. So what do I do? I make sure that I'm the one in control in all my relationships. I use men like George used me—to satisfy an addiction. That is sick and I know it, but I'm powerless to do anything about it."

Josie looked out the window at the blue haze that hung over the distant mountains. "I know now that's why I was so drawn to David. By his example he showed me what love between a man and woman should look like. Sex wasn't the ruling ingredient. Love and respect were and I was desperate to know what that would feel like. So I pursued him the only way I knew how. I enticed him."

He slowed down as they ran into a heavy downpour. "When I think of all the girls I've used, I hate myself. I wonder how many of them have been abused and are like us, looking for love in all the wrong places."

Josie shifted in her seat. "You know what else? I think sweet Nicolas felt sorry for me. I'm sure he would have taken me in even if I hadn't offered him my body, but that was the only way I knew to relate to a man. So even that relationship was tarnished."

She looked at her brother. "Jake, I hear what Dr. Metcalf is saying, but my body is protesting. I'm not convinced I will ever be free from my past."

"Josie, I'm still struggling with the physical desires too, but at least I understand why. Abuse taught us that sex was a physical means of satisfying a physical desire without any emotional or relational connections or commitments. That's why we've never had a meaningful relationship.

"We didn't become abusers like George and Felix, Josie. Instead, we became users. Ever notice there's only two letters difference in those two words? We don't violate wills, but sex is all about us. You say yours is about control, and that's an ironic delusion. You aren't in control of anything or anyone, least of all yourself. Mine has always been about satisfying an addiction. Both are sick reasons.

"Part of our challenge is to not only change our view and understanding of who we are, but what sex is and is not. We are too warped to accomplish that on our own."

Josie didn't respond.

"We can't give up, Sis. Look at Thelma."

Fourteen

The Roberts siblings were faced with some difficult challenges the rest of the summer. Their folks were doing all they could to help, but much of the outcome was dependent on their attitude and belief that what they were doing was worthwhile and right.

September summoned both of them back to campus and school life. Josie knew her days of abstinence were over the first day back. Her last remnant of resistance disappeared when she walked into her External Auditing class. The eye-catching, thirtyish professor had every female's heart rate doubled before he opened his mouth. Dr. Ted Jenson would be her next and possibly most challenging conquest.

To her delight, the interest was mutual. He baited and fished. She teased and nibbled. By the third week, the games were over and she was involved in the most passionate affair ever. Since he was faculty, their trysts were very secretive. And Josie wasn't confessing anything back home either.

As she was exiting his apartment the 5th of October, Ted stopped her at the door. "Josie, are you pregnant?"

She wasn't showing yet, but there were other indications. "As a matter of fact, I am, Ted. Four months and counting. Does it bother you?"

His countenance clouded. After spewing out some less than polite words, he seized her arm with one hand and her chin with the other. "Of course, it bothers me. You make love to me while carrying another man's child! What kind of woman are you?"

Josie smiled, pulled her arm free and continued walking towards the door. "Obviously, the kind men like you find interesting."

Ted moved between her and the door. "I find you more than interesting. You appeal to me as no other woman has, but this changes everything. Unless you have an abortion, don't come back."

Being around Melinda and Maria had convinced Josie there was a small person forming inside her body. She had already discarded one. Could she do it again?

One look at Ted and she knew her answer. "Don't worry, Honey. I'll take care of our little problem before the week is out. See you in class." And Josie glided out the door.

As she walked into the abortion clinic two days later, she could not stop the questions that were begging for answers. But being pregnant was a nuisance and she didn't need a little person next door who reminded her of Nicolas. Besides, she was enjoying Ted too much to let a pregnancy come between them.

Unlike his sibling, Jake had been diligently working with Dr. Metcalf. Three months of learning to live with a different mindset and identifying the lies that had accompanied the abuse had not been easy.

Madison's little pink book had been his companion many sleepless, tormented nights. Late calls to her and Henry had kept him from making a different kind of call on more than one occasion.

It was Friday, October 8, and Jake was impatiently waiting for his girl to get home.

The sound of Madison's car pulling in the driveway caused him to bid the determined box turtle he had been tracking *adieu*. *Remember, little friend, the race isn't to the fastest but the one who doesn't give up.*

He waved to get Madison's attention. "Hey, come swing with me before you head in."

After laying her books on the hood of the car, she joined him. The October air was brisk, the sun was warm and the foliage was radiant with the vibrant colors of autumn.

Madison spun around taking in the scene before them. "A friend suggested that I needed to enjoy life more. I think this may be what he had in mind."

Jake stopped the swing. "He? This wouldn't be a young, single doctor, would it?"

"Yeah, but being near him doesn't stir one butterfly. You, on the other hand, stir up a dozen colonies."

He pulled her beside him. "Guess what, my Butterfly Lady. Dr. Metcalf agreed we have earned our first night on the town."

She jumped up and twirled around. "Our first real date? Where are we going and what shall I wear?"

"Dress up, Sweetheart. I'm going to show you off." He reached for a hand and pulled her back on the swing. "I have other news. My tests continue to be negative."

A lone tear rolled down her cheek. She wrinkled her nose and playfully pushed him away. "I hate to leave you, but I have a date with this dreamy guy I've had a crush on for over four months. I need a beauty treatment or two."

He watched as she gathered her books and ran into her house. *How in this big, mad world did I end up with a girl like that?*

The vision that entered the Diamond's great room three hours later robbed him of what little intellect he possessed in her presence. He took a deep breath and let out a low whistle. Her hair, her eyes, her smile and all her feminine charms were showcased by a fashionable, sleeveless, V-neck, A-line, knee length, teal dress made out of some kind of soft, flowing cloth that begged to be touched. A single strand of pearls and matching earrings were perfect accents.

His reaction embarrassed her. "Am I overdressed, Jake? I can change."

Her blush and those long, curved lashes that swept over downturned eyes made her twice as appealing. He touched a hand and signaled for her to turn around. "Not a chance. Now I know what *dressed to the nines* means."

As if on cue, *Just the Way You Look Tonight* began to stream through the intercom.

Jake took Madison in his arms and danced and sang as if the words of the song were written for them.

Melinda heard Jake's voice and raced into the room. "Dance with *me*, Jake. Dance with *me*."

He released Madison and gathered the youngest Diamond in his arms and whirled her around the room.

"I like you, Jake. Do you like me?" asked the dark-eyed cutie.

He put her down and knelt in front of her. "Melinda, you are one of my favorite girls in the whole world."

Inquisitive eyes shifted from Jake to his date as a little finger pointed at Madison. "You like her too?"

"Yes, Sweetie, I like her too. Is that okay?"

"Uh-huh." Satisfied, she ran back to play with Henry who was sporting a telling smile.

"So what do you think of my number one princess tonight?"

Jake glanced between Madison and her dad. "Sir, I've waited months for a date with your daughter, and she shows up looking like …"

He opened his hands toward the object of the conversation. "*A princess.*"

Henry chuckled. "You two have a good time."

"Yes, Sir."

Jake helped Madison with her matching jacket and escorted her out the door.

Once they were out of sight of the family, Madison stepped away and began impishly circling him. "Hmm. Gray slacks, a soft blue turtleneck that matches your heart-stopping eyes and navy blazer never had this impact on me before. It has to be the man."

Jake sobered. "Lady, your butterflies are small creatures compared to the herd of wild buffalo you set loose in me. Unless you are prepared to elope tonight, you need to back off talk like that."

He tucked her hand in his arm as they walked to his car. "I'm game, in case you've wondered."

She hesitated when he opened her door. "Not yet, Jake."

"I'm making you aware of my intentions."

He helped her in the car and then slid in the driver's seat. During the ride, Jake confessed that he was struggling with his career path. "Have you always known you would be in the medical profession?"

"I've never wanted to do anything else. As challenging as the work is, Jake, I love what I do."

He pulled under the canopy, handed his keys to the valet and escorted his girl into the classy restaurant. While Jake was signing in, someone bumped his shoulder. "Where did you find that jewel, Jake?" asked one of his former basketball coaches.

Jake glanced at the woman being discussed. "She claims her family moved here from Kentucky, but I'm suspicious Heaven is closer to the truth."

The coach slapped him on the shoulder. "Don't tell me the love bug has finally sunk its teeth into Jake Roberts. Wait till I tell the others."

"Yeah, I thought I was immune, but that one proved I was wrong!"

Jake felt like a millionaire as he escorted Madison to their table. The woman was a tonic for his weary soul and evidence of God's love.

He admired her while she reviewed every item on the menu. "So what have you decided?"

She closed her menu. "Order for me, Jake, or I'm going to shut my eyes and choose."

He laughed. "That could get interesting."

He ordered the appetizer sampler followed by the house salad. At that point, Madison declared that was all she needed. Jake overruled and ordered the eight ounce serving of roast prime rib of beef for her while helping himself to the twelve ounce portion. He rounded out the meal with asparagus hollandaise and creamed corn with Applewood bacon.

"Next time, I'm just going to close my eyes and point," Madison teased.

They ate leisurely and talked much. Madison finished long before Jake folded his napkin. "Jake, are you famished?"

After savoring the bite in his mouth, Jake confessed. "I've missed more than one meal the last few months. Think my appetite has returned."

The next time the waiter stopped by, Jake ordered a sampler plate of their chocolate desserts and a glass of their best dessert wine.

As the luscious array of chocolates was placed between them, Madison's eyes lit up. Jake tempted her with a bite. "I believe chocolate is on your favorite list."

"You remembered." She picked up the fork provided and sampled every treat on the plate.

Jake was enjoying the dessert and the wine, but it was the woman at his table that filled his heart. She caught him admiring her.

"This was wonderful, Jake. Thank you. C–could we …" She trailed off.

"What's on your mind, Madison?"

"We've talked about everything except us."

He motioned for the bill. "I agree. After the symphony, we'll find a private place and catch up."

"Jake, I know we've spent time together the last four months, but this is our first date. There's so much going on in my head and heart. Would you mind if we skip the symphony tonight?"

"Are you sure?"

She nodded.

"Your house or mine?"

She giggled and wrinkled her cute nose. "Well, let's see. A house of four or a house of ten?"

"We can decide on the way," he suggested as he offered his arm.

As he was helping her into the car, Madison's eyes lit up. "Wait a minute. I know the perfect place. Mom's latest project has just been completed."

Most of the younger ones were in their rooms by the time they arrived. They chatted with her parents for a few minutes before Madison put in her request. "Would you two mind if we use the east sun parlor for a while?"

Henry's smile conveyed hearty approval. "That's a great idea."

Madison led Jake to the newly renovated, over-sized, sun parlor on the east end of their home. She eased into one of the chairs and waited for his response.

"What is this?" he asked, as he did a three-hundred-and-sixty-degree turn.

"It's Dad's answer to Mom's request for a prayer chapel and the family's need for a music room."

Thelma had converted this sunny space into the most unusual room Jake had ever seen. Twelve, soft, comfortable, high-backed, arm chairs were arranged in a circle. In the middle of that circle was another circle of padded kneeling benches. Inside the second circle was a rustic six foot cross with the same message burned into both sides of the horizontal beam. *I will always love you.*

In all four corners behind the seating were collections of various musical instruments, including a set of drums in one corner and a keyboard in another. Guitars, a cello, xylophone, violin, flute and saxophone filled in all the empty spaces.

Jake gently brushed a hand over the words on the cross. Slowly he faced her. "Maddie, Uncle George told me that he was teaching me about love. What a lie that was! He introduced me to the world's substitute for the real thing ... perverted love and lust. God sent David and you to show me the difference."

Madison patted the seat beside her. He joined her and laced their fingers together.

"Doc says I'm making good process. Your dad has been patiently answering my questions about the Bible."

Madison's face exploded with delight. "You and Dad have been talking?"

"Yes. When the urge to call a girl hit, I usually called you. But sometimes, I was so ashamed that I called your Dad. Your mom has talked to me a couple of times too. And when sleep avoided me, I'd read your little pink book like I promised. Henry told me to write down verses that spoke to me and questions that other passages provoked. We've been meeting weekly for months."

A stray tear broke out only to be followed by other escapees. "And all this time I thought you two were sharpening your chess game. So what is going on?"

He kissed her hand and then wiped the tears that were melting his stubborn will. "Your dad is a chess whiz, but he's a better listener and mentor.

"Something is definitely stirring, Madison. Henry says God's Spirit is hovering over the dark and desolate places inside me ... kind of like He did in Genesis.

"Right now, it's the claims of Jesus that I'm struggling with. I've always thought He was just another good man ... like Gandhi. Your dad has debunked that theory. The truth is either Jesus was who He said He was or He was the biggest fraud and liar that ever lived. I'm seeking truth, Madison."

He was holding her hands and searching her heart. "My question is ... where does that put us? I'm open and waiting, Madison, and I've not been with anyone since I met you. That's all I know to do. I'd like to put a ring on your finger in the near future and start making plans to get married as soon as you graduate. What do you say?"

Jake reached for a tissue from one of the conveniently placed boxes and wiped her tears.

"Jake, I want to say yes, but ..."

He placed a finger over her lips. "I need you to say *yes*, Madison."

He moved to his knees. "You once asked if I trusted you. Now I'm asking you the same question. Do you trust me? I know my track record is horrific, but I've had a definite attitude and mind change as far as love and intimacy are concerned. Marry me, Maddie."

She slipped out of his reach and fell on her knees on the closest kneeling bench. No words were spoken but the evidence of tears was abundant.

Jake had never bowed a knee to any deity. He looked at the cross. *I will always love you.* He knew her tears and prayers were for him. Slowly he lowered his tall frame until his knees touched the bench next to hers.

How does one pray? With his eyes glued to the words burned into the empty cross, he awkwardly took a leap of faith. "God, if You are who Maddie and her dad say You are, I could use Your help. If Jesus is who He claimed to be ... if He did die for my sins ... I need to know.

"I've done plenty of things I'm not proud of. I'm been left with habits and thoughts that torment at times. It's getting better but Henry says I can be healed from the damage of my past and freed from the addiction. It would be real good news to find out that what he's saying is true and the Bible is the story of Your love for me.

"So in case I've been wrong ... here I am ... mess and all."

Madison raised her head and stared at the man whose eyes were still glued to the cross.

"Yes," she whispered.

His face moved toward the sound. Hope questioned. "Yes? As in m-m-marrying me?"

She nodded and lunged at him so clumsily that they tumbled off the kneeling benches onto the carpet. Their bodies were too close and the temptation too great to linger. He helped her up. "God is alive and well and this strange room has become my favorite place in this miniature-Biltmore—maybe the world."

Jake touched his lips to hers and her response was more than he could handle.

He backed away. "Those kisses are off limits until our wedding night. Dr. Metcalf and your dad have helped me work through much. When I explained my desire to be with you, they smiled and said that was natural, not evil or dirty. But I don't trust myself yet."

He sat in the closest chair and his eyes clouded with moisture. "I don't know how to say what needs to be said at this point, but I have to try."

A pained expression shadowed his face. "If you had said no I would have been devastated, but I would have understood."

He planted his elbows on his knees and stared at the floor. "Dealing with the pain and shame of my past has plowed up disgusting and repugnant garbage inside me. At times, I wasn't sure there was any hope. If not for you, your little pink book, your dad and Dr. Metcalf, I would have given up."

As he looked up, Madison reached for a tissue and wiped his tears. "Maddie, the fact that you know my past and agreed to marry me ..." He couldn't finish.

Madison gently rubbed his back. "Jake, I've spent hours talking with Mom and Dad about you and us. Your past was as big a snag as your lack of faith. With tears, my mom often referred me to the story in Luke 7 of the town harlot who washed Jesus' feet with her tears and dried them with her hair. The costly perfume she used to anoint Him was probably earned by selling her body.

"The host condemned her and judged Jesus for allowing such an action, Jesus silenced him with a story about the size of debts forgiven and ended with mom's favorite verse in the Bible. *I tell you, her many sins have been forgiven—for she loved much. But he who has been forgiven little loves little.*"

Madison was now weeping. "Jesus told the woman, *your sins are forgiven ... your faith has saved you. Go in peace.*" She touched his chin. "Look at me, Jake."

He lifted his head as tear-filled eyes met hers.

Jake and Josie's Discovery

"God has forgiven you ... and so have I. You don't ever have to bring up your past again ... to Him or me. Live in the peace that kind of grace and love offers."

He swallowed her up in his big arms and they wept as the grace and love of God washed over him ... and them. Unaware of time, they soaked quietly and humbly in the Presence of their *in the beginning God*.

Jake brushed wet hair off her face and wiped the moisture from her cheeks. "I treasure you, Maddie."

His light kiss was almost reverent. "It's getting late and you need to get some sleep."

He looked around the room. "Do you think ...? No, it's too much to ask. I need to get home myself."

"What is too much, Jake?"

"It probably sounds crazy to you, but I was wondering if your folks would object to my sleeping here tonight."

Madison was glowing. "I'll go get a pallet, blanket and pillow. Dad will be pleased." She kissed him and hurried away. By the time he picked a spot, she had returned with all he needed. "There's a bathroom two doors back on the left. I'll leave the light on." As she walked out of the room, she whispered, "God and I will always love you, Jake Roberts."

At this moment he couldn't find words that came close to describing all that was lighting up in his head or awakening in his heart. He made his way back to the kneeling bench. *God, we connected tonight, but I have no idea what happened. So I'm going to read Your book ... and then just listen.*

He fell asleep ... listening.

A gentle rain splashing against the windows woke Jake the next morning. As his eyes adjusted to the light, he noticed Henry's form in one of the chairs. When he stirred, Henry looked his way.

"Good morning, Son. Madison told me I'd find you here. What's going on?"

Jake stretched and hauled himself out of his makeshift bed. "Something happened in here last night, Mr. Diamond. I can't tell you what it was, except it was a God connection. So much is going on inside my head and heart and I can't explain that either. But I know one thing. Unless I dreamed it, your daughter has agreed to become my wife."

Henry turned to watch the rain that was washing the outside world. "I wasn't aware that you planned to ask her so soon."

A look of panic darkened Jake's face. "I hope you don't disapprove, Sir."

Henry quickly dispelled his fear. "No. I'm just marveling at how quickly your mind and heart are changing. Do you have time to talk this morning or do we need to wait until our appointment?"

"It's Saturday morning. I can spare a couple of hours."

Henry handed Jake one of the Bibles and together they spent the morning contemplating the discussion between Jesus and Nicodemus regarding a new birth—a new beginning as related in the third chapter of the gospel of John.

"Much as the Spirit in response to God's Word brought forth a new physical creation, so the same life-giving Spirit brings forth a new spiritual creation in receptive hearts," Henry explained.

It was another wonderful Genesis morning!

When Jake ran into Madison two hours later, he not only knew there was a God who loved him, he now knew that Jesus was the Christ who came to earth to make all things new… and that included him.

A spiritual rebirth. A new beginning. He now understood that things of God cannot be comprehended until or unless the heart of man bows to the possibility that he is wrong and God is right. In that amazingly simple, yet powerful act of humility, the God of the universe weaves His way into a heart and life. Regardless of the situation or the status in life, God still comes to the open, welcoming, repenting heart.

His next step was baptism and Henry was arranging that.

When he shared that news with Madison, she squealed and leaped into his arms. Her delight warmed his heart and her tears soaked his shirt.

"Oh, Jake, I knew the doors were opened last night, but I didn't dream understanding would follow so quickly."

He pulled an index card out of his pocket. "Listen to the prayer from Psalm 25 that your dad gave me. *Show me your ways, O LORD, teach me your paths; guide me in your truth and teach me, for you are God my Savior, and my hope is in you all day long. Remember, O LORD, your great mercy and love, for they are from of old. Remember not the sins of my youth and my rebellious ways; according to your love remember me, for you are good, O LORD."*

His face lit up as he pulled out another card. "Then he gave me this from Psalm 103. *He does not treat us as our sins deserve or repay us according to our iniquities. For as high as the heavens are above the earth, so great is his love for those who fear him; as far as the east is from the west, so far has he removed our transgressions from us."*

"Kipling was right about the east and west never meeting, but the impossible can and did happen. I really am new on the inside."

He showed her a third card. "Look at these verses that confirm my new identity. I'm going to put them on my bathroom mirror so I will see them every morning and every evening. I want God's truth to become my reality."

All Madison could do was nod and reach for more tissues.

"When I expressed my doubt of being able to live the life, he handed me the fourth card. Philippians 4:13 *"I can do all things through Christ who strengthens me."*

They clung to each other ... and the promises of God.

Fifteen

Jake's goal was to get in and out of his house before anyone questioned his absence last night. The garage door was open and his dad's vehicle was missing. One down, two to go.

He managed to shower and get dressed without rousing the other two. With his book bag in hand, he quietly tiptoed out his door. Breakfast on campus would have to do.

As his foot hit the bottom step, Josie's voice stopped him in his tracks. "Not so fast, Lover Boy! Mom and Dad thought you were snug in your room last night. I, on the other hand, was aware that although your car was in the garage, you never entered this house. I cannot believe you scored with Madison."

"Look, Josie. It's not what you think, okay? Nothing happened and I have hours of research waiting for me at the library, so if you would take a rain check on this conversation, I'd appreciate it."

She tucked her arm through his and tugged him towards the kitchen. "Hey, you need breakfast. I'll cook. You talk."

"Sis, I don't have time. Let's make a date to spend tomorrow afternoon together and I'll answer all questions."

"Hey, you don't have to be so defensive about breaking the no-sex-for-now guidelines. I did that weeks ago. Promise you'll come clean and I'll tell you about my latest interest. I already know who yours is."

Jake was visibly shaken. "Who is it this time?"

She punched his shoulder. "Don't be so self-righteous, Jake. Exposing George and Felix didn't change who we are. I still need a man in my life, just like you need a woman. His name is Ted Jenson. He's my auditing professor."

Concern was added to his surprise. "You are fooling around with your professor? He can get fired. How old is he? Is he married?"

"Hold your horses! We are being careful. He's mature, not old, and he's not the marrying kind any more than we are."

She began gathering ingredients to make omelets. "Hey, want yours with meat or veggies or both?"

Jake sighed and set his books aside. "Both, please."

He set the table and poured the juice. "Tell me about you and Ted. Does he know about your pregnancy?"

Moving a hand to her abdomen, she told of her abortion. "Nick didn't want it, the Diamonds didn't need it and Ted wasn't interested in a pregnant woman. Three strikes and no more baby. Ted wants me back when I've healed."

She dished the omelets on their plates and sat down to eat. Snatching her napkin, she looked at him with a playful smile. "Now tell me the juicy details about you and the girl next door."

"Absolutely nothing happened between Madison and me last night, except I asked her to marry me and she said yes."

She slapped the bar and laughed. "Yeah, and I stopped by St. Rose and talked to the priest about becoming a nun."

"I'm not joking, Josie." He pushed his plate to the side.

"You married? Maybe when the hot place below freezes over."

He grabbed her hand and headed for the door.

"Hey, where are you taking me? What about breakfast?"

"Next door. Close your mouth. All the bugs will think you are inviting them in."

Thelma and Melinda responded to the doorbell. The little one leaped into Jake's arms. "Are you going to spend the night with us again, Jake?"

He hugged her. "Probably not, Melinda. Last night was very special."

He looked at Thelma. "Sorry to bother you, but would you mind showing Josie where I spent the night? The library is calling my name or I'd stay and enjoy this myself."

Thelma smiled as she caught the drift of Jake's intent. "You go on. I'll show her around and see if she's interested."

She reached for Melinda. "Come on, Sweetie. Let's show Josie our latest remodeling job."

The trio made their way to the converted sun parlor. As they approached, Thelma stepped aside and indicated Josie should go first.

Josie stopped at the door and stared at the strange setup. The place had Thelma's knack and talent throughout, but this space was troubling.

The walls were covered with famous paintings and tapestries of Bible scenes which gave it the appeal of an art gallery. The corners were set up for jam sessions. That was actually pretty cool. But two sets of circles surrounding a cross? That had the feel of a small cathedral or church. In a house?

She moved past the chairs to the wooden stands and picked up one of the books. It was a Bible. She starting flipping and stopped at Genesis 1:1. *In the beginning God created the heavens and the earth ...*

Something flickered inside. Those words were talking about David and Callie's God. She slowly turned to Thelma hoping there was a sensible answer to this strange room.

"Your brother slept on a pallet along the south wall last night ... alone."

Josie's eyes filled with unbelief. "My brother spent the night in here? Alone? On the floor? Was he drunk?"

Thelma chuckled. "Not with the wine of this world."

Alarm engulfed Josie's face. "You'll need to excuse me. I have to get back to the house."

As Josie neared Thelma, the discerning lady placed a hand on her arm. "When did you have the abortion?" Tears were gathering in her eyes.

"How did you know?"

"I'm not sure." Thelma moved to the xylophone where Melinda was laboriously trying to pick out the melody of *Jesus Loves Me*.

"How are you doing, Josie?"

"Me? Great!" She had to get out of there. This little powwow had given her the heebie jeebies.

In her hasty departure, she crashed into Donald. "Oh, hi. Sorry about that. Need to run."

Donald waited until she was gone and reached for Melinda. "Tell me Jake didn't sleep in our house last night."

"Uh huh, he did too, Donald. I saw him and Daddy talking this morning," little Miss Observant added.

Thelma walked with them to the kitchen. "She's right, Son. And while here, God showed up." She gave him a brief synopsis.

Melinda had left them for her dolls. "Do you think he's for real, Mom? Or just making a play for Madison?"

"It's real, Donald. Only God can accomplish what is happening inside Jake Roberts. He's been humble and honest in his searching. God's timing is always perfect. How awesome is it that he had his God encounter in our new family chapel!"

"He's probably going to end up being my brother-in-law, isn't he?"

She laid a hand on his arm. "Madison said yes last night."

He grabbed his book bag and headed for the door. "He'd better be good to her or he'll answer to me."

"Madison said you made that painfully clear early on."

As he walked out the door, Thelma thanked the Lord for her number two son and prayed for her number one.

Sixteen

Jake finished his research assignment early and stopped by Robbins Jewelers on the way home. A family conference was needed, but right now all he had on his mind was Madison. He had called and made arrangements to pick her up at seven o'clock. He specified casual this time.

Mandy was his greeter. "Come on in, Jake. Sis will be down shortly."

An enchanting piano melody began to echo through the house. "I'm no maestro, but that sounds like some serious music," Jake commented.

"That's Maria, our in-house, concert pianist. She is trying out the new baby grand Dad bought for her birthday."

"Mandy, I know Madison plays the guitar and sings some, but how good is she?"

She beamed. "The girl has talent. She and Maria played in the community orchestra back home. Those two were always singing and playing somewhere."

He gently knuckle tapped her shoulder. "Thanks."

Mandy smiled and rushed out as Madison walked in.

While Jake was checking his pocket for the ring, Madison softly kissed his cheek. "Either my vision is going bad or you get better looking every time I see you, Jake Roberts."

With a playful smile and taking on the stance and voice of Sylvester Stallone's *Rocky*, he responded, "Get outta here. That was my line, Babe."

"Sure it was, Rocky." she teased as she flicked her knuckles over her chest. "I've never seen you in a vest and long sleeves before. Add the jeans … and wow-zee."

His fists landed on his hips. "Wait a minute, Doll. Does that mean I gotta worry about other guys in long sleeves and vests tonight?"

She reached for her jacket and tucked her arm in his. "If they are as handsome as you, I'd say you'd better worry."

"Well, now, it's that word *handsome* that worries me most. Cause you see, Sweet Lips, I ain't never been known to be on the top of anyone's good-looks list."

She faced him. "Jake, I didn't choose a loser."

He hugged her. "That's what I love about you, Babe. You stand by your man."

He assisted her into the car and headed for Langdon's. As he pulled in the crowded parking lot, Madison commented about the quaint and inviting establishment.

Once inside it didn't take her long to realize that this was impromptu karaoke night. Her eyes lit up. "I love this place. Wait till I tell the family."

Jake's best entertainment was watching Madison. Not only was she enjoying the food, she was engrossed in the renderings of songs by the locals. She clapped, laughed and encouraged each brave soul summoned to the mike.

Near the end of their meal, Madison's name was called. She froze and then looked at Jake with questioning eyes. "Jake Roberts, you are the only person here who knows my name."

He stood up to help her out of her chair. "Not anymore."

She looked between him and the stage as the reality of the moment sank in. Folks were clapping and urging her to be a good sport. Jake leaned closed. "For me, Maddie."

She studied his face. "You set me up, didn't you?"

"Mandy spilled the beans about your musical talents. Don't you think the man you're going to marry should know such things?"

She gently pushed him away and made her way to the stage where she and the MC talked for a few moments. He disappeared and returned with a guitar which she strapped on and began tuning as he introduced her.

She eased back on a tall stool and began strumming the intro. "This song was written in the 30s by Jerome Kern with lyrics by Dorothy

Field. It was reintroduced by Frank Sinatra in the 60s. My escort offered his rendition last night." She leaned toward the mike and focused on Jake. "This is for you."

The audience whistled and applauded, but quietened quickly as the mike picked up on the talented guitarist and soloist who offered her rendition of *Just the Way You Look Tonight*. Jake sat spellbound as a voice with a haunting resemblance to Karen Carpenter's filled the place, but it was her ability to connect with the audience that blew him away. He had never seen her so relaxed and charismatic. She was better than good.

Silence reigned when the song finished, until she began to remove the guitar straps. At that moment the place erupted as folks pushed back their chairs, stood to their feet and demanded an encore. Her face went through several shades of red as she made her way back to their table. As she neared, Jake reached out and encircled her in his arms. "So can we elope tonight?"

The crowd wasn't giving up. The MC was back on stage. "How about another song, Madison?"

Jake leaned down. "Come on, Honey. I'll go with you this time."

Her head popped off his chest. "You'll sing with me?"

"And alienate this rambunctious crowd? No way." He grabbed a hand and led her back to the stage. The MC handed her the guitar while Jake moved to the microphone.

"Last night I asked this lovely lady to marry me and she said yes." That drew a round of applause from a rowdy crowd.

"Before she sings again, I have something for her."

He turned to Madison, reached for her left hand and slipped a beautiful marquise diamond ring on her finger. "Now it's official."

The crowd went wild when Jake kissed her. She blushed and began strumming a few notes of a familiar hymn as Jake walked back to his seat.

While playing the melody, she related the story of a slave trader who finally gave his heart to Jesus and later played a key role in helping abolish the slave trade in England. "This song is for everyone who understands what it's like to lose your way and stumble in the darkness."

And she reverently sang the words to John Newton's song of redemption. *Amazing grace, how sweet the sound, that saved a wretch like me. I once was lost, but now I'm found. Was blind, but now I see.*

"If you know the words, sing along." She led the patrons in the first verse again. More and more voices joined hers as she sang the last verse.

This time as she finished and stepped off the stage, a subdued applause began to echo through the place. The stage lights were turned down as a softer, quieter noise gradually filled the place.

After they finished their meal, Madison laid her left hand in her right one and admired her ring. "I will never forget this night, Jake. Thank you."

He was glad they were in a public place. "Are you interested in dessert?" When she shook her head, he motioned for their tab.

The ride home was filled with chatter and excitement. As he helped her out of the car, he gathered her in his arms. "You are not allowed to sing to me again until we are married. I wanted to ask if there was a preacher or justice of the peace in the place by the time you finished our song."

"Tonight was all your own doing, Sir."

"I know and I'm wouldn't change a thing, but I was ignorant of the impact you and music would have on me." He kissed her with the passion the night had stirred.

"Jake," she whispered, "that was a bedroom kiss and as wonderfully inviting as it was ... we agreed they are not allowed yet."

"So let's elope tomorrow."

She wiggled out of his embrace and headed for the Roberts' rear entrance. "Let's tell your family our good news."

William was the first to spot them. "It's about time you two showed up."

Virginia and Josie were perusing design magazines. Josie spoke up. "Wait until you hear your son's story, Dad. Go ahead, Jake. Tell the folks what you've been up to."

Jake led Madison to the love seat and lifted her left hand.

Josie sprang from her chair to examine his purchase. "Sheesh! You weren't joking about buying this woman a ring." Her attention shifted to Madison. "Don't be surprised if he changes his mind in a few weeks and breaks your heart."

Madison stood and hugged her skeptical, future sister-in-law. "I trust him, Josie."

Virginia got in line. "I couldn't be happier."

Jake stood and put his arms around his mom and Madison. "Thanks, Mom."

William slowly joined the circle. "You know I approve of your choice, Jake, but I am curious about last night."

Jake pulled Madison to his side in a protective manner. "It's not what you think, Dad."

When everyone was comfortably settled again, Jake reached for Madison's hand. "While it's true I slept under the same roof as Maddie last night, we did not sleep together. Truth is that I have not been intimate with a female since the day this woman moved next door."

"I told you he's gone off the deep end. Just wait until you hear the rest," Josie chimed in.

He gazed at Josie with compassion. "The traumatic revelations of our mutual abuse by Uncle George and your rape were the beginnings of radical changes in me, Sis. I've not only been seeing the counselor regularly, but I've also been talking with Henry on a weekly basis about questions I've had about God and the Bible."

Josie was hyper. "Now are you convinced?"

"Don't be so quick to judge, Josie. I find this interesting. Continue, Jake," Virginia said.

Jake squeezed Madison's hand. "Mom, have you seen the Diamond's east sun parlor lately?"

"No, but what do their renovations have to do with this?"

Madison jumped in and three pairs of Roberts' eyes reflected a gamut of emotions ... mostly disbelief ... as she described the family's newest room.

"It definitely has Thelma's touch, but she went overboard this time. A church inside a house?" the skeptic blurted out.

Jake picked up his story. "Last night, Madison and I went to the chapel so we could talk privately. For the first time in my life I bowed my knees and opened my heart to this *in-the-beginning-God* I've heard about the last five years."

He paused to look at his mom and dad. "Something happened to me during and after that prayer. When it came time to leave, I asked to stay. They graciously agreed. Henry joined me this morning for a couple of hours and the questions I've had about God were answered. I guess I'm what some folks would call a believer."

Josie was on her feet. "They have brainwashed him, Dad."

Virginia reached for her daughter's hand. "Josie, the Diamonds are not a cult. They are Christians who base their faith on a personal relationship with God, not the religion of man or a church."

Josie stared at her mom. "Have you joined the crazy club too?"

Virginia's eyes searched William's. "Josie, I was a believer long before the Diamonds moved next door."

Josie's naturally big eyes opened even wider. "You? Since when?"

"Before your dad and I married. Have you never noticed the Bible on my nightstand?"

"Yes, but I've never seen you read it or heard you talk about it."

William spoke up. "Your mother reads her Bible in the privacy of our bedroom as I have requested. She married me believing I was a man of faith. After we married, I shocked her by confessing my deception and insisting that God would not be a topic of discussion in our home and that she would not shove her beliefs on any children we would have. She has honored that request, but it looks like her silent prayers have been heard for one of our offspring."

He studied Jake for a few seconds. "You've surprised me, Son, but I respect your decision."

Virginia's tear-filled eyes were now focused on William. "Thank you."

Josie could not sit still. Her bouncing knees shook the sofa. "Has everyone in this family lost their freaking minds? Mom agrees with you and Dad respects your decision? I feel like I've just entered *the Twilight Zone*."

Suddenly her body stilled. "Wait a minute, Mom. Does this mean that you are against abortions?"

A few more tears rolled out of watery eyes. "I've grieved over the loss of our first grandchild, Josie, and I hurt for you. I've prayed you will allow the Diamonds to adopt your second baby."

Josie crossed her arms in a challenging pose. "Well, you might as well know that I've aborted grandbaby number two."

Virginia wept openly. Madison wept silently.

Unable to maintain eye contact with her grieving mom, she pivoted towards William. "Dad, do you think I've done wrong?"

"I think it's your body and your choice, Josie."

Catching Virginia's teary gaze, he offered apologetically, "Jake and Madison are your reward."

Still she wept.

William made his way to Jake. "Although I don't agree with the direction you are going theologically, I am extremely impressed with your choice of this young lady."

Jake shook his dad's hand. "Thanks. I'm probably not going to be as quiet about my faith as Mom's been."

William patted him on the back. "You are a man getting ready to start your own family. As long as you don't try to shove what you believe on me, we'll do just fine."

"Do you think we can still work together?"

"As in the insurance business?"

"Yes, Sir."

A wide grin slowly emerged. "You bet. Are you interested?"

"Yes. I've decided I enjoy insurance more than the legal field."

William put his arm around Jake's shoulders. "The timing couldn't be better. Clayton told me last week that he was going to retire at the end of the year. So I'm in the market for a new partner. Looks like one just walked in the door! Roberts and Roberts. I like the sound of that!"

"Me too. Let me get my girl home and we'll continue this conversation when I return."

As soon as they were out the door, Jake grabbed Madison's hands. "Can you believe what happened in that house tonight?"

She was wiping the stray tears that were still escaping. "It's been your mother's prayers all this time. Wonder if Mom knows."

"Knowing Thelma she probably figured that out weeks, if not months ago."

Madison put a hand on his arm. "Talk to Dad about the wisdom of being in business with an unbeliever, Jake."

"Are you concerned about Dad and me?"

"A little."

"Your dad is a wise businessman. I promise I'll talk to him."

He stopped her before she opened the door. "Maddie, I was teasing about eloping, but is there any chance that you would consider marrying before you graduate? Maybe Christmas break? I know that wouldn't give you much time, but will you at least talk with your folks and pray about it?"

"Yes ... to both those questions."

His hug lifted her feet off the ground. "What a day it has been!"

Seventeen

Madison shared Jake's marriage idea with her parents the next evening. "Dad, do you think Jake is ready for marriage?"

Henry looked at his daughter for a few seconds before answering. "Honey, Jake Roberts is probably more prepared for a healthy relationship than most men who have grown up in church.

"He has responded well to Dr. Metcalf's counsel and suggestions as well as mine. Exposing his and Josie's abuse was the pain God used to get his attention. His faith became the catalyst for pulling it all together."

He looked at his wife. "What do you think, Thelma? You can identify with Jake."

She turned to her daughter. "First of all, this is short notice and that eliminates a big wedding. Are you okay with that? Secondly, are *you* ready? I agree with your dad. Jake has been diligent and honest about the changes that needed to take place. Have you seen enough or do you need more time? More proof?"

Thelma put her arm around Henry's waist. "Your dad helped me understand early on that my identity was not based on my past, but on my relationship with God. He kept telling me who I was in Christ, because we live out of what we believe to be truth, Madison.

"Jake is learning to walk in truth, and like the rest of us, he will spent the remainder of his life doing that."

She reached for her daughter's hand. "It's your decision."

"Thanks, Mom. I'll let you know … when I know."

October 15, Madison asked Jake to meet her in the family chapel at seven o'clock in the evening. She was playing the melody of a song that had been sung at her folks' wedding. Jake walked in as she finished. "I've never heard that tune. Is it a new one?"

"Actually it's a song based on Ruth 1:16. *Don't urge me to leave you or to turn back from you. Where you go I will go, and where you stay I will stay. Your people will be my people and your God my God.*

"Listen." She began to play and sing *Whither Thou Goest.*

It took a full four lines before he caught on. His eyes filled with anticipation as he placed his hand over hers ... interrupting the song. "Maddie, are you saying yes?"

She was biting her lips to hide her smile. "I was just wondering what you're doing December 11?"

"Getting married?" The eagerness in his eyes stopped any further stalling or teasing.

"If we can find a preacher."

Jake Roberts carefully lifted the guitar strap off her shoulder and placed the instrument in its rack. He pulled Madison to her feet. "Are you sure about this?"

"I'm sure."

Jake kissed her with adoring passion. "Let's name our first daughter Grace." He clutched her hand and started jogging down the hall. "Come on, we have to tell our families."

After sharing with her folks, they followed the stepping stones that now joined the two houses.

His folks were enjoying the outdoors from the comfort and beauty of their renovated sunroom. William and Virginia were delighted and supportive.

"Maybe your news will excite your sister, Jake," William chimed in.

"Is she home?"

"Yeah, but she's hibernating again."

"Come on, Maddie. Let's go rouse the bear."

Jake knocked. No response.

"Hey, Sis! Open up. I've got some great news to share with you."

All was silent. Jake banged louder. "Come on, Josie. This is me."

He heard shuffling towards the door, but wasn't prepared for the person who greeted him. Josie was a wreck ... and smelled like a brewery. "Hi Jakey! How's my big brother? Still using women and breaking hearts? That's what men are best at, you know." Her words were slurred and her steps unsteady.

Jake turned to Madison. "Go get Mom, Hon. Warn her before she gets here." With that Jake walked into Josie's sitting area and began looking for her choice of escape.

"What's going on, Sis?"

She staggered. "Do you love me, Jakey? Every male that says that just wants my body. Is that what you told the girls you used?"

She staggered towards a half-empty bottle, but he moved faster. "Wrong solution, Sis."

Virginia had been standing in the doorway. "I'll take it from here, Jake. You and Madison have plans to make. Go!"

William and Madison were discussing the current Cavalier basketball team and their prospects for the season when Jake joined them.

"Dad, Josie is drunk."

"Drunk?" He rose from his chair. "I'd better go help your mother."

"Before you do—what would you say if I drop out of school and start working with you immediately?"

"The job is yours when you are ready, Jake."

Jake breathed a sigh of relief. "Come on, Sweetheart. Let's see how fast we can get ready for a wedding."

With a notepad in hand, they went to the kitchen nook and began making lists and plans. The more they talked, the quieter the man became.

"What's on your mind, Jake?"

"David and Callie."

He filled her in on his and Josie's history with them, including the night of the seduction that led to their broken engagement.

"Maybe you should call him."

"I'll add that to my list of things to do."

The next item was housing. "This is my biggest concern, Maddie."

"Dad offered our furnished guest suite which has an outside entrance. The decision is yours."

He hem hawed around. "I like your family, Honey, but I'm not sure I want to live in a house with nine other folks."

"Well, if nothing else works out, at least we won't be on the streets. You could talk to Dad about the privacy issue."

Jake studied the calendar. "Maddie, in nine weeks we will be married. Are you sure that gives you enough time?"

"We'll make it simple, Jake. I was a bridesmaid for a couple of my friends, and before it was over both wished they had opted for a smaller, simpler wedding. Besides, my family is so new to the area that we don't have many friends outside the church anyway. Only nine weeks of stress sounds good to me."

"Honey, I'll make it my goal to be your stress reliever."

EIGHTEEN

While Jake's life was filled with wedding plans and a new direction, unbeknownst to anyone, Josie had been keeping an eye on Ted. Those reconnaissance missions had prompted the purchase of her own stash of Jack Daniels.

Four weeks after her second abortion, she knocked on his door. Communication had been kept at a professional level the four weeks she was healing.

Ted greeted her with a big smile and a warm hug. "I've missed you, Josie."

Seeing the desire in his eyes convinced her she could never walk away from this kind of life. It was who she was. Having that kind of power over a man fed the need inside her like nothing else.

When she slipped off her jacket to reveal a seductive blouse, he made no attempt to hide the passion she aroused in him.

He moved close and kissed her on the neck. "You are a man pleaser, Lady."

She jerked away. "Not so fast, Ted. Don't you want to know how I'm doing?"

He took in every inch of her. "Honey, my eyes tell me you've never been better."

Ignoring him, Josie parked herself on his sofa.

"Tell me what you've been up to while I was taking care of business. You've been rather cool the last four weeks." She crossed her legs to expose more flesh.

He settled beside her. "You know I couldn't risk anyone finding out about us."

With her delicate fingers spread in front of her, she examined her recent manicure. "I saw you a couple of times with the dark-haired, grad assistant in the department. Nice looking girl. Anything you want to tell me?"

He rose and paced and stuffed his hands in and out of his pockets a few times before finally settling back on the sofa.

"Look, Josie, I've been with a couple of girls while you've been healing. What did you expect? You were carrying someone else's baby. Besides, neither of them compared to you. We have something special between us. I'm hoping you'll agree to move in at the end of the term."

Josie deliberately checked him out ... the way he had her. Without a doubt he was the most appealing man she had ever been with, but he was controlling this relationship. And she could not tolerate that.

She moved off the sofa and gathered her belongings. "I don't think so, Ted. I'm sure one of your other girls will jump at your offer though. Take care. See you in class."

As she moved towards the door, he grabbed her wrist. "Where do you think you are going? You play around but I can't."

Josie turned on him like a wounded she-bear. "I suggest you get your hands off me, Dr. Jenson. I am not yours to use when you please, if it doesn't please me. And suddenly you don't please me."

His hands shot in the air. Struggling to control his anger, he stepped in front of her. "There's the small matter of your grade, Miss Roberts."

Josie showed off her best fake laugh. "Oh, I'm confident I'll pass or you'll be looking for a new position next semester. Your choice, Ted. It matters not to me. See you in class."

Though she left with a smirk, her head high and an appearance of triumph, inside she felt like the loser she knew she was. And with an ever-growing sadness and emptiness, Josie headed for her next class. Ted's years and experience gave him an advantage she wasn't comfortable with.

That encounter threw her into a tailspin. While Jake was living in some kind of dream world, hers felt more like the nightmares that still haunted her.

As her despondency mushroomed, so did her dependency on Jack Daniels.

Hounding Jake became one of her pastimes. "You're dreaming, Jake. This magical spell you've fallen into is going to erupt like a volcano one day and spew you out. You and me? We have signs tattooed on our souls. *Used and damaged goods.* You'll get tired of Madison and trash her like all the others. It's just the way we are."

"At one time I would have agreed with you. I now know change is possible. Give God a chance, Josie."

She slammed the door in his face.

Four days later, the Roberts siblings were called into the study. William was shuffling through some papers on his desk. "Family conference time again."

Josie sauntered to the window overlooking the front lawn and street.

"The private investigator finished his report," William announced as he handed Jake a copy and held one out for Josie. She moved close enough to take it and ambled back to the window.

Both were scanning the summary sheet. Josie's face lit up. "I see Felix is already where he belongs. What did he do? Rape someone else?"

William's face turned an ashen gray as his eyes met hers. "Sweetheart, he not only raped her; he killed her."

Josie went pale as the memory of her own ordeal and the reality of what another girl had endured met head on.

"So do we file more charges against him, Josie?" William asked.

She bit her lower lip as tears collected in her eyes. "I'm glad to know that he's not going to hurt anyone else. I never want to hear about him again."

"Good."

William drew in another deep breath and picked up the other case study. "George is another story. As far as the investigator could find, his trail is clean. So what do we do?"

"What about you, Dad? This is your brother," Jake asked.

"True, Son. But more importantly, you are my children. For that reason alone, I know I have to personally confront him. I would like the two of you with me when that happens. I guess his response will determine our next step. What do you say?"

"What do you think, Sis?"

Still battling tears, she threw the papers on William's desk. "I have no desire to confront George in person or in the courtroom. Count me out."

She stormed out of the room. Virginia followed.

William waited for Jake's response.

"I want to go, Dad."

"Good. I'll make the arrangements."

Nineteen

December greeted Charlottesville with a cold, torrential rain. Raincoats and galoshes had been pulled out for the Diamond bus riders.

Thelma, along with her little helper, was attending to the never ending responsibilities connected with being mom and chief administer of house and family management.

They were in the laundry room singing about the wise men when Maria walked in with the mail. Seeing Ethan's handwriting caught Thelma off guard. "It's been so long since he's written."

Maria lingered in the doorway. "Maybe this is good news, Mom."

Thelma pressed the letter to her heart. "Maria, I don't think I want to open this until Henry is close by."

She returned the envelope. "Would you mind putting it with the other mail on his desk?"

"Sure."

Maria soon joined them and the individual laundry baskets filled fast as two washers and two dryers kept the ladies busy. Melinda's job was to sort the bathroom linens according to colors into the five baskets. Her folding efforts were lacking, but she had her colors down pat.

Thelma kept busy the rest of the day, but her heart was never far from the letter on Henry's desk. She breathed a sigh of relief when the kitchen crew finished up for the evening.

Without delay but with some apprehension, she walked into his office. "Did you notice the letter from Ethan?"

He folded the paper and patted his lap. "Let's read it together."

She settled and put her arm around his neck.

"Are you nervous?" he asked as he slit the top.

"Yeah, with a measure of curiosity thrown in."
"Me too." He pulled out a single sheet of notebook paper.

Dear Mom and Henry,

I just wanted you to know that I'm tired of living this way. I don't think I can take it much longer. I'm a rotten son and a born loser. Nothing I do ever turns out right. Besides everyone would be better off without me.

I never intended to end up here, and now I can't figure a way out except to end it all. I'm sorry for all the trouble I've caused. This way you won't have to worry about me anymore.

Sorry, Mom. I know you'll be sad, but you don't understand what it's like inside my head and inside these walls.

Tell the others I love them.

Ethan

Thelma grabbed the letter and jumped off Henry's lap. "Is he telling us that he is going to end his life?"

Henry was already flipping through their rolodex. "Yes, I think he is." He dialed the facility where Ethan was housed and asked to speak to someone in charge of the prisoners. He explained the letter they had just received.

The voice on the other end informed them that they did not put stock in such letters. He claimed that most of the long term prisoners wanted to end it at one time or another but usually got over it.

Henry hung up ... frustrated and concerned. "What about the others, Thelma? Do we tell them?"

"Maria is the only one who knows the letter came. If she hasn't told anyone else, I think we should ask her to keep it quiet. Let's not trouble the other children with this."

He nodded and called Maria into his office to read the letter. "We're asking you not to tell the others."

"Not even Madison?"

"She's trying to finish this semester and prepare for her wedding. Let's not say anything."

Maria agreed.

It was late afternoon on Saturday, December 4, when the phone rang. Daniel answered and notified his mom that the call was for her. As Thelma listened to the information being shared, she grabbed Daniel's arm and collapsed in the closest chair. Tears were streaming down her cheeks. She said little, but listened intently to the voice on the other end.

"When can we see him?"

She was quiet for another brief moment. "I see. Will you keep me informed of his condition?" More silence. "Thank you, Chaplain."

"Mom, is it Ethan?" Daniel's concerned was evident.

"Yes, Son, go find your dad and the others and have them meet me in the chapel." Grabbing a handful of tissues, she hurried down the hall.

Within five minutes the crew that was home had been rounded up. They found their distraught mom in her favorite chair. Henry knelt in front of her. "What is it, Thelma?"

The kids crowded around ... touching a shoulder, patting her back, rubbing an arm.

"That was the prison chaplain. A guard found Ethan hanging unconscious in his cell last night. They were able to revive him, but he refuses to eat. That's all I was told."

She was no longer the only Diamond weeping. Maria moved to a kneeling bench. Without a word, the other siblings followed her lead. All except Melinda. She crawled in Thelma's lap and snuggled close. "Don't worry, Mommy. They can't keep Jesus away."

Thelma held the little one closer. "You're right, Sweetheart. Prison walls can't shut out Jesus."

As she grieved and prayed for her oldest child, she thanked God for her youngest.

Slowly the children filtered out of the chapel, leaving Thelma and Henry with Melinda sound asleep on his shoulder. "Are you going to be okay, Hon?"

She nodded. "I feel like a failure where he is concerned, Henry. I was young and too messed up to know how to parent a child. I'm counting on the promise that God redeems our messes."

"As long as there is life, there is hope," Henry added. "Our hands are tied, but as Melinda wisely reminded us, they can't shut out the One who loves him most."

Thelma lingered in the chapel while Henry carried Melinda to her room.

It wasn't long before Madison and Jake walked in. "We just heard, Mom, and I have an idea. Why don't we get a photo of Ethan and attach it to the cross?"

Thelma bounced out of her chair. "I know just the one we need." With renewed hope Thelma headed to the library. By the end of the hour, she had attached a beautiful cord to a framed photo of Ethan that had been taken several months before he went to prison.

She looped the cord over the center upright of the cross, then knelt in front of the photo and thanked the Lord for saving his physical life.

While Thelma was praying, Jake and Madison made their exit. He headed home and she went to the kitchen to help with the meal.

Donald walked in to grab a hold-over until supper.

"Now I know why they call your kind grease monkeys. What did you do? Take a bath in the drain oil?" Madison teased.

He wiped his finger on a greasy spot and swiped it on her cheek. "I happen to like this image, Miss Clara Barton. You wear white. I wear black. The world needs both of us."

He jumped back as she tried to flick flour from the dough board on him. Both watched as the white dust drifted to the floor. "You know Mom's rules. You make a mess. You clean it up."

Madison fanned the air with her hand. "Donald, you not only look dirty, you reek. Why don't you go clean up before we eat?"

He sniffed his armpit and staggered ... dramatically ... out of the room.

Madison laughed until she remembered the phone call. "Wait a minute."

She washed the biscuit dough off her hands and caught up with him. "Mom got some tough news today." She relayed the phone call.

Donald stared at the winter scene outside the set of triple bay windows surrounding the offset eating area. "How are she and Dad coping?"

"Hurting. Do you ever watch Melinda with those two? Somehow that child knows how to encourage them when the rest of us are tongue-tied."

She punched his shoulder when he didn't respond. "Penny for your thoughts."

He turned slowly with penetrating blue eyes that reminded her of Ethan. "Are you sure about marrying Jake?"

"I knew that question was coming sooner or later. I'm not ignorant of his past, Donald. I've had many long, tearful conversations with Mom and Dad and more sleepless nights seeking the Lord. The answer didn't come quickly or painlessly, but yes, I'm sure."

"He'd give me a run for my money, Sis, but I believe I can take him down if the need ever arises."

Madison studied her caring, protective brother. "Your offer warms my heart."

"I'm going to clean up and go find the folks. Better get back to that tray of biscuits. Why don't you make an extra dozen? The thought of biscuits and molasses and the aroma coming from that pot of ham and beans make me mighty hungry. Think Paul Bunyan, okay?"

Twenty

Jake shared the disturbing news of Ethan's suicide attempt with his family.

The update rattled Josie. "You mean they wouldn't let him die? Why? So he can go back to the closest place to purgatory on planet Earth? Why do other folks think they always know what is best for the rest of us?" She stormed out of the room.

Virginia was visibly shaken. "How are they, Jake?"

"Hurting, but not giving up." He told about Ethan's photo and the cross.

Virginia moved beside her husband. "I'm concerned about Josie, William."

He reached for her hand. "Me too, Honey, but where she is concerned, I feel like a man without legs trying to run. I'm open to suggestions. Any thoughts, Jake?"

"I recently heard of a Christian organization called Teen Challenge that has long term rehab for folks like Josie, but getting her to agree to go—that's a horse of a different color."

"How have you walked away so easily?" William asked.

"Although my attitude about sex took a one-eighty turn the day our secrets were revealed, I have scratched, clawed and dug my way out of the pit inch by inch with the help of others and being open to the possibility that God was real and cared."

He played with the keys in his pocket. "Josie's story is harsher than mine. Somewhere deep inside your abused and used daughter is an innocent little girl who had to hide to survive, Dad. Lies keep her there. When she realizes that, she won't need to medicate the pain—or try to end it."

Tears were pooling in Virginia's eyes. "Son, I'm sorry I never shared with you two about a loving God."

Tenderness radiated from Jake's eyes. "You're forgiven, Mom, but with Dad being a nonbeliever, I'm not sure it would have turned out much differently. I'm mighty grateful you prayed."

William was drumming his fingers on the nearby end table. "Enough of this religious talk. Have you found a place to live yet, Jake? Time is running out."

Jake squeezed the bridge of his nose and glanced towards the house next door. "It looks like we're going to be your neighbors. It's not what I want, but it's what we can afford right now."

William smiled. "Not wanting to share your bride with her large family?"

"You were young and in love once, Dad. You ought to understand."

William winked at his wife. "I may not be as young, Son, but I'm still very much in love."

Jake grinned and went to the kitchen for a snack. Virginia lightly touched William's leg. "Think I'll let you reminisce by yourself."

He grabbed her hand. "Are you sorry you married me, Virginia?"

She looked at him with the same compassion that was birthed the day she discovered his distorted view of God. "I love you, William. I'm sad that we haven't been able to share life on a deeper level."

He pulled her onto his lap. "I've sensed that sadness and have tried to make up for it in other ways. I can't imagine my life without you and our children." His kiss left no doubt.

She blushed and scooted off his lap. "William, you need to behave. We have children in the house."

"Yeah, and our son is reminding me of the delight of being in love."

"Me too. Maybe I should go brew a pot of tea."

"You do that, Dear."

As she entered the kitchen, Jake interrupted his hot chocolate making. "Mom, tell me about you and Dad."

As they puttered around the kitchen preparing their drinks, Virginia began to reminisce.

"Your dad and I met the winter of my last semester at UV. My best friend begged me for weeks to double date with her boyfriend's best friend. I finally agreed.

"The next Friday night William showed up at my door while Betty and Rob waited in the car. It wasn't just his John Wayne size and rugged good looks that got my attention; the man oozed with the charm of a more mature man."

She smiled as a memory surfaced. "I can still see that lopsided grin as he backed up a few steps to get a better look. 'Well, now, what have we here?' was his greeting.

"I'm sure I turned ten shades of red, but with the poise of a man accustomed to talking himself out of a corner and knowing how to make a woman feel comfortable, he soon had me laughing at him.

"The guys took us to the Black Angus Steak House and the movies that night. By the time the evening was over, I felt certain he was as interested as I was."

Jake filled his cup. "And?"

"When the phone was silent for a week, I called Betty to see if Rob had mentioned William's response. She laughed. William told Rob he had met his future wife."

Virginia poured the rest of the tea in her cup. "After four weeks of silence, I gave up. The fifth Sunday after our first date, I walked into church and found myself staring at the backs of William, Betty and Rob three or four rows from the back. That scene caught me so off guard that I lingered in the back until the service started.

"When they stood to sing, I walked to the pew where William was perched closest to the aisle. He nudged Betty and Rob toward the inside and made a spot for me. Without a word, he shared the songbook and rejoined the singing."

She looked at Jake with curiosity. "Have you ever heard him sing?"

"Can't say that I have, Mom."

"He has a rich, deep bass voice that I've not heard since he quit going to church."

She paused. "We had lots of fun dates after that, and without fail he showed up every time the church doors opened. I never questioned his faith. He spoke *Christianese* quite well.

"Hard to believe, isn't it? He pursued me fast and furious from that day in church until the day we married. Love can make one blind, Jake.

"The first Sunday after our honeymoon I dressed for church. William did everything he could to distract me. I wasn't prepared for what followed. He spent the next hour sharing his heart about his religious upbringing."

Tears were added to her story. "His dad had been so strict and condemning that William's image of God was pretty much summed up in his own father. I felt sorry for him, Jake. He had never seen God as a loving Father or Jesus as the forgiving Son."

She pushed her tea cup aside and reached for a napkin to wipe her tears. "When I asked why he didn't tell me, he looked at me with an expression that bore into my heart and hasn't left.

"He told me he knew I wouldn't date him, let alone marry him if I knew." She was twisting her napkin into dozens of spiral shreds at this point. "So he decided he would do what he had to do for as long as he had to in order to win my heart and hand ... and the church plan was birthed."

"What happened that morning, Mom?"

"I was angry at myself for allowing my love for William to blind me to the truth. I was angry at him for deceiving me, but the emotion that eventually won out was compassion for a young man with a distorted view of God and himself. I couldn't get past the hurt inside him.

"He told me that he never intended to step foot inside a church again and that religion was a topic we would never discuss. I wept for both of us that day. I was married to a man who didn't believe in a God whom I loved. I didn't believe in divorce except for adultery, so I turned to the only source I knew ... God."

She wiped her tears and blew her nose. "I looked up a passage I had read before, but rarely heard anyone comment on in I Peter 3. It instructs wives of unbelieving husbands to live in such a way that without words—that was the phrase that stuck in my head and worked its way into my heart—but by our lives our husbands might have a change of heart. That became my mission in our marriage.

"The other passage that gave me direction was in I Corinthians 7. It bids us stay with, not leave an unbelieving husband if he chooses to stay. It suggests that by staying my life may have an influence on him."

Virginia stood up, leaned across the bar and touched Jake's hand. "Son, I may have been wrong, but later that day, I knelt in front of my new husband and asked him to forgive his dad for presenting an unloving God. I told him that to the best of my ability I would respect his request and try to love him like God loves me."

She kept dabbing the moisture from her eyes. "I've kept a Bible in our bedroom and he has often seen me reading it. I've been part of a ladies home Bible study for years. He's never said a word to discourage any of that."

Jake moved around the counter top and pulled his mom into a hug. "Mom, I'm confident now that you prayed David Henderson into my life, and without a doubt, the Diamonds have been a godsend for this family. I'm not convinced you missed God."

He picked up their cups and rinsed them before opening the dishwasher. "Your story gives me hope for Josie and Dad."

A smile broke through the smudges caused by all the tears. "And yours, Son, has renewed my faith."

They continued to talk while cleaning the kitchen. "Have you told Thelma any of this?"

She chuckled. "What do you think we do those mornings we have coffee?"

TWENTY-ONE

Though December 11 dawned bright, but unusually cold, Jake Roberts was unaware of the chill. His thoughts were on his bride and the plane tickets in his suitcase. The two dads had pooled resources and prepaid for a two weeks honeymoon in Hawaii.

The house next door was busy preparing for the two o'clock wedding. The phone rang. Hoping it was Jake, Madison volunteered to answer.

"Don't you dare," Maria interjected as she slid in front of her and snatched the phone. "Hello. You've reached the Diamond residence. This is Maria."

Maria's eyes widened and her mouth dropped open. Putting her hand over the mouthpiece, she whispered, "Go get Mom, Madison. It's Ethan."

"Hi, Maria."

His sister was fighting tears. "You scared us out of our wits, Ethan."

"Sorry about that. I was convinced everyone would be better off without me."

"I'm glad God disagreed with you." Thelma rushed into the room. "Here's Mom."

Thelma's hand was trembling as the phone was transferred. "Ethan, what is going on?"

"They tell me I'm going to live."

She could hear the emotion in his voice.

"I just wanted to tell you how sorry I am for all the trouble I keep causing you, Mom."

He hesitated and then made an unusual request. "I was just wondering if you could send me a Bible. I think I need one."

Tears were racing down her cheeks. "I'll see that one heads your way as soon as possible, Son. Why did you do it, Ethan?"

"Four months ago I was attacked by a gang. I was so beat up they transferred me to the medical ward. That sounded pretty good until I found out that meant twenty-three hours a day in a cell by myself. I know they did it to protect me until I healed, but with so much time to think and nothing to do, I decided that life behind bars wasn't worth living and everyone would be better off without me.

"I finally figured out a way to hang myself ... and almost succeeded. A nosey guard found me. I was so angry when I regained consciousness that I refused to eat.

"While lying there four nights later, it hit me that there had to be a reason I wasn't dead. I began to wonder if God was real and didn't want me to die yet. I cried out to Him, Mom. I don't remember everything I said, but something happened inside me. And the next day I got a Thinking-of-You card from a lady I've never heard of. Besides that, I never get mail. I took the card as God's confirmation.

"I decided it was time to eat again. And I've been thinking that maybe if I had a Bible I could learn about God. Anyway, I just wanted you to know I'm sorry."

Thelma struggled through a deluge of emotions. "Ethan, you are forgiven."

Her voice broke. "Will you forgive me ... for not being the parent you needed growing up?" She could hear sniffles on the other end of the line.

"Yeah, Mom. I know now that you did the best you knew how to do under the circumstances. Will you and Henry come see me soon?"

"We'll make it a priority. Maybe we can arrange to bring one of your siblings with us."

"That would be great. Tell the family hello and to stay away from drugs and folks who use or sell them."

"I will, Ethan. Hey, before you hang up ... Madison is getting married today."

His voice broke. "Send me a photo of her and the lucky guy. My time is up. Talk to you later." The dial tone followed.

Thelma and Maria hugged. "Run and tell the family to meet in the chapel."

Maria broadcast the latest family bulletin. "Ethan just called. Meet Mom in the chapel."

Thelma stood in the doorway and hugged each child as he or she entered the family's newest gathering place. Melinda was the last and reached for Thelma's arms. "What is it, Mommy? Did Jesus find Ethan?"

Thelma lifted the trusting child into her arms. "It seems they have met, Sweetie."

She related Ethan's story to the family. Tears were plentiful. Smiles and hugs were spontaneous.

Madison wept uncontrollably.

"Maddie, if you don't quit crying, your wedding photos are going to be awful. You need some cold compresses," Mandy suggested.

Henry spoke up. "We do have a wedding to attend."

Mandy seized Madison's hand and proceeded to the kitchen.

Thelma raised her hand to get everyone else's attention. "I've set out sandwiches in the kitchen. You are on your own for lunch. Just clean up what you mess up."

With that the chapel emptied and individual preparations for the wedding continued.

Next door, Jake was challenging his dad to a game of pool. "Come on, Dad. I need to do something to help with these jitters."

William chuckled and selected his favorite cue. "Rack them up, Son. I need to humble you one more time while you're living under my roof."

Virginia set a tray of finger foods on the card table. "Better grab something, Jake. You didn't eat much breakfast."

He groaned as he scratched on his first shot. "Mom, do you think Madison is as nervous as I am? Can't I call her to be sure she's okay?"

Virginia smiled. "I'm pretty sure she's faring better than you are, Son."

He pulled his checklist out of his pocket. "Dad, I've already packed the car. I moved my belongings to the guest apartment yesterday. Can you think of ...?"

He slapped his forehead and laid down his cue. "Can you believe I forgot to set out a change of clothes to wear after the wedding?"

Jake and Josie's Discovery

William kept taking his shots while listening to Jake's random ramblings. "At this point, I'm glad your head is attached. Too bad you're not playing. I'm on a roll."

By one o'clock both families were at the church. All of the Diamond family were in the wedding. Josie had refused to take part, but promised to show up sober.

In the room of females, all the talk was about Ethan's call. Virginia got so excited she began to cry.

"Don't get us started again, Friend. We don't need red, swollen eyes for our kids' wedding photos," Thelma warned.

"Where's my uke, Maria? Did we remember to bring it?" Madison asked as she rummaged through the paraphernalia in the room.

"We didn't, but I did. It's in the case by the door. Are you sure you can do this?"

"I'm sure."

Virginia picked up on Madison's plans. "Jake Roberts may have a coronary before he gets married. The man has been a basket case for two days."

On the men's wing, Henry had shared the good news about Ethan's call with William and Jake.

"What a wedding gift for Madison!" Jake added.

Henry laughed. "All the women had cold compresses on their eyes the last half hour before we left."

A friend helping with the wedding alerted both groups that it was time for the mothers to light the unity candle. William and Henry sneaked out and watched as their wives made their way to the front to the music and words of *Sunrise, Sunset* from *Fiddler on the Roof*.

"I'm identifying with Teyve right now, William. I remember meeting my bride at the altar not that many years ago. Now I'm giving my daughter to your son. Say, shouldn't you be with Jake?"

"Yeah. I think that boy is in worse shape than I was twenty-four years ago."

As soon as William joined the groom and the three Diamond sons, the minister led the men to their designated spots. When the bridesmaids were in place, Maria slipped to the piano and joined the organist in a classical rendition of *the Hawaiian Wedding Song*. Soft strums of a ukulele joined the duo. Jake's attention was drawn toward the balcony and there stood his radiant bride serenading him with a song of forever love.

He took a deep breath trying to dispel the onslaught of jitters that were racing up and down his spine as she sang her vows to him. It didn't work. He clasped his moist hands tightly to keep from fidgeting. That didn't work either. He was feeling a little faint and wondered if a man ever passed out at his own wedding. *We should have eloped.*

When the serenade ended, Maria and the organist continued playing as Henry escorted his daughter to the interior stairs. The second Madison glanced at Jake, he left his spot and moved to the foot of the stairs ... waiting for his bride.

The attendees stirred. Henry looked at Madison. "Either he is eager or doesn't trust me. I'm leaning towards eager."

She put her hand over her mouth to stifle the laughter. Jake smiled. When her foot hit the floor, he pivoted to her left and offered his right arm. "I warned you not to sing to me again until we were married."

She leaned close. "I couldn't resist. Just be glad I didn't add the hula."

"The hula? I wouldn't have survived."

"Yeah, that's the only thing that saved you."

When Henry kissed his daughter and stepped out of the scene, Jake moved to her right.

Their attention was now on the pastor whose words were challenging them. When the exchange of vows and rings concluded, the minister stepped behind the kneeling bench that Madison insisted they use for their prayer of dedication and blessing.

As his knees touched the pad, Jake remembered the first time that happened. By an act of his will and the words of his mouth, he had given himself to the God who made him. This time, he was giving himself to a woman who had demonstrated God's love as a friend and now as a wife.

After the minister's blessing, he stepped away to give the couple a few minutes of privacy for personal prayers.

Jake whispered, "Lord, I'm grateful for a new beginning and the bride by my side."

Madison responded, "Father, may we love and treasure each other as you do us."

As their eyes met, Jake kissed his wife affectionately before helping her up. There was a quiet stirring and subdued mirth among the attendees.

The minister chuckled. "You are the first groom to beat me to the punch line, Jake. Why don't you kiss your bride again? For me this time."

Gone were the jitters, the sweat and the nerves. "Hello, Wife." He helped her to her feet, dramatically swept her backwards and kissed her soundly to the delight of the folks watching.

The small reception and photo shoot were blurs for Jake. All of that disappeared when he was instructed to change into street clothes and meet back in the reception area in twenty minutes.

Jake showed up fifteen minutes later in jeans, vest and long sleeve shirt. Madison appeared wearing a sundress with a jacket. Obviously, she had Hawaii on her mind.

"You may get a bit cold, Babe." Framing her face with his hands, he kissed her lightly. "Are you ready to leave?"

"If you are."

Thelma handed Madison a lovely winter white coat. Jake grabbed his top coat and they slipped out quietly.

The engine was running and warmth greeted them when Jake opened Madison's door. "So this was why Henry asked for my keys."

"Dad probably felt sorry for me when he saw my sundress."

As Jake shifted into drive, he leaned close enough to kiss his bride. "This all feels like a fairy tale, Madison. I cannot believe we are married."

"Me either."

They chatted about the wedding, Ethan and a dozen other things as they drove towards Richmond. When Jake zipped past the airport exit, Madison sounded the alarm. "Honey, I think you missed our turn."

"You are not the only one with a surprise up your sleeve this day, Mrs. Roberts. Our plane doesn't leave until eleven o'clock tomorrow morning. We have a honeymoon suite at the Jefferson Hotel Richmond tonight."

"You mean ... we ..." Her words trailed off.

"Do you mind?"

"I like your surprise. Does anyone else know?"

"Nope."

As they approached the hotel, Madison's delight and interest in history surfaced. "Jake, tell me about this amazing architectural beauty."

"I knew you'd ask, so I did some research. It was built by a lover of all things Renaissance named Lewis Ginter. The multi-million-dollar project took three years to complete and opened in 1895."

"Wow! It's in marvelous condition to be that old." Madison was enthralled.

"There have been several renovations, and in 1969 it was added to the National Registry of Historic Places. It is considered by some to be one of the best examples of Beaux Art in the country."

As they made their way inside, Madison did a three-hundred-and-sixty-degree turn as she took in the breath-taking public spaces. "That marble staircase could have been in *Gone with the Wind!* Dad has to bring Mom here for their next anniversary. Tell me more, Jake."

"It has over three hundred guest rooms and thirty more for on-site employees. Many of our Presidents, including our current President Carter, and scores of entertainers and famous folks, including Elvis, have enjoyed its grandeur."

She reached for his hand. "Your bride is impressed."

"This is my wedding gift to you, Maddie. Having you as my wife makes me feel like the richest, most blessed man in God's universe."

He tipped the bell boys, thanked them and shut the door. Before she could speak, he kissed her without restraint. "Just practicing, Sweetheart."

She took a deep breath. "Jake Roberts, if we weren't married, you'd have to go home for such behavior."

"I am home, Maddie. Where you are is home from this day forward." He swept her up in his arms, carried her into the bedroom and deposited her on the bed. With a hint of anticipation, he winked as he turned to leave the room. "I'll get your things."

She watched as he placed her luggage close by. "I'll be in the sitting area."

A blend of nervousness and excitement caused her to linger—though she and Thelma had talked. Twenty minutes later, she took a deep breath and opened the door. The lights were dim and Frank Sinatra was singing *Just the Way You Look Tonight*.

A peek revealed a shirtless husband attending to the wine glasses. He turned. All six feet five inches of him. A smile that matched the twinkle in his eyes let her know he was pleased.

He placed his hand over his heart, breathed deeply and pointed to her choice of attire. "Where did you get ... that?"

In spite of the modesty that would have normally prompted her to look down, she kept her eyes on him. "Mom."

His eyes danced as he lifted his wine glass. "To my mother-in-law. That explains the Diamond population next door."

She blushed. He set aside his glass, reached for her hand and bowed. "Mrs. Roberts, I believe this is our song. May I?"

Love for this man quieted her hesitation. "Yes, Mr. Roberts, it is ... and you may."

She slipped into his arms ... and the dance of love began.

Twenty-Two

Back in Rugby Heights, Josie was foremost on everyone's mind. Since Jake's wedding she had slipped into deeper depression while her sober times were fewer and further apart.

Thelma identified with her pain and continued to reach out. The young woman remained a closed book until the day Thelma mentioned Ethan.

"Would you mind sharing his story?"

Thelma divulged Ethan's journey and watched as the saga of her wayward son opened the previously impenetrable door.

"So now he's gone religious? Did he have a vision? Or did something freaky happen while he was unconscious?"

"No, nothing like that." Thelma shared his explanation and his one-hundred-and-eighty-degree shift regarding life and God.

While Josie wrestled with those thoughts, Thelma probed. "Is there someone you love more than anyone else? Is there anyone who loves you unconditionally?"

She didn't answer immediately. "The only people I love are my folks and Jake. I always felt closer to Jake than my parents. I think they love me unconditionally, but at times it doesn't feel that way."

"What are your thoughts about Jake and Madison?"

An expression Thelma had noted several times recently darkened Josie's face. Moving to the window, she peered at the scenery with no thought of the spring green waiting to burst forth or the brilliant summer colors hidden beneath the gray cover of winter.

"Jake has changed, but I don't think it'll last." She faced the person who came closest to understanding her. "He and I are messed up, Ms. Thelma."

Thelma smiled. "No one can deny that Jake has changed. Is it possible that he has discovered a way to be free from his past, Josie? Is it possible that he has discovered what love and sex between a man and woman was meant to be?"

Josie crossed her arms and began to shuffle her feet.

"The truth is, Josie, that neither of you are beyond God's love or goodness and generosity."

Clearly uncomfortable with the direction the conversation was going, Josie moved towards the door. "Think I need to get back to the house and clean up my place. Mom's been after me for a month now."

Thelma followed her to the door. "If you ever decide to redecorate your suite, let me know. I'll assist any way I can."

Josie halted abruptly and spun back around. "Really? I love what you've done and continue to do with this place, and the sunroom renovations you recommended for Mom and Dad have made it the family's favorite place to gather. I've had the same décor since I started high school. Maybe a change is needed."

Thelma smiled. "Let me know."

That thought took root as Josie walked home. She approached her dad.

"Great idea, Honey. Run your ideas by your mom. She'll be living here long after you are gone."

Josie and Virginia spent the next evening tossing around ideas.

The following day, the Roberts women invited Thelma to join them in Josie's suite. "William put a ceiling on our expenditures, but I think we can accomplish the changes she wants within that budget. What do you think?" Virginia asked.

"Being creative is half the fun of design. We might even save him a dime or two. You two nail down what you want, then we'll work on the design together. That will enable you to decide how much you want to do and what needs to be hired out."

Josie's enthusiasm was evident. "I want to do as much as I can. I like dabbling in paint and working with layouts. Even shopping for accessories sounds like fun."

Thelma was pacing off the width of the sitting area. "Josie, have you ever considered design as a career?"

The rootless young lady perked up. "Not until you moved next door. How would I get started?"

Thelma had moved to the windows. "I'd recommend finishing your degree. An accounting background is a great asset for going into any business venture. In the meanwhile, you could begin checking out some design schools. You have a unique knack for utilizing space plus an artistic flare for mixing beauty with purpose. I'd consider going into business with you at some point if you get your degree and license."

Josie squealed and spontaneously hugged Thelma. "This is not some kind of therapeutic excuse to get me out of my drunken stupor, is it?"

Thelma laughed and returned her hug. "I can't lie. It seemed like a logical place to jump start a change."

"What do you think, Mom?"

"I've never seen you this excited about adding and subtracting numbers."

Thelma turned to leave. Josie followed. "Were you really a wild child, Ms. Thelma? Was your life as complicated as mine?"

"Yes, and remember I had a son."

They walked down the stairs and out to the breezeway.

"I meant to ask. Have you heard from Ethan lately?" Josie quizzed.

"As a matter of fact, I have. He calls two and three times a week now. He's like Jake. The changes just keep coming. He's looking forward to being transferred to a federal facility soon."

Josie looked down at her feet and kicked at the stone on the patio. "Do you think it would be okay if I wrote him sometime?"

Thelma didn't try to hide the excitement her question stirred. "Oh, I think that would be wonderful for both of you. I'll get his address to you."

Molly delivered Ethan's address later that day.

Writing him was easier than Josie imagined. They were sort of like family with her brother married to his sister, and with his family living next door, she had plenty to write about.

She wondered if he would answer.

Twenty-Three

Christmas Eve arrived and the Diamond's cooking traditions were in full swing with three clusters of activities in their remodeled, industrial-equipped kitchen. The place smelled like a candy shop.

Virginia was helping Mandy and Maria with fudge. Josie, Molly and Melinda had the ovens filled with trays of Christmas cookies. Melinda was showing Josie how to decorate the different shapes.

Daniel and Dennis were making wassail, eggnog and the family's favorite punch, while Donald was assisting Thelma in the divinity department.

About an hour into the projects, the phone rang. Mandy was closest and answered.

"Hello. You've reached the Diamond residence. This is Mandy speaking."

"Merry Christmas, Mandy."

The fifteen-year-old squealed. "Ethan, is this you?" She tried to catch her mom's attention by waving a chocolate covered spatula in the air.

"Yeah, it's me. What's all the noise in the background?"

The spatula was still waving while Mandy explained what each group was doing.

"Wish I could be there."

Her excitement gave way to a sad reality. "Me too, Ethan."

All activity ceased as Thelma made her way to the phone.

"Here's Mom."

As the phone was transferred, a chorus of voices shouted Christmas greetings.

"Did you hear them? Everyone is here except Madison."

"Yeah. By the time I get out of this place, they'll all be grown and gone. Drugs not only robbed me of my youth, Mom; they stole my future too."

"The others have heeded your warnings, Ethan."

"I'm glad to hear that. Listen, Mom. I've kept something important from you and Henry."

Silence filled the phone line for a few seconds. "You have a five-year-old grandson. His name is Morgan."

Tears began to trail down Thelma's cheeks. "You have a son?"

With those words the family began to gather around. "Is he with his mother? Can we see him?"

"Actually, his mom is in jail and Morgan has been in a foster home outside of Lexington for the last three years. I was wondering if you and Henry might consider becoming his foster parents."

Tears were now racing down her cheeks. She placed her right hand over her heart and took a deep breath. "Someone find your dad, please."

Thelma assured Ethan that they would be at the Department of Human Resources the first day they were open. "We will do everything within our power to get him as soon as possible, Ethan. Thank you for asking." One of the kids handed her a tissue.

"Sorry I've waited so long, Mom. My head is beginning to clear and I'm trying to right some wrongs." His voice choked up.

"Try not to fret, Son."

"Several guys are in line behind me, so I need to hang up. I know it's a long way, but could you and Henry come for a visit again soon?"

"Sure, Son. We'll make arrangements to visit the next time Henry has business in Kentucky." She held the phone away from her ear and the room filled with words of love and greetings again. "Love you, Ethan. Merry Christmas."

"Merry Christmas, everyone." And the phone went silent.

Henry walked in the room and the crowd divided as he made his way to Thelma. "I hear we have a grandson." A lone tear wandered down his cheek. "Ethan wants us to get custody?"

She could only nod and walk into his open arms. Seven other pairs of arms joined theirs. A grandson and nephew for Christmas! As the group dispersed, they began to buzz about the new family addition and started making plans for his arrival.

Josie and Virginia had quietly moved into the background and noiselessly slipped out the door. William was in the kitchen enjoying a glass of eggnog when they walked in.

"What in the world is wrong with you two? Tears on Christmas Eve? Did the Grinch show up?"

"Quite the opposite, Dad. Watching that family is like being on the set of *the Waltons*." Josie shared their exciting news.

Ethan had written to her about Morgan and his decision. She couldn't wait to tell him how excited his family was.

William placed his empty cup in the sink. "Rosa Lee Fite is over Children's Services in the county. I wonder how difficult it is to get a child from another state."

"Their adoptions took place in Kentucky. Maybe that will expedite the process some. Besides, they are his blood kin and I think that makes a big difference," Virginia offered.

She placed a gentle hand on William's arm. "They invited us to go to a candlelight service at their church this evening. Will you go with me?"

He covered her hand with his. "You go. I'll stay with Josie."

She kissed his cheek. "I look forward to the day we go together."

"Don't give up on us, Dear."

Twenty-Four

While most of the family were at a Christmas Eve service, Jake and Madison's flight arrived in Richmond. They hitched a ride on the airport shuttle to their vehicle, paid the parking fee and headed home. "Earth to Mrs. Roberts."

She laughed and scooted close. "Actually, having to come back to earth after two weeks in paradise is going to be difficult."

"My thoughts exactly."

Madison was leaning on Jake's shoulder. "Jet lag is no joke. My stomach is as confused as my brain. Mind if we grab something to eat on the way home?"

"Eat in or take out?"

"Let's take it home. Doesn't that sound wonderful? I can't imagine life without you, Jake."

He moved his arm around her and pulled her close. "That's good to hear because I don't fancy the idea of you being anywhere else."

As they relived their days in Hawaii, he confessed, "Hawaii and you? Only heaven could be better. Don't forget to send your hula outfit to your Hawaiian friend in Kentucky."

She snuggled. "She will be pleased."

Jake pulled into an open parking space at Whitt's Barbeque. A young lady on roller skates took their order. They continued to reminisce until the roller derby queen delivered a tray of food balanced on one hand. Jake paid the bill and smiled when an excited squeal alerted him she had found her twenty-dollar tip.

The smell of barbeque permeated the car as they drove home. After parking in the spot designated for the guest apartment, Jake and Madison grabbed the food and necessities and made it as far as the door.

"You stand right there," Jake ordered.

He came back and unloaded her arms. "Stay put, Mrs. Roberts."

The next time he swept her in his arms and closed the door with his foot.

"Jake, are you aware that one of the reasons for carrying one's wife over the threshold was to help her with any reluctance she might have at that point in the marriage?"

A teasing smile lit up his face. "I like that better than the one about keeping her from tripping over the threshold and bringing bad luck to the marriage. Must have been some crudely fashioned thresholds or extremely clumsy women back then."

Both laughed as she slid out of his arms.

After getting some solid food in their confused tummies, Madison cleaned their small kitchen while Jake toted the rest of their luggage into their new abode.

After everything was cleaned up and put away, Madison looked at her husband of two weeks. "How does the first night together in our first home sound, Mr. Roberts?"

"Heavenly." He swept her off her feet and carried her into the bedroom. "Just in case you're nervous or clumsy."

Twenty-Five

It was mid-morning before either of them stirred. Jake was trying to slip out of bed to retrieve the Christmas present he had hidden before they married.

"Sneaking out on me, huh?" came a sleepy voice that was becoming wonderfully familiar every morning.

"Guilty, but I can repent and make up for it." He crawled back under the covers. Just as he pulled her into his arms, the phone rang. "Let's ignore it."

"I recognized that sound, Jake. Earth is calling and we have to answer at some point."

The fact that she had started massaging his shoulders didn't help. "Okay, if that is earth and you expect me to answer, then you need to take those magical hands off my body."

She threw her hands in the air and fell back on the bed.

"You didn't have to concede so easily."

"Jake, the phone."

He grabbed the one on the nightstand. "Merry Christmas from Jake and Madison."

He melted as Madison began massaging his neck and shoulders again.

"Hi, Melinda. I missed you too."

A puzzled look caused his forehead to crease. "You got a brother and nephew for Christmas?"

The massage ended abruptly as Madison moved in front of him and mouthed, *a brother and nephew?*

"Tell you what, Sweetheart. We'll see you this afternoon. Okay?"

He smiled as he listened to the youngest Diamond relate all he had missed. "Yeah, you tell your mom we will see you later."

Jake pulled Madison back onto the bed. "That's what your four-year-old sister said. Do you think Thelma is pregnant again or have they found another baby?"

"Knowing my folks either answer could be correct, but a nephew would mean Ethan has a son."

After glancing at the clock, Madison jumped up, grabbed some undies and headed for the shower. "We promised your folks we'd be there for brunch this morning."

"I'll make the bed and put on a pot of coffee." He tousled her hair. "Bedhead becomes you."

She flipped him with the garment in her hand. "Sure it does. Think I'll wear it all day."

After retrieving Madison's gift, Jake straightened the covers and placed the package on her pillow. By the time she strolled out of the bathroom, the aromatic smell of coffee was filling the air.

Madison panicked when she noticed a gift on her pillow. She was in the middle of a frantic search when he crept in and grabbed her from behind. "Looking for something?"

Startled and frustrated, she turned to face him. "You need to disappear for a few more minutes."

With a cocky confidence he pointed towards the closet. "Middle shelf."

She punched him. "You saw it?"

"Yes, but I didn't open it."

After hauling down his gift, she placed it on his pillow. "I'm ready when you are."

"Ladies first."

She tore into the package only to find another package inside. After ripping apart the smaller package, she discovered a small ring box. "What have you done?"

A flip of the top revealed a beautiful emerald and diamond ring. After slipping it on her finger, she leaped into his arms. "You are spoiling me, Jake Roberts."

She kissed him with wifely affection. "Tell me about the ring."

"First things first. Honey, please don't kiss me like that when we have places to go and people to see."

Jake took on an exaggerated air of aloofness. "Let me demonstrate the three types of kisses allowed in such circumstances. Number One." He kissed her lightly on the cheek.

She frowned. "Nah, those bird pecks are for Mom and Dad. What's number two?"

He kissed her lightly on the forehead.

She put her hands on her hips. "I can't even reach your forehead, Jake. Number three had better be good or you're stuck with wifely kisses."

He bowed and kissed the back of her hand while flashing a cheesy smile.

"Come on, Jake. Those are FT kisses." She jumped on the bed and stood up.

"What in the world are FT kisses?" he asked as he put his hands on her waist.

"Fairy tales. I have a better idea," Madison said as she extended her right hand.

He grinned and clasp the offered appendage.

With a vigorous motion, she shook it. "Thanks for the beautiful gift, Mr. Roberts."

He laughed and pulled her into his arms as they collapsed on the bed. "Don't you think that's a little impersonal?"

"It's that or WKs."

She held out the ring. "So tell me about this surprise."

"I wanted to give you something to remember our first Christmas. The emerald represents the beginning of our life together, and the diamonds represent the name you gave up to become mine."

"Keep up that kind of talk and I'll have to kiss you like a wife again."

"Not until I open my gift."

She wiggled out of his arms and handed him the odd shaped package. As he tore into the wrapping he discovered two separate presents. Tearing into the smaller one, he withdrew a box that held a beautiful navy, leather-bound Bible with his name and the words, *A New Beginning,* embossed on the front. "How did you know?"

She reached for the New Testament she had given him months ago. "Besides the fact that you're still carrying around my *pink* New

Testament? This is your first Christmas as a believer and you needed a Bible of your own."

He rubbed the leather cover and traced the engraved words with a reflective expression. "If not for the God in this book, there wouldn't be a Mrs. Roberts. I shudder to think that I could have missed it all."

"Open the other gift."

He ripped the paper away to reveal a wall plaque with the phrase from the cross repeated multiple times. *I Will Always Love You.* On the back, Madison had added the dates of his first God encounter and their wedding and signed it—God and Maddie.

He hugged her affectionately. "What a difference He has made in my life!"

"Yeah, and He'll do that in any heart that yields, Jake."

"This the best Christmas of my life, Mrs. Roberts."

"Me too, Mr. Roberts."

And she kissed him with wifely kisses.

Twenty-Six

They made their way to his folks' place later that morning. When Jake started to barge in without knocking, Madison grabbed his hand. "Hey, you don't live here anymore. Don't you think you owe your folks the same respect that you are asking of them?"

She rang the doorbell.

"But this is … was … my home for twenty-three years. I've never knocked."

"Is this your home today?"

Understanding dawned and a teasing smile accompanied his dancing eyes. "No, it's not, Mrs. Roberts. Ring the bell again. I don't think they heard it."

He leaned down to kiss her just as Josie opened the door. "Ah, the Love Birds have returned. How does it feel to have to knock, Jake?"

"It's different, but I like the reason." He put his arm around Madison's shoulders and kissed her again.

"Good grief," Josie sputtered and turned back into the house.

His folks were in the den. "Glad to have you two back home. How was the trip?" Virginia asked.

"Except for the jet lag which seems to be worse coming home than it was leaving, it was perfect."

William smiled. "Most folks find it easier traveling west than east."

Jake pointed to the addition of a manger scene to the usual Christmas decorations. "Nice touch, Mom."

She cast a grateful glance toward William. "Your father bought it for me last week."

Jake's and Madison's eyes darted to the man of the house.

"Don't ask," William answered before he could be questioned.

Virginia rescued him. "Let's go eat. I happen to know these two have no food in their cabinets. They have to be hungry."

Jake patted his tummy. "Yeah, we need to do something about that."

Talk of work and Josie's new plans for renovating her suite occupied most of the conversation during the meal.

"I'd like to see what you and Mom have come up with, Josie." With that the two younger Roberts women scurried upstairs.

William and Jake took their eggnog into the game room. "How was Hawaii, Son?"

"Paradise, Dad, and loving that woman is beyond incredible. Thanks for your part in making it possible."

William chuckled. "I told you she'd be worth the wait." They shared about life and work … and the women in their lives.

Upstairs, Josie and Madison were pouring over her design drawings and color palettes. "This won't look or feel like the same place, Josie. Bet Mom's been in seventh heaven working with someone who shares an interest in her world of design."

Josie looked up. "Have you talked to your folks since you left?"

"No. Jake had a short conversation with Melinda this morning, but that's all. We're headed there next."

That was the moment Jake tapped on the door and stuck his head in. "If we're going to make your folks by two o'clock, we need to get moving."

He walked in and put an arm around Josie's shoulder. "I highly recommend married life, Sis."

"Jake Roberts, I never thought I'd see you so daft over one girl."

"It's a wonderful change, Josie."

Twenty-Seven

As they approached the Diamond's rear entrance, Jake stepped in front of Madison and rang the doorbell.

"You are a quick study, Sir."

Before Madison could respond, the door opened and Melinda ran into Jake's arms. "You're my brother now, aren't you, Jake?" As he lifted her, she latched small arms around his neck and squeezed.

"You bet I am. How's my favorite little sister?"

Madison stayed by the door to watch Jake's welcome into the family. Henry was the last to offer his greetings. "I see you've gained a number of brothers and sisters, but I think you've misplaced a wife."

Jake turned. "Sweetie, this will not do." He knelt on the floor. "I've lost my wife."

Melinda giggled and pointed to Madison. "There she is. I'll get her." She ran into her big sister's open arms. "Jake lost you, but I found you."

She studied Madison's face. "What's a honeymoon?"

Keeping the youngest family member in her arms, Madison stood. "Well, it's like this. Many, many years ago, when people married, the couple went away by themselves for a month. The bride's father would give them enough honey wine to last the thirty days. Back then, calendars were based on the moon, so as time passed it became known as the honeymoon."

Melinda framed Madison's face in her hands. "So you and Jake drank a lot of that honey stuff?"

Jake's smiling eyes and priceless expression were matched by her dad's.

Dodging youthful bullets was Thelma Diamond's specialty. Madison followed suit. "What is this I hear about a new little brother?"

Melinda's eyes got big. "Tell her about Morgan, Daddy. I'm going to be an aunt and sister all at the same time."

Madison carried Melinda into the sitting area with the others. Henry reached for the pint size, dark-haired, heart stealer. "Both of you are aunts and will soon have another brother."

He relayed Ethan's phone call, the news of Morgan and the request to seek custody.

"How did Mom take the news?"

"You know your mom. She's thrilled that God is entrusting us with another life."

Donald stood and stretched his hand towards his brother-in-law. "I'm calling a truce. Welcome to the family, Jake."

The newest addition playfully wiped his hand across his forehead and then shook the hand of a brother he now appreciated. "Thanks, Donald. You can't resign yet. You have four other sisters that bear watching."

The Guardian looked at his assignments. "Yeah, I'm keeping my eyes on them ... and their male friends."

Thelma moved past everyone and hugged Madison and then Jake. "Welcome to the family."

"Glad to belong, Mrs. D."

After joining the exciting chaos of the large family's celebrations, Jake and Madison shared some of their Hawaiian adventures, including an afternoon at Pearl Harbor. Their suntans spoke of time spent at the beach.

"Jake neglected to tell me that he had spent a couple of summers working at Virginia Beach and learned to surf. I crashed more than I surfed, but I had fun."

"She's being modest. She's a fast learner."

He looked around the room. "Are you aware this woman can hula?"

"Yeah and you should see Mom," Mandy offered.

"What's a hula, Jake?" Melinda asked.

Maria spoke up. "Remember that large ring you try to spin around your waist, Melinda? It's called a hula hoop."

Bright eyes enlarged. "Maddie, will you teach me to hula?"

"Great idea, Melinda. I think the Diamond and Roberts women should have a hula party."

Looking at her younger siblings, Madison whispered. "See if you can talk Santa Claus into spending Christmas in Hawaii next year. Forego the gifts and opt for the trip."

From then on something was always happening. After a few hours of never ending conversations and activities, jet lag plus all the commotion was getting to Jake. "Anybody know where my wife might be?"

"I think she may be in her old room picking up a few more items to transfer to your place. The other girls are divvying up what's left," one of the boys explained.

With that, Jake bounded up the stairs. He knew the girls lived on the second floor and the boys camped out on the third. As he hit the landing, he emitted a fair rendering of Tarzan's jungle cry. Five female heads popped out of the third door on the left. The scene looked like a human staircase. He beat on his chest and did an even better imitation. "Tarzan looking for Jane."

Madison was trying to stifle a belly laugh as she stepped out of the room. "Honestly, Jake, that was embarrassing."

"Then why other girls laughing so hard, Jane?" He swept her off her feet. "Tarzan ready go home, but want Jane go with him."

"If you'll put me down, you can help me get some more of my things to our place." She whispered, "Please behave."

He kissed her lightly and set her down. "Tarzan try behave."

The girls were taking in the scene and giggling behind hands covering their whispers. All except Melinda. She rushed him. "You are not Tarzan. You are Jake. She is Madison." She pointed to each.

Jake abandoned Tarzan for the moment. "I do believe you are right. Guess I need to help Madison get some of her things moved to our place."

Melinda scrutinized him a few seconds. "Madison lives here, Jake. You live next door. The honeymoon is over. You need to go home."

Grabbing the items Madison had set out, he headed for the stairs. "I'm leaving, Sweetheart. I'll let you handle your own exit."

He left whistling a tune from *Snow White and the Seven Drafts. Hi-Ho, Hi-Ho, It's off to Work We Go.*

Jake had been home about an hour when he heard a bump on the door. "Jake, my hands are full. Please open the door."

As he swung the door wide, Madison hurried in laden with food and drinks.

"Honey, why didn't you call or ask for help?"

"I thought I could manage." She deposited her goodies on the small counter.

"I was ready to leave when Mom offered to share their food. Since our cupboards are bare, I accepted. It took us a while to divide it out. Sorry I'm late."

"Tarzan hungry." He started rummaging through the containers and bags and found the ham and rolls.

"How did you explain your departure to Melinda?"

She snickered. "I left her with Mom."

He put the food down and pulled her close. "I know you are accustomed to living with a swarm of people. I hope you'll adjust to just the two of us for a while."

"Jake, I belong with you."

"You don't miss your big family?"

"Haven't so far."

He sorted through more of the food and helped himself to some sweet potato casserole.

"Your honeymoon story was interesting. Can you imagine a month in Hawaii? Not sure about the honey wine every day though."

"Back then, honey was considered a fertility food. They hoped the little woman would be pregnant by the time the honeymoon was over," Madison added.

"That's strange information to know."

"It's part of my love of history, Jake. The origin of such phrases and traditions intrigue me. When we started planning for our wedding, I researched the history behind some of them."

He grabbed a Coke and took his ham sandwich and sweet potatoes to the small table. "Want me to fix something for you?"

"You eat, Tarzan. Jane fix her own plate."

"Tarzan loves Jane."

She put her right hand over her heart and blew him a kiss with the other. "Jane crazy about Tarzan."

"Tarzan glad no place to go."

Twenty-Eight

The rest of December passed with the speed and noise of a fast moving freight train. Except for the Diamonds who were wading through a quagmire of legalities in their efforts to gain custody of Morgan, January brought a quieter and less hectic routine for the families now joined by more than a foot path and property lines.

Josie's involvement in home renovations was a welcomed redirection. Her interest in booze was less, but unknown to those around her, the need to conquer another male was front and center. She noticed a new name on Ted's old office as she hurried to meet her latest flame, Dan.

Her sibling was working hard for his dad and studying for his license, while Madison's last semester of nursing involved the ER and Trauma Unit. It was her third day back.

She was in the cafeteria with friends. A nurse at the next table asked if they had heard about the wedding in ICU today. Another nurse spoke up. "I witnessed it. There hasn't been a dry eye on our floor since then. He's not going to make it, but she married him anyway."

Someone else chimed in. "I heard he was one of the star players on last year's basketball team."

Madison's heart quickened. "Are you referring to the Cavaliers?"

"Yes, that's what they say."

Her heart began to race. "Do you know his name?"

"Henderson. David Henderson."

Madison's hand flew to her mouth to silence the groan that slipped out. When she was able to catch her breath, she asked," Would you happen to know his wife's name?"

Another nurse spoke up, "Callie, I believe."

A wave of nausea hit Madison's gut. Excusing herself, she quickly dropped off her tray and hurried to the closest restroom where her body expelled the food even as her mind refused to digest the news she had heard.

Except for the day Ethan was sentenced to twenty-five years in prison and the day she learned of Jake and Josie's abuse, she could not remember being so shaken. Her body and mind were in such turmoil that she wasn't sure how she made it through her assigned duties.

How was she going to tell Jake? *What* was she going to tell Jake? She couldn't face him yet. She rushed into her parents' house praying at least one of them would be available. Fat chance. Her mom was surrounded by bodies of all sizes asking a dozen questions. Her dad wasn't home.

Madison waved as she moved towards the renovated sun parlor. "I'll be in the chapel for a while." She collapsed on the closest kneeling bench and lifted her eyes to the words on that cross. *I will always love you.*

God, how can You allow this to happen? To them? It's not fair. It's not right. Where are You?

She wept and groaned and struggled with words—and God. Her compassion for the newlyweds ran deep.

The struggling sapped her energy and left no peace. She reached for the Bible tucked in her bench and opened it to Job 14:5 *A person's days are determined; you have decreed the number of his months and have set limits he cannot exceed.*

This hasn't caught You by surprise, has it, Lord?

She noted the cross-reference and turned to Psalm 139:16. *Your eyes saw my unformed body; all the days ordained for me were written in Your book before one of them came to be.*

Before we take our first breath, You know the day we will take our last, don't You?"

Immediately James 4:14 came to mind. *Why, you do not even know what will happen tomorrow. What is your life? You are a mist that appears for a little while and then vanishes. Instead, you ought to say, 'If it is the Lord's will, we will live and do this or that.'*

She remembered her dad's words when Donald's girlfriend died. *The number of our years is not nearly as important as the impact of our life.*

She turned to Psalm 116:15. Her grandmother's funeral was the first time she remembered ever hearing it. *Precious in the sight of the Lord is the death of his faithful servants.*

Madison broke. *David wasn't perfect, Lord, but his heart was always Yours. Evidently You are eager to have him home. Help Callie and his folks understand that. Help Jake too.*

Seeing death from God's prospective brought a calmness to Madison's heart. She returned home praying for Jake.

The minute she caught a glimpse of her happy hubby, she lost her composure. He dropped his briefcase at the door and wrapped her in his arms.

"This is a first. What's going on?"

She looked at him and thought of David. Quiet tears continued to flow and she shook her head wanting this conversation to go away.

"Maddie, you are scaring me."

Grabbing a tissue and blowing her nose, she pulled him onto the sofa. Between the tears and nasal clearing, she managed to share the story she had overheard in the cafeteria … minus the names.

"That's tragic, Honey, but things like that happen every day at hospitals. You've been taught that you cannot get personally involved in the lives of your patients, haven't you?"

She took a deep breath. "Jake, it is someone you know well."

The shock and fear that engulfed Jake replaced his composure. He clutched her closest hand. "Someone I know is dying?"

She nodded and stared at the crumbled tissue in her free hand.

"For crying out loud, Madison, who is it?"

She knelt in front of him and placed her hands on his knees as tears dripped on his pants. "David … Henderson."

Jake's countenance paled as he grabbed her hands and leaped to his feet. "David? You're mistaken, Madison. It can't be him."

"Jake, it's David Henderson from Lynchburg, and he married Callie Adams today."

As all doubts were silenced, Jake closed his eyes and curled his arms over his head as he began to take deep, long breaths. Slowly his arms descended and his eyes grew stormy.

Jake and Josie's Discovery

It was a cold evening, but Jake Roberts headed out the door. He ran the streets of Rugby Heights until his legs could barely move and his body was begging for rest. When he walked back into their apartment an hour later, he was exhausted, but it was the guilt and regret that were smothering him.

He made it as far as the lounger where he collapsed and wept. Madison knelt beside him. Her tears joined his.

Finally he spoke. "She forgave him, Maddie. Callie … forgave … David."

And he wept and clung to his wife. In desperation he asked, "Can I go see him?"

She shook her head. "Only immediate family."

Jake fingered his wedding band. "Josie's seduction blew their original wedding plans to smithereens. What if they are spending their honeymoon in ICU because of Josie and me? What if his death is our fault?"

He was pacing the floor of their nine-hundred-square-feet apartment. "Why didn't I call him when I realized he had been right and I had been wrong? Why didn't I let him know that his life made a difference in mine?"

With that he buried his head in his hands and moaned. "God, I feel so guilty. I'm living the charmed life while David is dying. He's the good guy. I'm the rotten sinner."

A bewildered man faced her. "Where is God in all of this, Maddie?"

Taking his face in her hands, she searched for words to explain what she had experienced today. "Do you know that before we take our first breath that God knows when we will draw our last?"

She shared the verses she had read in the chapel earlier. "Ultimately, life and death are in His hands, Jake. Aren't you glad God put David in your life before He took him home? And think about it. As sad as folks are to lose him, God and heaven are calling it a precious event. Didn't you tell me his mother died during his freshman year at UV? Imagine her joy and anticipation."

He snatched her hand. "I need to go to the chapel."

Thelma kept the children away.

The time there was unlike any either of them had ever experienced. Jake confessed and repented of each memory involving David and Callie that surfaced. He offered thanksgiving for the man's impact on his life. He wept and grieved for their suffering and loss.

He recalled a recent teaching from II Kings 19 and 20 about Elijah's influence being passed to Elisha. As surely as he knew his name, he realized that he wanted his life to impact other young men like David's had his. He rose with a new passion and purpose.

When he shared that impression with Henry and Thelma, they suggested fasting one meal a day with a time of prayer for David and Callie.

Madison spoke up. "Doctors, nurses and medical staff all over that hospital are being impacted by those two. It's like God has given them a megaphone to broadcast the message of His love. Medical folks attending them say that his room feels like a cathedral."

David had been alive when classes ended Friday afternoon. One look at Madison's face Monday evening confirmed Jake's fear. Callie Henderson was a widow.

"He died yesterday afternoon, Jake."

It was a quiet and sobering night. Jake called the Lynchburg paper for funeral arrangements, then he and Madison went next door to tell his family the news. As the story unfolded, Josie fell apart.

"It's my fault. They would have been married months ago if it wasn't for me. The only decent man I've ever known and I killed him."

She would not be consoled.

On the 12th of January, four of David's teammates and a medicated Josie headed to Lynchburg. Jake used that time to share the goodness of God in his life since they graduated, and the part David's life had in it all.

The guys were shocked when he boldly identified himself as an *in-the-beginning-God* believer. All listened. A couple questioned. It was a reflective trip.

Jake wasn't surprised by the crowd streaming in and out of the funeral home, but he wasn't prepared for the sight of David's widow standing beside a casket. Knowing his past was forgiven didn't lessen the pain his actions possibly played in this scene. He could find no words to offer other than "I'm sorry for your loss, Callie."

"Thank you for coming, Jake."

She recognized him and was gracious. What would she do now? What would he do if Madison died? That question was so upsetting that he had to move away. Josie on the other hand was determined to hang close.

David's dad introduced himself and thanked Jake for coming.

"I'm truly sorry, Mr. Henderson."

The man placed his other hand over Jake's. "I believe that, Son."

Jake couldn't speak. He withdrew his hand and spotted Josie talking to Callie who looked ready to bolt.

Before he could respond, Mr. Henderson quickly stepped between the two and escorted Josie in his direction. Jake grabbed her hand and ushered her out the door.

"What was that about, Josie?"

She placed a hand on his arm to stop him. "Don't you understand, Jake? David is dead and Callie is a widow because of me."

She was crying uncontrollably by this point. "I hate myself ... I hate George and Felix and his friends ... I hate men who see me only as a body for their pleasure ... I hate the God who allowed all of this to happen."

He put his arm around her shoulders and drew her close. "Sis, if you want to honor David, give his God a chance."

The trip home was filled with questions about life, death, and God, as six young people faced their own mortality. To the best of his ability, Jake shared how his life had changed since he opened his heart and mind to the possibility that God might be the real deal.

Later that evening, Madison listened as he related the events of the trip. "Josie is tormented, Madison. She knows her life is messed up but she hasn't figured out God is the missing ingredient yet. Why are humans so resistant to the idea of God?"

"I don't know, Jake, but I've heard my dad say that God will allow us to experience the full consequences of our choices in order to bring us to a place of admitting our need, because only then can He help us."

"What's it going to take for her?"

"Only God knows."

She leaned her head on his shoulder. "How is Callie?"

"Numb, I suspect."

He enclosed her in his arms. "I wanted to share her pain, but didn't know how."

"You didn't tell her about your God encounter?"

"It didn't seem like the time."

"Do you think there will ever be a right time, Jake?"

"I pray so, Maddie."

Twenty-Nine

A cold and snowy January gave way to an even colder and snowier February, and like the snow, Josie's depression deepened. While the rest of the families were skiing, skating and sledding, except for classes, she was hibernating. David's death had further eroded her already shaky world.

After receiving her last letter, Ethan alerted his mom. "I'm concerned about Josie, Mom."

"How much has she told you, Son?"

"She's getting pretty desperate. I share about my own experiences, but I'm so new at this. I don't feel like I have answers for her."

"Ethan, you keep sharing what God is doing in your life. He'll take care of the rest. I'll alert Virginia. By the way, it looks like we will be getting Morgan by the eleventh of the month. We have a photo now. I can see you in him."

"Sorry I didn't speak up sooner." He hesitated. "Mom, do you think it would be okay if I call Josie?"

Tears pooled. "Yes, I'm sure it would be."

Thelma shared Ethan's concerns with Virginia the next day. They prayed.

Friday morning the social worker knocked on the seldom used front door of the Diamond residence. Thelma and Melinda responded. Holding Mrs. Vaughter's hand was a tow-headed youngster with a heart-stealing smile and his dad's blue eyes.

Those eyes were fixed on Melinda. Thelma invited them in and in spite of her resolve, tears began to trickle down her cheeks as she led them to the formal living room.

The case worker introduced Morgan who looked from Melinda to Thelma. "Are you my *for real* grandmother? Is she my sister or my aunt? I thought aunts were big people."

Kneeling in front of the child and reaching for his hands, Thelma assured him she was his *for real* grandmother. Before she could explain that Melinda was his aunt, he jumped into her arms.

"I've never had a *for real* anyone before. My real mom and dad had to go away without me. Granny Gray has been my pretend mama." Leaning back and looking in her face, he asked, "Can we call her some time? I like her."

"I'd like to talk to the lady who has raised such a fine young man."

He hugged her again and then turned his attention to Melinda who was also checking him out. What a *Kodak* moment.

Thelma sat down and lifted Melinda into her lap. "Morgan, this is our youngest child, Melinda. Including your daddy, we have nine children."

His eyes got big. He held up his right hand with all fingers spread wide and four half bent ones on his left hand. "Five plus four?"

She laughed and reached for his little hands and counted the small fingers with him. "Yes, nine and you make ten."

He opened up both hands. "I make ten! That's a really big family." He looked at the room that was larger than the house he had lived in the last three years. "And this is a really big house."

He crawled on the seat beside her. "Granny Gray's house is little. This looks like a castle. Do I have a room all by myself?"

She set Melinda on her feet and looked at Mrs. Vaughter. "Yes, why don't we go check it out?"

He started jumping up and down and clapping. "A room of my own? I had to sleep on the pad on the floor at Granny's house."

"Hope you like stairs. You'll be on the third floor with the other boys." Two different little hands found hers.

The time she had spent fixing up Morgan's room was worth the look in his eyes when he walked in. "This is all mine?" He pointed to a photo on the wall. "He looks like me."

Thelma almost cried. "That's a picture of your daddy when he was your age."

Jake and Josie's Discovery

Big eyes studied her and then the other photos she had grouped together. "Are all these my daddy?"

She was crying again. "Yes, Morgan."

"Was this his room?"

Thelma knelt by the grandchild who was finally making a connection with his family. "No, we haven't lived here long, but I tried to make this an Ethan and Morgan room. Is that okay?"

He hugged her long and hard. "I miss my daddy. When will he be home?"

"It will be a while, Morgan."

As Thelma lifted him into her arms. Mrs. Vaughter indicated she needed to leave. Thelma hugged her sweet grandson and set him back down. Melinda's eyes were shooting darts at the newest family member. Thelma lifted the jealous one into her arms. "God sent Morgan for us to love. I need you to help me do that. Okay?"

She laid her head on Thelma's shoulder as they walked to the door. Morgan hugged Mrs. Vaughter. "Tell Granny I have a big room and a big *for real* family and grandmother now."

She smiled and bid them good day.

Thirty minutes later, Thelma grabbed both children and headed to the elementary school to register the latest family addition. By the time they returned, Henry was home.

Morgan saw him in the kitchen grabbing a bite to eat. "Are you my *for real* granddaddy?"

Henry was so overcome, he struggled to answer. He knelt in front of the lad. "That ... would be me."

It had been a long time since a little man had run into his arms. Henry held him close. "I'm glad you are here, Morgan."

"Me too. I start little school Monday."

Henry caught a glimpse of Melinda and realized his oversight. "Morgan, what do you think of my baby girl?" He put an arm around her.

"She's not a baby, but she is a girl."

Henry rumpled the youngster's hair. "That she is, Son."

The foursome spent the rest of the day getting to know each other. They were all in the game room when the bus delivered more Diamonds. The scene that followed was priceless.

Morgan reached for Henry who picked him up and one by one introduced him to four more of his *for-real* family members. The child's delight over his growing family endeared him to their hearts immediately.

By the time Maria arrived home, a stranger wouldn't have guessed that Morgan hadn't been part of the family all his life.

When Donald walked in, Morgan stared. "Holy Moly! You are big. Are you my dad's brother too?"

Donald stooped and swept his nephew in his arms. "Big seems to run in our family, Morgan, and I have a feeling that one day you'll be as big as I am."

"Does my daddy look like you?"

Donald's eyes were collecting moisture. He set him back on the floor and crouched beside him. "Some folks say we do."

Morgan smiled and hugged him again. "Now I know what my daddy looks like."

Those two hugged while the others wiped a few tears.

"We're going to be special buddies, Morgan," Donald promised. "Your room is next to mine and if you ever need anything or have a bad dream, you let me know. Okay?"

"You mean when I have scary dreams about getting lost and being alone, I can come to your room?"

"You betcha."

Morgan stayed close to Donald most of the evening.

When Jake and Madison dropped in, Morgan checked him out from head to toe. "Wow! You are bigger than Donald. Are you my dad's brother too?"

Jake went to his knees but was still towering over the boy. "No, I married your daddy's sister, Madison, but we can be brothers if you want to be."

"Oh, I do." Morgan looked at Madison and leaned close to Jake. "She's pretty."

Jake whispered. "I agree."

Suddenly everyone's ears perked up. The sound of a siren was getting louder and closer. Several ran to the window to look out.

"Mom! Dad! An ambulance just pulled into the Roberts' driveway," Molly announced.

Madison was out the door before anyone else. Jake was close behind. By the time they reached the door, the medics were pulling the gurney out of the ambulance and hurrying in the house. William was manning the door.

"What's going on, Dad?"

"It's Josie. She's not responsive and her breathing is erratic." Madison knew Josie's condition was serious.

As they wheeled her to the ambulance, Jake moved beside Madison. "Go tell your folks what's going on. I'll grab my keys and meet you at the car."

The four Roberts arrived soon after the ambulance, but had to wait for an hour or so before a doctor called their name. Dr. Beckley introduced himself. "Your daughter is suffering from alcohol poisoning. We pumped her stomach. Was she using any kind of drugs that you are aware of?"

Virginia told him about the sedative.

"That would explain why she has not roused yet. We'll put her in ICU until she regains consciousness. If she does okay, we'll move her to a medical wing. In the meanwhile, she needs to be encouraged to seek help."

"Believe me, we've tried. What do you suggest?" William asked.

"Sometimes, these experiences shake them enough to prompt a change of attitude. Let's hope that will be true for her."

By Saturday morning, Josie was coming around. One of the older doctors with years of experience informed her that if her parents had not called an ambulance when they did, she would be dead. "Were you trying to take your life, young lady?"

"No, I was trying to escape it."

He looked at her with the wisdom of decades. "What's the difference?"

She hesitated. "I'm not sure."

"Out of one hundred and thirty-six cases of alcohol poisoning a day, an average of six people die. You came close to being one of those six. Young lady, it's time to quit running and face your giant. Looks like you need a David in your life."

Josie's head snapped in his direction. "Why did you say that?"

"Because you are facing something bigger than you and you need to give someone who knows how to slay the giant of addiction access to your life."

With tears slowly rolling down her cheeks, she looked at his wrinkles and the gray hair. "I know I need help."

"Good. I'm going to keep you for twenty-four more hours, but I'll be making you an appointment to get back with Dr. Metcalf by next week."

"Thank you." Tears were plentiful. She didn't want to die. She just wanted free from the turmoil inside her head and the pain in her heart. Alcohol and drugs offered temporary relief but solved nothing. Was there a David for her?

By Sunday afternoon, Josie was home and sober. William had personally cleaned out every trace of alcohol he could find in her suite. "If your mom or I smell alcohol on your breath again, you will have to move out, Josie. We love you too much to watch you kill yourself."

"I'll try, Dad."

Later that night she heard the phone ring but ignored it. Virginia tapped on her door. "Josie, the call is for you."

"I don't want to talk to anyone."

"Not even Ethan?"

"Ethan?" A butterfly sensation hit her stomach and her heart skipped a few beats. "I'll take it in here."

She picked up the phone and suddenly the letters had a voice. Their initial uneasiness soon gave way to comfortable conversation between friends.

"You are going to seek help, aren't you, Josie?"

"Yeah, would you believe Dr. Beckley compared my addiction to a giant? Prison took care of yours. What do you suggest I do?"

She was getting tangled in the phone cord.

"You know my story, Josie. Prison made me want to die. God gave me a reason to live."

"I'm sorry to state the obvious, but what good has that done you? You're still locked up."

"Physically, yes, but Josie, I'm free on the inside and my head is clearer than it's been in my life. Can you say that?"

He halted briefly. "Right now, you're in a prison worse than mine."
He's not as bright as I thought he was.
"You still there?" Ethan's voice was kind.
"Yeah. You don't beat around the bush, do you?"
"Not any more. I was a rebellious kid set on living life my way, Josie. I ended up an addict because I didn't want anyone telling me what to do. The drugs made me feel good in the beginning. I lied and stole everything I could get my hands on to buy them. They soon took over my body, soul and spirit. I knew it was wrong to rob that bank, but I had to feed the demon of heroin. I'm in this place, Josie, because I listened to the stupid lies of stupid people. And that's why I will spend many more years behind these bars.

"So yes, I'm going to tell you the truth every chance I get. I learned the importance of that the hard way.

"But you know something? It took this place to break me. I thank God for these walls and bars. I wish I wasn't here, Josie, but the truth is—if I wasn't, I'd be dead."

"You really mean that, don't you?"

"Yeah, I do. Promise you'll think about what I said? I don't want to lose you and I don't want you to mess up your life. Do you hear me?"

Josie was trying to unknot the phone cord. "I hear you. Do you think we will ever meet, Ethan?"

"In order for that to happen, you'll have to come to me, and a lot of miles and barriers separate us. But miracles do happen. Think I'll add your name to my visitors' list. If you are half as pretty as this photo I have on my mirror, I can understand your men problems. Is it okay if I call you when I can?"

"If you promise not to quit writing. I re-read your letters almost every day."

"Same here. I'll call when possible, but let's give those postal workers something to do. Okay?"

"Yeah."

Long after they hung up, Josie was still pondering the conversation. She didn't believe in God but she couldn't explain the changes in Jake and Ethan. Was it possible she was wrong?

Ethan and Josie continued to stay in touch via phone and letters for the next few weeks, then suddenly all communication ceased.

She approached Thelma.

"We haven't heard from him either, Josie. Did he mention that he was being transferred in the near future?"

"Yeah, but wouldn't he give us notice?"

"He can't. He doesn't know exactly when it will happen. Did he tell you he can't take anything with him?"

Josie's eyes widened. "No. Does that include the letters I've written and the books he's been reading? Even his Bible?"

"Yes. A friend of ours back home is going to pick them up and send them to me. Would you like to have your letters back?"

Josie actually blushed. "Yes. Ethan has become a special friend, Ms. Thelma."

"You'll hear from him soon."

She was tracing the mortar joints between the stones with her foot. "Do you have a photo of him I could have?"

Thelma patted Josie's arm. "Sure. I'll have one to you by tomorrow."

"Thanks."

A week later, both women received a letter from Ethan informing them of his move to the United States Penitentiary in Atlanta and his new address. Visits would involve a five-hundred-and-forty-mile road trip.

There were more letters than phone calls at this point because calls were limited. But the man was excited about the new freedoms he had at his new location. Josie cried as she read about his being able to go outside without shackles and cuffs for the first time in two years.

Then he shared about his newest pen pal. A six-year-old girl named Hope. She and her family had been praying for him for some time and now Hope was making special cards for him. "Getting a card from Hope feels like a card from Jesus," he had included in his last letter.

His letters were filled with excitement and freedom, not imprisonment and despair. And he talked about his Bible study groups and Sunday services like they were Michael Jackson concerts.

Theirs was a crazy relationship. She could lie to him and he'd never know, but for reasons she couldn't explain, she didn't want to.

She trusted him and she wanted him to trust her. So when she was tempted to drink or struggled with the counseling session, she grabbed her writing tablet and pen and poured out her heart to a man she had never met.

When she had a really good day, she spent the evening writing him about that too. For the first time in her life, she had someone who knew everything about her and accepted her, but wasn't about to allow her to stay that way. She had a best friend.

Thirty

The last of February, William approached Jake. "Son, I've contacted George and arranged to meet him at the Gunter Hotel in downtown San Antonio, March 4, at 7 p.m. I didn't mention that you might be coming. Are you sure you want to do this?"

Jake turned to take in the view outside his dad's office before responding. "I'm sure."

William's expression relaxed. "Good."

Jake watched the pedestrians and drivers scurrying to their next appointments while dodging the miniature hills created by the snow plows and series of winter storms that had been hitting the area. "Dad, I have no idea how George will respond, and that's a little scary."

He walked back to the chair in front of William's desk. "Do you think he was abused?"

"That's the first question I intend to ask."

Though some had labeled the snows of 1977 as the *White Hurricanes*, March 4, hinted of spring. Their flight left Richmond at noon and arrived at San Antonio International Airport four hours later. William called George to let him know he had arrived and to confirm the meeting. By the time they got settled in their suite and ordered food, it was time to face the past.

"Jake, I'd like for you to stay in the bedroom while I talk to George. I find myself torn between wanting to tear him apart and wondering what happened to him. Leave the door cracked. I think we'll know when it's time to confront."

"I'm nervous, Dad. More than I thought I'd be. Just thinking about seeing him makes me feel dirty and guilty ... and ashamed."

Jake and Josie's Discovery

"The child was not at fault, Jake. I can vouch for the fact that the man has dealt honorably with the fallout. Don't allow seeing and confronting George to undo any of that."

Jake relaxed some. "Thanks for the reminder and approval, Dad."

When a knock sounded at the door. Jake slipped into the bedroom as his emotionally charged dad opened the door and stared at his grown-up, baby brother. The age difference, plus William's rare trips back home once he left at age eighteen, made blood the only thing that connected them ... until now.

Evidently George picked up on the tension. He hesitated. William gained enough control to step back and invite his guest inside. "Come in, George. How are things going for you?"

From his uniform to his speech, George mirrored military. He entered with an air of confident cautiousness. "I can't complain. I finally earned my wings and hope to one day be a flight instructor."

They took seats facing each other. "I'm impressed. Earning your Air Force wings puts you in an elite group of pilots. Were you always interested in flying?"

George relaxed. "I can't remember when I didn't want to fly. After landing a part-time job out of high school at the local municipal airport, I worked my way through college. Afterwards I enlisted in the Air Force for the sole purpose of becoming a pilot. It's been a long haul, but the career of my dreams is now a reality. I recently married and we are expecting our first child. How about you and your family?"

All the time William was sharing the highlights of his own life and family, he was scrutinizing his brother. Nothing about his appearance or speech would make one suspect he was capable of such appalling behavior.

William deliberately rose from his seat and approached the window overlooking downtown. He could not pretend any longer. He pivoted and with all the control he could muster, faced the abuser of his children. "George, my primary motive for meeting with you has more to do with the past than the present."

"The past? Our age gap and your rare visits home robbed us of that."

William picked up on the resentment in that statement and moved in front of a man that could match him in size and was probably in better shape. "Some disturbing information has come to my attention within the last year."

With a slight air of defensiveness, George rose to his feet. "Why don't you quit beating around the bush and get to the point?"

William didn't budge from his spot ... or his purpose. "Were you ever sexually abused as a child, George?"

Anger clouded his face immediately. "You brought me here to ask about my sex life?"

George headed for the door.

"I wouldn't advise leaving, Brother. Either you answer my questions or my next stop will be the base military police."

George whipped around. His face was flushed and his hands were clenched. "Are you threatening me, William?"

"Nope. Making you a promise."

Confused and furious, George moved into William's personal space. "Why would you ask such a personal question? And if I was, what business is it of yours?"

William stepped around George and nonchalantly positioned his body against the door. "It became my business when I learned you had molested my children. Now you can answer my question or I may ignore the fact that we are related and beat you within an inch of your life."

Mocking laughter countered. "Look, William, I don't know what Jake and Josie have told you, but it's a lie. Mom and Dad would never have tolerated such behavior, and you know it."

William stayed between the man and the door, but edged towards him until they were within inches of each other. He was aching to unleash the pain and anger inside him. "You are not listening, George. Were you abused or introduced to sex at an early age?"

With a sarcastic tone and defiant body language, George retorted. "Listen, long-lost Brother. I agreed to meet you, because I thought you wanted us to get to know each other. I resent your accusing me of things your kids made up. And I might not be the one beat up if you don't back off."

William never flinched. "You can come out now, Jake."

George's head jerked towards the bedroom and his rigid body slumped as his six feet five inches, two hundred fifty pound nephew joined them.

While the two were observing each other, William didn't miss a beat. "The kid grew up, George, and I'm pretty sure he's not real happy that you've called him a liar."

With his protective father instincts gathering momentum, William wedged between the two and put his hand on George. "All I can picture in my mind right now is you robbing both my children of their innocence—repeatedly—to satisfy something gone haywire inside you. I expected you to protect and defend them, not use and abuse them."

He pushed George back a step. "You are going to be a father soon. Do you want some sick pervert to molest your child, or God forbid, would you do so yourself? My children's lives have been majorly impacted by the damage you inflicted on them. And yet, you deny your behavior and the soul sickness that spawned it."

William glanced at Jake and remembered the day his children came to him. "George, if I could have gotten my hands on you the day I found out, you would be minus your manly parts. But the more I thought about it and the more I talked with a counselor, the more convinced I became that you too must have been a victim."

A slight softening was evident in his voice and expression. "Seeing what being a victim did to Jake and Josie instilled a small measure of compassion for you. That is the only reason I haven't already turned you in to the authorities. Getting through this conversation is not going to be easy, but I am determined it will take place. Either you talk now or we'll go to the base police and file a report. The choice is yours."

William moved back to his chair and Jake settled on the sofa. "Now, let's try again."

George lifted his head and his eyes sought William's. "You're not going to tell anyone about this, are you? I would lose everything."

William had witnessed the pain of his children's confession and it appeared there was more heartache to be revealed. "That's going to depend on you."

George began pacing. Jake and William watched quietly.

"You were gone by the time the Masons moved to town and joined our church. Mr. Mason and Dad became close friends which put our families together often. Both Masons had been married before and each brought a child into the marriage.

"Kenneth was two years older than me and we became as close as our dads. I was twelve when he first introduced me to sex. He started with a stash of girly magazines under his old man's bed. Those images lit a fire in me that begged to be fed.

"Next thing I knew we were sneaking into his ten-year-old stepsister's room. Scared me to death the first night. He told her that we had come to play. The girl cried and trembled the entire time. I kept telling him that we'd get killed if she told on us. He laughed and said she had no one to tell. Seems his old man visited her more often than Ken did.

"That continued the three years the Masons stayed in town. They had moved away the first summer Jake and Josie came for a visit."

He glanced at Jake. "I thought you enjoyed it."

All the memories came rushing back, and the lust and stirring of his flesh filled Jake with guilt and a fresh sense of loathing. He jumped up, grabbed George by his coat lapels and pulled him close. "Enjoyed it? You aroused the sex drive that God meant to bless and bring beauty as well as pleasure in the union of a man and his wife, not a young boy with another boy. The demons I have had to fight this last year could fill a corner of hell."

George was visibly shaken.

"What about Josie? Did you think she was enjoying it?"

Trying to put some distance between them, George put his hands on Jake's chest. "No, but Kenneth said girls don't like it at first but if I'd be patient, they'd change their minds at some point. I thought she enjoyed it the last two summers."

Jake yanked George close to his face again. "You knew it was wrong every time you walked in her room. You used your own niece to satisfy a perverted sickness in you. How did you justify using Kenneth's sister?" He gave him a slight push and then grabbed him again.

George tried to resist and Jake flipped him over the back of the sofa. He jumped up and dusted himself off. "That girl was so messed up by the time I got to her that I didn't figure I was doing her any damage."

That brought William to his feet on the other side of the man. "I still may redesign your body parts. How do you think she got so messed up, George? Could it be that beasts like you treated her as less than a human being for their own sick pleasure? Don't tell me you didn't know it was wrong. Does the word *respect* have any meaning to you?"

George glared angrily at William. "Respect? Where would I have learned that? Dad had no respect for us and less for Mom. I never understood respect until I joined the military. That's one of the reasons I was so determined to earn my wings and make a career with them. Folks respect me now."

Jake's emotions were vacillating between anger and compassion. "You haven't answered my question. Did you or did you not know it was wrong?"

George hung his head. "I knew, but after four years with Kenneth, I didn't know how to put out the fire. I was addicted."

That statement hit Jake with the force of an f-5 tornado. He backed away from George and collapsed on the sofa with his head in his hands. "I understand about the fire of addiction and using others to satisfy the cravings ... thanks to you."

He searched George's face. "Is this the first time you've ever faced the ugliness of your depraved lifestyle, George?"

His military toughness was giving way to personal pain. "I've admitted it to myself, but never anyone else."

"Have there been other victims?"

George sank into the nearest chair and nodded.

William spoke up. "Right now I'm torn between wanting to rip you apart and trying to help you find a way out of your debauchery. Although Jake is climbing out of his inferno of sexual abuse and the addictions that followed, my daughter is still fully engulfed in its flames."

George lifted his head. "That's me. I've tried, but it never lasts. I thought marriage would help, but it hasn't. I'm addicted to porn to the point that Sarah has threatened to leave me."

He stood up. "The thought of anyone abusing my child nauseates me, but in all honesty, I keep wondering if I'm capable of doing it myself."

An emotional Jake moved in front of his abuser. "I have good news for you, George. Change is possible, but you have to hate what you have become enough to allow God and folks who care to help. You're looking at the proof."

Jake put his hands in his pockets. "I wish with all my heart that you had resisted Kenneth's perverted influence in your life. I wish I had known to resist yours or at least told someone. I wish you and I didn't have a sexually immoral past.

"Wishing can't change what was, but God can change us. Admit your need, George."

Jake turned towards William. "Tell him his choices, Dad."

"Here's the deal, George. You have to get gut honest with at least two other people. I want you to see a counselor. Jake insists that you include a person of faith. If at any time, contact with you or those two ceases, we will contact the authorities in your area. You chose to do wrong. Now you can choose to do right or face the choices of your past in court."

William handed him a business card. "On the back is also my home phone number and address. "I expect to hear from you and your accountability partners twice a month."

A relieved George rose and reached for the card. "Thank you."

He studied William for a moment. "Jake talks about the things of God. You don't."

William considered his son and then his brother. "I grew up hating God and the church, George, but I'm learning that Dad's view of God was warped and twisted. My dear wife has quietly and lovingly presented a caring and compassionate God for twenty-four years and recently this son of mine has loudly confirmed she has been right all the time. I can't say I'm a believer, but I'm not angry anymore."

George handed William a card with his personal information and headed for the door. "I need to get home. Sarah will be wondering what happened to me. I confess to you that I'm plenty scared about what lies ahead. If she or the military finds out about this, life will be over for me. Thank you for giving me a chance."

Jake stepped forward. "George, for your sake and theirs, at some point get honest with the other victims."

George paused. "I guess I ought to start with you." He reached out his hand. "I'm sorry, Jake, for dragging you into my world of perversion and addiction. Had I known what those first days with Kenneth would lead to, I would have run from him. I wish you had known to run from me. Will you tell Josie that I'm sorry?" Tears were gathering in his eyes.

He looked at their clasped hands. "If you hadn't come along, I'd never had the courage to face this demon I've lived with since I was twelve years old. As unexpected and disturbing as this confrontation has been, you have given me hope."

All three were stuffing down emotions as George exited the room. "I'll be in touch."

Quietness and reflection occupied the remainder of the evening. When Jake announced he was going to take a walk, William decided to join him. The sights and sounds of a night on the streets of a big city reminded them of the sexual revolution and the epidemic of abuse that accompanied it.

Jake walked and reflected. William walked and wondered.

Thirty-One

Once back in Virginia, William and Jake shared the details of the trip with their wives and waited for the first contact from George.

In the meanwhile, winter offered one more Currier and Ives setting. The Diamonds were making paths down the hill at the back of their house on sleds, inner tubes and Thelma's large cookie trays. Morgan and Melinda had persuaded Jake to join them. He left a note for Madison.

Thelma was preparing a large kettle of homemade hot chocolate and a pot of hearty chili when her phone rang. It was Madison's supervisor trying to locate Jake. Thelma grabbed a coat and scanned the area. He was sledding down the hill with both little ones in front of him. Daniel was close by. "Son, would you tell Jake I have an important message for him?"

She watched as Daniel fulfilled his mission and Jake began scanning the landscape and bodies for her. She motioned him in.

He moved as fast as the snow and the hill would allow.

"How can I help you?"

She handed him a phone number. "Madison's supervisor wants you to call."

Concern creased his face. "What's going on?"

"She didn't say."

Jake hurried to their apartment and placed the call. His heart took on a new rhythm and his knees went weak as he listened to the supervisor explain that Madison had been placed in intensive care within the hour. "Her symptoms hint of meningitis. We need to determine if it is viral or bacterial. We are doing a spinal tap now."

"How serious is meningitis?"

The brief silence that followed beckoned a recent memory of other newlyweds.

"Bacterial is more serious than viral, Mr. Roberts. We're crossing our fingers. We have caught it early which is tremendously important either way."

He shucked off his snow apparel and quickly donned some suitable clothes before going next door. Tears clouded his vision as he shared the news with Madison's mom. Thelma hugged him. Her eyes were leaking too.

As Jake headed for his car, he heard Thelma's request for everyone to meet in the chapel.

The trip to the hospital took twice as long due to the snow and ice on the hills. Jake wanted to believe and trust that Madison would be okay, but he could still see David's body in the casket. Tears were free falling and fear was having a heyday by the time he arrived.

He hurried to the ICU, gave his name and asked about Madison. "She's in isolation until the results of the spinal tap come back. Let me check with the head nurse."

While Jake was waiting, Henry exited the elevator. "Any word?"

Jake shook his head and breathed easier. He was not alone. Henry motioned toward the sitting area. "Come sit down, Jake."

"I can't. I've never been as scared in my life."

"What are you afraid of, Jake?"

"Losing her!" He stopped in front of his father-in-law. "Aren't you?"

Henry pulled his bifocals and a small brown New Testament out of his pocket and read Psalm 56:3. *"When I am afraid, I will trust in you."*

"Being afraid is human and comes naturally, Jake. Trusting God comes from learning to live in relationship with Him. When we begin to understand the depth of His love for us and the measures He took to prove it, our trust level increases."

Jake sat down beside Henry. "Well, my relationship must be in the basement right now, because I'm filled with fear."

"Son, do you believe that God brought Madison into your life for your good?"

"You know I do."

"Has He forgiven your sins and given you a new life? Is He continually changing your mind as you soak in His Word? Do you find your relationship with Him helps you resist the lies and behaviors of your past? Are you living a miracle every day?"

His eyes lit up. "Yes ... to all."

"Then dare to trust Him for what is happening today."

"So you don't think this is punishment for my past?"

"No, Jake. This is the result of living in a world where sin and disease exist, because we have an enemy whose goal is our demise.

"Let's choose to trust Madison to the God who made her and loves her more than we do. There's no peace anywhere else."

Jake prayed silently. *Lord, I admit I love Madison more than anyone else, including You. I don't know how to change that and I'm filled with fear right now. You gave her to me. Guess now I need to trust her to You.*

A nurse interrupted them. "Mr. Roberts, the doctor is with your wife now and has asked for you to join them."

Jake introduced Henry. "You may come too, Sir."

When they entered the room, Jake's eyes inspected every inch of Madison. Other than an IV drip bag, she looked tired, but normal. With a groggy grin, she offered her hand. Touching her was like breathing after holding his breath for an impossibly long time.

The doctor was looking at her chart. "Good news, Jake. It's viral. We're going to move her out of isolation, but I'd like to keep an eye on her for the next forty-eight hours. We don't want pneumonia to set in. You can stay with her if you like. Two to three weeks and she should be fully recovered."

"Thank you, Sir."

Gratitude overwhelmed Jake. He refused to leave Madison except to shower and change clothes the next two days. By the time he got her home, he had arranged with his dad to work out of their apartment for a week.

The next two weeks was a season of much reflection for Jake and Madison. A growing awareness of God's grace and love throughout their lives was generating a mixture of repentant and grateful hearts.

Thirty-Two

Josie Roberts hadn't missed a session with Dr. Metcalf since being released from the hospital. They had finally finished the ones she had ignored or missed months ago.

"Today, Josie, we are going to address what I believe to be the root of your struggles. We live by what we believe to be true, and too many times that is not in line with what is true. Have you ever heard the quote that suggests that truth will set us free?"

She twiddled her thumbs and smiled. "Yeah, Jake and Ethan tell me that regularly."

"Well, if truth sets us free, what do lies do?"

Her eyes lit up. "Imprison us?"

"Good answer." Her conversation with Ethan on this subject resurfaced.

"So how does one determine what is true and what is not?"

She shifted in her chair. "Doesn't it depend on the situation?"

"Are you suggesting that truth is changeable?"

"Dad says truth is relative. Isn't that what relative means?"

"Yes, it is."

He handed her a dictionary. "Would you look up the words *true* and *truth* and summarize their definitions?"

She flipped through the pages and studied both words. "Both definitions indicated that if something is true then it agrees with facts or what is."

"Where in that definition does changeable or relative fit, Josie?"

"I don't understand."

"Is the sun shining today, Josie?"

She looked out the window. "No."

"You have agreed with the *facts or what is* in our neck of the woods. You have spoken truthfully."

"But can't something be true for me and not you? The sun is shining somewhere today."

"Yes it is, but has the truth changed or simply revealed the fact that different locations are experiencing different weather conditions?"

"I'm with you so far."

"Let's try something else. Is alcohol addictive?"

"It depends on the person. See. It's relative."

"Or does truth reveal the fact that alcohol is addictive to some people and not addictive to others?"

"My mind is running through a dozen scenarios. I'm going to have to think about this."

Dr. Metcalf picked up his clipboard. "Good. Those truths are definable and explainable in our physical world. My assignment for you this week is more difficult.

"Is there ultimate truth that governs our lives and relationships? If so what is its foundation? If not, then how does one determine the principles to live by?"

He removed the sheet of paper from the clipboard and slipped it into her file. "Ask folks you know. Read. Study. Investigate. Bring your collected materials and thoughts to our next session."

"Dr. Metcalf, I've avoided this line of thinking all my life."

"As a friend of mine often asks, 'How's that working for you?'"

"Not so well."

As soon as she got home, she grabbed a notepad and began to systematically interview folks. Her dad and several of her professors and classmates were convinced that truth is relative.

One of her professors and a couple of random students she interviewed agreed with her Mom, Jake, Madison and Henry that God is the source of truth. Ethan added that Satan is the father of all lies. But it was Thelma's answer that caused her to ponder.

Thelma handed her an apple. "What is the apple's source, Josie?"

"Probably Kroger or Junior's." She took a bite.

"No, those are the distributors, not the source."

"Oh, you mean an apple tree."

"Yes, and just as the apple has its source in an apple tree, if ultimate truth exists then it too must have a source. Any ideas?"

Josie pondered before answering. "Is that why you believe in God?"

"Guess it's time to tell you my story. When I met Henry, God occupied zero percent of my thought processes. I was angry at the world and out to prove I was more than a body to please a man. After all, God had never done anything for me.

"All I ever wanted was what every girl longs for. To love and be loved. To be accepted and valued for who am I. To find a niche in life and be happy. I decided that being the life of the party was the way to accomplish all those goals. And that's where I met Henry's wild brother.

"I knew Henry was different the first time we met and I was drawn to him like a moth to a flame. He asked questions that made me think. After several weeks, he challenged me with the very question you are asking.

"Because of my attraction to him, I began an honest search for truth. Up front I realized that if God wasn't the source of truth then each person becomes their own god or allows some other human that role in their life. I knew I wasn't qualified for such a task and didn't know anyone who was. So with Henry's help I spent six months checking out the possibility that the source of truth might be God.

"The Bible affirms that truth has a source and a name. Jesus made the statement in John 14:6 that *He is the way, the truth and the life*. And he added *no one comes to the Father, except by me.*

"That brought me to a crossroad. Does truth have a source? Is it God? Is Jesus the embodiment of truth? If not, how does one determine what is true and what is not?

"Henry challenged me to be honest with God about my doubts, but to give Him permission to change my mind. I did and the rest is history. God always responds to a seeking heart, Josie."

The inquisitive young woman put her notepad away. "So the Doc's question really involves my belief system?" She was studying this lady who had intrigued her from the first day they met.

"Yes, and if you decide God doesn't exist, then you have simultaneously decided that ultimate truth does not exist. The absence of ultimate truth, means one person's truth becomes another person's lie. What does that sound like to you?"

"Confusion and chaos."

"I'm going to challenge you to give God a chance, Josie. John 16:13 tells us that *the Spirit of truth will guide us into all truth*. God is eager to prove that fact to you personally. A heart that admits a need and cries out for help will never be turned away. Let me get something for you."

She returned with a little pink book. "God's written word reveals the source of truth. I challenge you to read the gospel of John with an open heart and mind. Question Him about things you don't understand. Ask your mom or come to me. You will find the answers when you seek with all your heart."

Josie returned to Dr. Metcalf the next week with her pages of comments and a seeking heart, but no answer.

"So what is your conclusion, Josie?"

She flipped through her pages of notes. "That I need to give serious thought to the idea of God as the ultimate source of truth or accept the fact that I'll never know whose truth or lies to believe."

"Then I'm going to leave that between you and God. I'll check on your progress weekly. Our next area of concern is relationships. Let's talk about yours."

He listened as she spoke of her dad, mom, brother and sister-in-law. She mentioned the growing relationship between her and the lady next door.

"What about friendships with peers, Josie?"

She admitted that she had never had any friends her age, except Jake and maybe Nicolas at one time. "But now I have a best friend. His name is Ethan."

"Tell me about him."

She shared how the connection occurred and the communication that had been taking place between them. "You don't think it's weird that my best friend is in prison?"

He smiled. "Actually I find it intriguing. All the other males in your life have been possible targets for conquest. You knew from the beginning that would not be the case with Ethan. That opened the door for you to find out what a relationship without sex could be like. Tell me the difference."

"I've been thinking about that. I can't conquer him. He can't use me. Our relationship had to be built on something other than sex and

I'm surprised. I really care for this guy. I find it easy to talk to him about everything. I trust him. And you know what? He trusts me.

"I didn't know that having a friend would be so neat. Sometimes I think I want to meet him and other times I'm afraid it will mess everything up."

"Why is that, Josie?"

"Because all my life it's been my face and body that have appealed to men. I need someone to care about the person inside, Doc."

The good doctor chuckled. "No red-blooded man can ignore your beauty, Josie, but give him a chance, and I think you'll find Ethan is genuinely interested in you as a person."

She looked up with hope in her eyes. "You really think so?"

He nodded and closed her chart. "I'm going to suggest that you make plans to visit Ethan if at all possible. Your assignment for the next two weeks is to seek out another friend. One you can interact with face-to-face."

Josie saw Thelma the next day and asked if she could join them sometime when they visited Ethan. "We have an appointment to see him Sunday. Be ready at 7:00 a.m."

"Do we have to tell him that I'm coming?" Josie asked.

"We have to alert the prison, but we'll ask if they will keep your visit a surprise."

It was Sunday morning, April 10, 1977. When Josie's alarm went off at five o'clock, she sprang from the bed with more excitement than she had experienced in years. All through her shower and breakfast, she tried to imagine what seeing Ethan would be like.

Thelma had explained that they would be flying out of the Charlottesville-Albemarle Airport. Josie was shocked when they approached a Beechcraft Super King Air 200 and Henry climbed in the pilot's seat.

"Henry uses the plane for business, but it also enables us to visit Ethan. It's a clear day so we'll make it in less than three hours. Have you flown before?"

Josie's eyes were huge. "No." She chose a seat and spent the trip gazing at the earth from a different perspective. For the first time in her life she realized how small her little corner of the world was. That led her to seriously ponder Ethan's even smaller spot.

The flight was mesmerizing; the prison was intimidating. Even though Thelma had advised her about the security clearance, she was a bit embarrassed by the body search. The entire process of passing through gates and being locked out and in ... of being confined in such a place shook her.

She had never felt claustrophobic before but she was experiencing tinges of something pushing in on her. The words *prison* and *freedom* suddenly took on new meanings.

This was Ethan's world and she felt physically sick. Twenty-three more years within these walls? Tears were rolling down her cheeks by the time they entered the meeting room.

Thelma noticed. "Try to be brave for him, Josie." She handed her a tissue. "Why don't you sit in the corner? Henry and I will talk to him for a spell and then I'll motion for you."

Josie nodded and moved to the designated spot. A couple of playful hummingbirds joined the swarm of butterflies that were playing tag or red-rover in her midsection.

The inmates began entering the room and connecting with their visitors. She recognized Ethan the second he walked through the door. Tears rolled down her cheeks as she watched the greeting between him and his folks. She watched as much as possible, but always ducked her head when he glanced her way.

He was eight years older than Madison. That would make him ... thirty or thirty-one. She looked around this place and realized this was the extent of his time and the only place he would share with family or anyone outside these walls for many years to come. No wonder he tried to end it all.

But he doesn't want to die anymore. Instead he insists he has a purpose in living—even in this place. She considered his daily existence and watched in complete amazement. He was happy.

He glanced her way at that moment and instinctively she smiled. He shot out of his chair and glanced between her and his folks who were smiling and nodding.

That was when he turned all of his attention on her. She knew he was admiring the view, but he was also seeing his friend. Emotions she couldn't explain or control were pulsing through her body.

Thelma stood and motioned her to come forward. She didn't remember walking the distance between them. She just remembered looking into his blue eyes and seeing the face of the only friend she had ever had. Tears were trailing down her cheeks.

"Hi, Ethan." Without giving it a second thought, she hugged him ... and their hearts collided.

Shyly Josie backed away and took the seat beside Thelma. Ethan had yet to speak. He slowly sat down but his eyes never left her face.

Henry reached for Thelma's hand, and they moved to the back of the room.

"Are you trying to kill me? I almost had a heart attack when I realized you were the girl in the corner." She watched him drink in every feature of her face. He briefly glanced at her body and gave a low whistle. "Maybe I did have a heart attack and am in heaven. Your photo doesn't do you justice. No wonder you have men problems."

"Is the face and body all you see, Ethan?"

"No. I know what's inside that beautiful wrapping. If you looked like Gravel Gertie, you would still be my best friend."

He leaned back and grinned like a Cheshire cat. "But since you and Gertie don't have anything in common, I'm going to enjoy God's wondrous creation as long as I can. When I put you on my visitors' list, I dreamed you would come, but I never believed it would happen. I still can't believe you are here."

With that, the two took up where the last letter or phone call ended. They chatted and laughed like old friends. Thelma and Henry watched and wiped stray tears.

When the time came to leave, Ethan choked up. "I will never forget this day or you. Just think, Josie. If I hadn't messed up my life, we would be neighbors ... and maybe much more."

She couldn't stop the tears. "Take care, Ethan."

When she stood, he placed his cuffed hands on her arm. Their eyes locked and she watched as moisture gathered in his eyes. She backed away as the guard indicated his time was up.

When he was out of sight, Josie fell in Thelma's arms and wept like a baby. "How do you deal with this pain? How does he?"

"Come on, Sweetheart. We'll talk on the way home."

Leaving wasn't any easier than entering. She felt like she was leaving half her heart inside the walls. She had a new understanding of the heartache the Diamonds lived with every day.

The first half of the return trip, she peppered Henry and Thelma about Ethan, their lives, their family, their faith. The second half she snuggled in the comfortable seat and let the events of the day settle. She was emotionally exhausted and finally fell asleep.

"What do you think our boy will have to say about his visit with Miss America?" Henry asked.

"He's falling in love with her, Henry, and that breaks my heart. She needs more than he can give. I think they would have made a grand couple." Thelma wept for both of them.

"They are friends, Hon. We have to let them work out the rest."

THIRTY-THREE

Josie's visit with Ethan kindled the flames of their friendship. They called it that, but both knew that if circumstances were different, it could be more.

Because of their growing closeness, Josie was wrestling with Dr. Metcalf's assignment of making another friend. Saturday morning, she half-heartedly dialed the number of the only other possible friend she had ever had.

She was about to hang up when Nicolas answered. "Hello."

Hearing his voice after all these months stirred a butterfly or two. She hesitated. "Huh ... this is a friend ... a voice from your past."

There was a long silence. "Hi, Josie. Believe it or not, you've been on my mind lately."

"I have?"

"Yeah. Could we get together sometime soon and talk?" There was a gentleness in his voice that wasn't there the last time.

"I'd like that."

"I need to stop by Mom's this morning. What if I drop by your place this afternoon? Say around four o'clock?"

"See you then, Nick."

"I'm looking forward to it."

Although it was an assignment that prompted that call, Josie realized she was a little antsy about seeing Nicolas again.

Shopping seemed a good way to calm the unexpected jitters she was experiencing. All the time she was shopping for some outfits with a more tailored look, she wondered if seeing Nicolas was a betrayal of Ethan.

By the time she heard his vehicle arrive later in the day, she had lost count of the number of *Tums* she had consumed.

Nicolas and her dad were fully engaged in conversation when she walked in. Being the recipient of his heart-stopping smile made her feel like she had hit the first drop on a roller coaster ride.

"Hi, Josie." He kissed her cheek and stepped back. "I like the new look."

"Thanks. It's good to see you, Nick."

Virginia's entrance disrupted the reconnecting moment as she offered a tray of snacks and drinks. "Enjoy."

Nicolas intercepted the delivery. "Thanks, Mrs. R. Looks delicious." He cast an inquiring glance at Josie.

"Oh, let's head to the game room," Josie said as she led the way down the hall.

Nick set the food tray on the card table and turned to Josie. "Thanks for letting me stop by. I've wanted to talk to you but have been too chicken to call."

"A lot has happened since I left, Nicolas."

He reached for a bottle of Coke and a brownie. "You too, huh?"

"Yeah. How about racking up and we can catch up while I humiliate you?"

He laughed as he exchanged his cola for a cue stick. "As I recall, you have never been considered a pool shark, Miss Roberts."

She chalked her tip and grinned. "Like I said. A lot has happened."

It didn't take long for the strain between them to give way to the years of knowing each other. After discussing his work and her schooling, Josie shared about Jake and Madison.

"You wouldn't believe the changes in him. He blames it on Madison and God. Sometimes he freaks me out."

She missed her second shot. "What about you? Any serious girlfriends? How are your sisters?"

His countenance clouded as he called his shot. "You remember, Bella and Gina?"

"Sure."

He made his shot and faced Josie.

"Long story short. I found out Christmas Eve that my step father had sexually abused both of them. Mom refused to believe it until Gina turned up pregnant. I convinced the girls to file charges and since Gina is a minor he is in jail where he belongs."

"Oh, Nick!" Tears of understanding and compassion were pooling in her eyes.

"Mom had a nervous breakdown and Gina isn't far behind. She doesn't want to keep the baby, but is determined it will live. She's interested in adoption."

Josie's waterlogged eyes met his. "Adoption? Are you serious? When is the baby due?"

"The end of June."

Josie's breathing accelerated and her eyes lit up. Tiptoeing, she kissed his cheek. "Excuse me. I need to make a phone call."

She dialed the house next door. "Yes, Molly. This is Josie. Is your dad or mom home?"

She was wrapping the cord around her wrist while pacing as far as the line would allow. "Ask them if I can bring a friend over."

Nicolas' quick response spared Josie a fall as her feet tangled in the phone line. "Great, we'll be there." She hung up.

"Have some folks I want you to meet."

Nick sat on the sofa and patted the spot next to him. "Before we go, I need to talk with you."

Josie left plenty of space between them. "What's going on?"

"I've attended a few of the counseling sessions with Gina and Bella. Learning what that monster did to my sisters and the impact it is having on their lives has shaken me up. Dr. Ransom pointed out that our culture has conditioned men to see women primarily as objects to satisfy desires rather than a whole person to be respected."

He reached for her hands. "I always hated how other men used you, Josie, and somehow thought because I cared for you that I was different."

Josie was stunned. "You never forced yourself on me, Nicolas."

"No, but instead of treasuring you and trying to help you see that you are more than a body for a man's pleasure, I used you to satisfy my own. I'm asking for your forgiveness and a chance for us to start over."

Tears were streaming down her cheeks by the time he finished. "I forgive you." She reached for a tissue "You've changed."

"Learning of my sisters' abuse caused me to take a long, hard look at my life, Josie, and it wasn't pretty."

"You sound like Jake."

Nicolas's eyes widened. "In what way, Josie?"

With that opening, she relayed hers and Jake's summers of abuse and her drug gang rape.

By the time she finished, Nick was raging. "Is there some kind of sickness among the male population? What is wrong with us?"

"I don't know the cause, but when statistics prove that one out of every three or four girls and one out of every five or six five boys will be violated at some point in their lives, something is horrifically wrong in our society."

He gently pulled her into his arms. "Are you prosecuting them?"

"Felix is in prison for life, and Dad and Jake have confronted George."

"Give me his address. I'd like to *confront* him."

"Right now, I'm concentrating on getting help, Nick. I've not handled it as well as Jake."

"Why didn't you call me, Josie?"

"I figured I had worn out my welcome. An assignment from my counselor prompted my call this morning."

He moved his hands to hers. "Remind me to thank your counselor. Will you visit Bella and Gina sometime?"

"If you'll go with me."

He checked his watch. "After we visit the Diamonds?"

"Sounds good to me."

She explained as much as she could about the family next door as they followed the foot path.

Nick rang the doorbell. "How many kids?"

"Ten, including their grandson."

"And you think they will consider another one?"

"They wanted ours, Nick."

"Ours?" That revelation obviously shook him.

Daniel's response to the doorbell prevented her explanation.

As they exited two hours later, Nick was shaking his head. "Gina is not going to believe this story. I'm not sure I do."

He halted half-way between the houses. "They wanted our baby too?"

"Yeah, and I knew they would be good parents."

Nicolas enclosed her hand in his. "Come on. Let's go tell the girls about the Diamonds and then you can share your story with them. They need a friend as much as you do, Josie."

He helped her in his truck. "Miss Roberts, would you consider going out with me tonight after we leave Bella and Gina?"

She smiled. "You mean ... like a date?"

"Yes."

After visiting with his sisters, Nick managed to get tickets to the university production of *Pippin* for the evening. As they were leaving the theater, Josie reached for his hand. "I'm not sure I would have appreciated Pippin's search for the meaning of life this time last year, but tonight I listened with interest."

As he tucked her in the passenger seat, he kissed her cheek. "Have I told you how stunning you look tonight, Miss Roberts?"

"Oh, only about a dozen times."

"I'm slipping."

They chatted like old friends all the way back to Rugby Heights. "Thanks for letting me drop in today. I'd like to do the same next Saturday if you'll agree."

"I don't know if I can take *Pippin* again."

He chuckled. "I meant being together."

She laughed. "I'd love it, Nick."

"See you next Saturday afternoon at four o'clock then. Plan on eating out and then a surprise."

He left without as much as a goodnight kiss. A date without sex. That was her first since she was fourteen years old.

Virginia and William were out for the evening. While grabbing a drink before heading to her suite, Josie checked the answering machine.

There was a call from Ethan's area code. That information put a chill on her evening as surely as the ice was cooling down her Pepsi.

She would not be sharing the events of the day ... or Nicolas ... with Ethan. Nor would she be sharing Ethan with Nicolas.

Confusion accompanied her upstairs.

Thirty-Four

Spring and graduation coincide in the hills and valleys of Virginia as the promise of new beginnings fills the air and campuses.

The young Roberts' graduates were excited about the new directions their lives were taking. Josie had accepted a junior accounting position with one of Mr. Diamond's offices in town. Design school plans were on hold.

Unable to find a job in a local doctor's office or clinic, Madison had signed on at the university hospital—in spite of Jake's protests. As he predicted, that decision brought the honeymoon to a screeching halt. Madison was now working the second shift which included every other weekend.

That meant five evenings every week, Jake Roberts now spent alone or with their folks. His story book marriage had taken an unexpected turn and he was trying to figure out a way to revise this chapter. So far all his proposed revisions had been rejected.

Inside the big house, renovations to convert Melinda's room into a nursery were wrapping up and Melinda had been moved to a big girl's room on the second floor. Maria, Mandy and Molly were out of school for the summer and helping their youngest sister adjust to the change.

The warm June weather found Jake joining the Diamond clan often in the pool or tennis court and other family activities. A typical conversation with Madison regarding the situation went something like this.

"Honey, I like your family, but I didn't marry them. The weeks you work the weekends and add a double shift, I see your family more than I see you."

"Folks get sick or have emergencies, Jake. I have to do my part."

"Well, maybe they need to hire more people."

"True, but it's not going to happen."

And that was the end of the discussion until Jake brought it up again.

Exciting news roused the Diamond clan in the wee hours of the morning on July 1. The newest family member was on the way. By five o'clock that afternoon, Gina had given birth to a beautiful seven pound eight ounce baby girl. Mary Gina Diamond.

By the next morning the preliminary paperwork for adoption was ready to be signed. "Gina, are you sure this is what you want to do?" Thelma asked as she took the baby from the nurse.

"I'm ashamed to tell you what is going through my seventeen-year-old mind right now."

Thelma prodded. "I think my forty-five-year-old brain can handle it, Gina."

"I love Mary, but she looks like her father and that reminds me of the last two years of my life which I'm desperately trying to forget. I think I would resent this little innocent girl if I kept her.

"Please don't hate me for being honest. I'm so grateful that she will have a loving family. Do you think she will ever forgive me?"

"I'll remind her that you fought to give her life."

Thelma glanced between the baby and her mother. "Henry and I ask you abide by your decision and not try to uproot her when you start your own family."

Gina was crying softly. "I promise."

After the Diamonds brought Mary home, Josie found herself dropping in often. By the end of the first week, she knew the source of the growing sadness inside her. Two aborted babies.

The days and weeks that followed found her and Nick regular visitors of little Mary. They babysat several times, and Josie kept her overnight the weekend Henry took Thelma to the Jefferson Hotel in Richmond for their anniversary.

"I look at this infant and know Gina made the right decision," Nick admitted on his recent Saturday visit.

He fingered Mary's tiny toes when Josie picked her up. With sad eyes he asked, "What do you think happened to our babies?"

Tears filled her eyes as the miracle named Mary nestled close. "I don't know. I'm glad you didn't push Gina to have an abortion. What changed your mind?"

"She's a good Catholic who believes life and death are in God's hands." He bowed his head. "And I couldn't fight her after all she had been through."

Nicolas reached for his niece. "Josie, can you forgive me for my part in our abortions?"

She hugged him and the baby that was allowed to live. A major tear flow erupted. "Yes. Now if I can just forgive myself."

Every weekend of July and August, Nick showed up after visiting his family, and he and Josie spent the afternoons and evenings together. As their relationship grew, she shared more and more of her life and struggles with him. He shared his dreams with her.

The summer was nearing an end and Nick had joined Josie's family for a cookout. They were enjoying the privacy the breezeway offered while William manned the grill. Their conversation turned to their college days.

"Nick, do you remember David Henderson?"

The look on his face surprised her. "Sure, I do. Three years of jealousy makes that name stand out. Why do you ask?"

She swatted at the mosquito that was buzzing near her ear. "He died last January."

"David is dead? What happened?"

"He got broadsided by a drunk on New Year's morning." Tears accompanied her story.

She paused and gazed at the picturesque valley below them. "What are your thoughts about God, Nick?"

He looked at her and then the scene in front of them. "I'm confident He is out there, Josie, but I don't think He has time for us."

She studied his handsome face. "How did you arrive at those interesting conclusions?"

"There's too much order and design to all of this for it to be accidental, but there's too much chaos in the world to believe He's interested in us."

She turned her attention back to the scene before them. "I would have agreed with you a few months ago, but the changes in Jake and

Ethan have made me wonder if I'm wrong." Too late she realized her slip of the tongue.

Nicolas' head jerked in her direction. "Jake I know. Mind telling me who the blazes Ethan is?"

Before she could decide the best way to answer, he leaned close and cradled her face in his hand. "Josie, are you seeing someone else?"

"Not ... exactly."

He withdrew his hand and rose from his chair. His Italian temper surfaced. "Forgive me if I seem a bit confused. I thought something serious was finally growing between us, and all this time you have been *not exactly* seeing someone else?"

She felt a warmth invade her heart and spread through her body. "Serious? You and me?"

He stopped in front of her and pulled her to her feet. "Well, one of us is, but the other one is questionable. So who is Ethan?"

Her eyes never left his. "Madison's oldest brother."

That news jolted him. "How? When?"

She backed out of his space ... wondering how to describe their relationship. "It started by exchanging letters, and then the phone calls were added. He knows everything about me—except you."

His blue eyes were seeking answers. "Let me get this straight. All the time we've been dating, you have been writing and talking to Ethan? Am I to believe that you've never dated him?"

"Yes ... to both questions."

Nick was fighting to keep his temper under control. "Your relationship is more than friendship, isn't it?"

Crocodile tears began to roll down her cheeks. "It can never be more than friendship. Ethan is in prison ... for a long time, Nicolas."

He squeezed his eyes shut and leaned his head back. "The Diamonds' oldest son is in prison?"

He walked to the edge of the breezeway and then turned to face her. "Does your relationship with him pose a problem for us?"

"Us?" Her tears would not stop.

"I've been waiting for the right time to tell you that I love you, Josie."

She placed her hands over her heart and took a deep breath. "You love me?"

He reached for her hands. "What do you think these weeks and months have been about? I've tried to show you the respect of a man in love with the whole woman, not just her body."

Her tear output increased. "Is that why you haven't even kissed me all this time?"

He hugged her. "Yes. When I think of all the men who have abused and used you for their own selfish purposes, two things go through my mind. I want to beat them up ... one by one, and then I want to spend the rest of my life making up for what has been done to you. Josie, I want to marry you."

Her hand flew to her mouth. "Marry? I thought you weren't ready for marriage."

He brushed her hair away from her beautiful face. "You keep echoing my words. A man can change his mind, you know."

She considered this man who had worked his way into her heart the last few months. "I can't and won't walk out of Ethan's life, Nick."

"What about me, Josie?"

"I've fallen in love with you."

Before she could finish her thoughts, he was kissing her with a new depth of passion that addled her senses and weakened her knees.

"Oh, I think it's a good thing you didn't kiss me before now." She was stunned by the feelings he stirred in her.

He smiled. "So, are you saying yes?"

Her eyes were pleading for understanding. "There is a small problem."

He stepped back. "That sounds scary, but let's hear it."

"I really want to go to a design school. Would you object?"

"Object? Honey, I'll finance it. Is this a yes?"

She leaped into his arms. "Si, lo farò!"

"Ahh, I can tell you've been working on your Italian."

He kissed her again. "I love *you*, Josie, and I plan to spend the rest of our lives proving that fact."

There was excitement in his eyes. "Want to go pick out your ring or want me to surprise you?"

"I love surprises."

Grasping her hand and heading in the direction of the others, they shared their news. William flashed a knowing smile between Virginia and Josie. "Told you so."

Virginia grinned. "Any date in mind?"

Nicolas looked at Josie. "This wasn't exactly planned. I still have to buy the woman a ring. How much time do you need, Hon?"

Her accounting brain was counting off the weeks and months. "How about Thanksgiving or Christmas holidays?"

"Let's make it the Saturday after Thanksgiving."

Josie glanced at her mom. "Can we handle a small wedding by that time?"

"Sure, Honey."

Josie hugged her mom and then Nick.

"Walk me out," Nick requested.

He leaned against his truck, pulled her into his arms and pointed to the full moon. "I hurt for Ethan, Josie."

"He's had a God experience, Nick, kind of like Jake. He's an amazing person who has helped me more than he'll ever know. Telling him is going to be one of the hardest things I've ever done."

He kissed her. "I trust you, but I don't trust me right now. I need to head home."

Josie's joy was overshadowed by the task in front of her. It took her two days of writing and crying and ripping up and starting over to get it on paper. There was no easy way to convey the message.

She gave the letter to Nick to read the next time they were together. "If he weren't in prison, he would already have a ring on your finger."

Her response surprised him. "I don't think so. He's like Madison about not marrying someone outside the faith. That reminds me—I've not told you about Mom and Dad's big secret, have I?" With that she shared their story.

"Man, your dad lied to her all the time they dated. She seems so devoted to him."

"She is, but she never gave up her faith."

"Well, whether Ethan would marry you or not, he's in love with you. Mailing this letter is going to make me feel like a heel."

She pushed away. "That makes two of us. So shall we call the whole thing off?"

He seized a hand. "Not on your life. Do you ever think about all *the ifs* in life, Josie?"

"Interesting you should ask. Ethan says they are quicksand pits. The more we struggle with them, the deeper we sink."

He kissed the top of her head. "He's a smart man to be locked up."

"He claims it took walls and bars for God to get his attention."

Thirty-Five

Nicolas knew Josie was struggling with Ethan's silence more than she admitted. He also knew her feelings for this man were more than friendship. He tried to understand, but truth was ... he was jealous.

It was Friday, September 23, and they were at the Clifton Inn where he had made arrangements to include a ring with her dessert. That fell flat when she didn't order one. Adjusting his plans, he ordered a sample box to go. Ring inside.

To Nicolas' delight, Ethan's name was not mentioned the entire meal. Ten minutes into the trip back to Rugby Heights, the ghost reappeared.

"Do you think I'll ever hear from Ethan again?"

Though his eyes were on the road and his hands on the wheel, his mind was all over the place. Answering that question was filled with potholes he'd tried to avoid, so he remained silent.

She turned towards him. "Other than you, he's the best friend I've ever had. What do you think I should do?"

"I don't know, but it needs to be soon. He's between us, Josie."

"What do you mean?"

"If he were free and you had to choose between us, who would it be?"

"That's never going to happen, so why even bring it up? Ethan said ..."

He interrupted her Ethan quote. "I don't give a hang what Ethan said. I asked you a question and I'd like an honest answer."

Neither spoke until he pulled in her driveway. "Your silence answers the question, Josie. I love you, but until Ethan's ghost is not part of our lives ... this engagement is off."

Her blue eyes were sparkling with moisture. "Nick, please don't do this to me. I not only love you; I need you."

He melted and handed her his handkerchief. "If our babies don't have blue eyes, we'll have to send them back."

"Babies?" She sniffled. "First you changed your mind about marriage and now you speak of babies?"

He exited his door and opened hers. "I've changed my mind about a lot of things lately."

She leaned close and hugged him. "Me too."

"Hey, grab that dessert box. Maybe your folks will enjoy it."

After greeting her folks, Nicolas suggested Josie make a pot of coffee or other drinks and set out the desserts.

"Give me five minutes." And she disappeared into the kitchen.

Nick waited until she was out of hearing range. "She doesn't know it, but her engagement ring is in that box. Let's go watch."

Josie's squeal echoed through the rooms. "Sounds like she found it," Virginia said.

Nicolas sprinted to the kitchen where Josie sat staring at her surprise. Those blue pools had sprung a major leak this time. He moved behind her, reached for the ring and slipped it on her finger.

She spun around to face him. "I thought you said …"

Before she could finish he kissed her. "So I changed my mind."

She hugged him affectionately. "I'm glad."

The foursome enjoyed the gourmet desserts and shared a few wedding ideas.

Later, Nick and Josie settled on the sofa to watch the *Tonight Show* with Johnny Carson after her folks called it a night.

"Do you know that I haven't been with another girl since you walked out on me?"

She shifted so she could see his face. "You haven't dated?"

"I dated a few times, but nothing happened. How about you?"

Josie scooted off the sofa. "I've been with others."

"Like sexually been with others?"

She looked at him with regret and shame. "Before you, Nick, that was the only way I knew to be with a man."

He turned off the television. "Before or after the abortion?"

"Both. But I've not been with anyone else since you came back into my life."

He was upset. "You crawled in bed with someone else while carrying my baby?"

"You didn't want it or me, so why did it matter?" For a girl who rarely cried, she was beginning to resemble a dripping faucet.

He faced her. "And you've been with someone since the abortion?"

"It was brief, but yes."

He put his hands on her shoulders and it was not an affectionate gesture. "I will not tolerate your old ways, Josie. I'm trying to understand how you got there, but now that you know—there is no excuse."

She was close to panic. "I'm really trying."

He pulled her close. "I know. Sometimes I get scared about us."

"I don't deny that I've lived a messed up life, Nick. You know that better than most. When Dr. Metcalf asked me to make a list of the people and events that were prompting my change of mind and attitude, you were on my list. Your love gives me hope that I can change." She clung to him and wept.

"Was Ethan on your list?"

She pulled away. "You know he was."

"So being on your list doesn't make me anymore special than anyone else in your life, does it?"

"Look, Nick. I don't know what you want from me but I'm doing the best I can right now. Do you want this ring back?" She took it off and offered it to him.

"Wear it this week. Both of us have some serious thinking to do."

"No, I don't want it until you have no reservations."

"Touché, Josie." He accepted the ring and dropped it in his pocket. "I don't want to be your second choice or your fall back guy. I want and need to be your one and only—without any reservations. Looks like we both have impediments to this marriage."

He turned to leave. "Shall I come next Saturday?"

Tears blinded her vision and pain paralyzed her vocal cords. She shook her head and walked out of the room.

She watched his truck pull out of the driveway and crumbled on her bed. If there had been any booze in the room, she would have drown herself in it.

THIRTY-SIX

The next morning Josie informed her mom and dad that the engagement was off, but refused to discuss any details. She was fighting a strong urge to spend the weekend with her old friend, Jack.

Instead she decided to join Jake on his morning jog since Madison would probably be sleeping. After donning her running garments and lacing her Nikes, she headed out the door just as Jake emerged from his paradise suite.

"Hey, wait up and I'll give you a run for you money this morning," she called.

"Morning, Sis. Are you challenging me to a race?"

"Not really. I could never keep up with those long legs of yours. Just making conversation."

They jogged and chatted about everything except what was on their minds. As they were on the downhill stretch, Jake ventured out. "How are the wedding plans coming along?"

Josie's response threw him off. "Race you the rest of the way home." And she lit a shuck.

Jake stayed a few yards behind and watched her push her body with a punishing pace. By the time they turned into the Roberts' driveway, she was bent over and her lungs were begging for more oxygen than she was able to pull in. She began to stagger and then fell to the ground.

Jake swept her off her feet and carried her into the house "Mom, are you close by?"

Virginia rushed in. "What is going on?"

"I need some icepacks and water. If she doesn't come around quickly, we'll have to call for help."

Jake and Josie's Discovery

Within a few minutes of applying ice packs under her armpits, behind her neck and her inner thighs, Josie began to stir. Virginia began administering water as soon as she was able to swallow.

"What happened, Jake?"

"I asked her about the wedding and she shifted into overdrive and crashed."

"Something happened after William and I went to bed. He gave her a ring last night, but she announced this morning that it's been called off."

"What h-happened" Josie quizzed.

"Oh, you had visions of competing with Wilma Rudolf that last mile."

"Oh, I remember."

"Josie, you finally got a letter from Ethan this morning," Virginia announced.

She shot up and had to lie down again. "Oops, I'm still woozy. Jake, would you mind getting it for me?"

When Jake handed her the letter, he and Virginia left the area to give her some privacy. It wasn't long before they heard sniffles.

Jake grabbed a bottle of Gatorade and went to the rescue. "Bad news, Sis?"

"First Nick and now Ethan. Those two are going to drive me to drink again, Jake."

"Whoa, Sis. What's going on?"

"Nick is jealous of Ethan and all the other men that have ever been in my life and Ethan tells me that if I don't get serious about my search for truth instead of making wedding plans that I'll end up back where I started. Friends like that ... I can do without."

Jake sat down beside her. "Why not give God a chance? Come to church with me the next few weeks. What can it hurt?"

Other than an occasional wedding, Josie had never stepped a foot inside a church. And she was a nervous wreck as they entered the building Sunday. Madison patted her on the arm. "Josie, either this stuff is real or it's not. Just relax and keep an open heart"

Josie relaxed some. "I'll try."

She spent most of the first service watching Jake. She couldn't believe this was the same person she had grown up with. The second week she paid more attention to the other people. The third week, she began to listen to the words of the songs and pay more attention to the teaching. By week four Josie felt at home and pastor's topic intrigued her. *The Power of Forgiveness.*

Pastor Worthington indicated forgiveness originated in the heart and actions of God toward us. He quoted a passage from Romans which stated all have sinned against God, and therefore, all need His forgiveness.

Josie didn't question her need of forgiveness anymore, but did God really expect her to forgive George and Felix? She hated them for what they had done to her, stolen from her and the impact it was still having in her life.

Could her hatred and unforgiveness keep her tied to them and their part in her life? She sought Jake's response on the way home.

"Two things stood out to me on this issue, Josie. Forgiveness isn't saying what the persons did was okay. It is a releasing of them and their wrongdoings to the One who forgave me. To the human mind that doesn't make much sense at first, but making that choice is an amazingly freeing decision."

Thirty-Seven

Jake was pleased Josie had been going to church and asking some good questions the last few weeks, but he was guilt-ridden for hiding the on-going conflict between him and Madison.

A stubborn streak that made most mules look compliant had surfaced in his wife since she started working. Not only was her job wreaking havoc on their marriage, now it was taking a toll on Madison's health. The last month she had been working double shifts at least twice each week. Would she listen to reasoning?

"Honey, this is not working. Our marriage is falling apart and you are past exhausted."

"So what are you saying, Jake? You want me to quit? Who is going to take care of those sick folks if I do that?"

"Who is going to take care of you when you pass out on the floor?"

She grabbed her lunch and walked out the door to work another double shift.

Add unreasonable to stubborn.

And so their days passed. It was Friday evening and Madison was working from 3:00 p.m. to 7:00 a.m. He was bored and lonely. Add angry. That was the emotion he experienced much too often lately.

Early Saturday morning, the exhausted, dedicated nurse snuck in quietly and headed for the shower while Jake was still in bed. As she was putting on her nightgown, he walked into the bathroom.

"Good morning, Wife." He encircled her from the back. "Hmm, you smell delicious!" He started nibbling on her ears and neck.

She turned in his arms and ignored his overtures. "I'm sorry, but I have to go to bed before I pass out."

He was beyond frustrated. "What am I supposed to do in this little place today ... besides be quiet? We have no life together anymore, Madison. All you do is work and sleep."

"Jake, I've tried to explain that this is the life of a beginning nurse." She wearily crawled into bed.

"Then quit nursing and be my wife again." He sat down beside her and began running his fingers up and down her arms.

She turned her back to him and pulled up the covers. "Jake, somebody has to take care of the sick folks. I'm sorry life is hard on us right now."

He jumped up. "Right now? I don't see a light at the end of the tunnel, do you? I feel like your job is more important to you than me or our marriage. You've changed since you've started working. There's not some cute doctor who has caught your eye, is there?"

She bolted up in bed. "Jake Roberts, you ought to be ashamed of yourself!"

He knelt beside her. "Maddie, I'm miserable and angry. You are exhausted and stubborn. Can you honestly say that you are happy with the way things are between us?"

She ran her fingers through his messy hair. "No. I'm concerned, but right now I'm too tired to even think about it. I have to work a double shift again tonight and have less than seven hours to sleep before I have to sign in again."

He snatched both her hands and yanked her out of bed. "You can't be serious! You'll pass out on the floor before morning."

Looking at her with the same frustration he had experienced too many times to count, he made a decision. "If you work a double shift tonight, I won't be here when you leave or get back."

She jerked her hands out of his and turned back to the bed. "Jake, that's not fair. I can't call this late and tell them no."

He shifted out of angry into furious. "I'm the only person you say *no* to Madison. You're wrecking our marriage and ruining your health to please everyone else. Well, I hope you sleep well and have a great night at the hospital. I plan to have some fun myself—without you—or either of our families. I may paint the town."

He grabbed his clothes and headed for the bathroom. She fell into bed ... crying and exhausted. Fifteen minutes later, she heard the door slam. She dragged her weary body out of bed and put on a bathrobe.

Breaking the cardinal rule, she entered her folks' place through the interior door and found her mom and dad in the kitchen with Melinda, Morgan and Mary. "Good morning," she offered, while losing her battle to control the tears.

Surprised described her parents' responses. Melinda and Morgan ran to hug her. Madison knelt as little arms wrapped around her neck. The tear flow increased.

"Why are you crying, Maddie?" Melinda asked as small fingers wiped her tears.

"My heart is sad. I think I need a mommy chat."

Thelma's concern was evident. "What's going on?"

She motioned her mom closer to her dad and spoke softly so little ears wouldn't hear. "Oh, Jake's upset because I have to work a double shift tonight."

Thelma stopped her activity. "Again?"

"Somebody has to, Mom. Jake doesn't understand."

Henry was buttering toast but also listening to the conversation. "Actually, Madison, I think the young man has been patient with you and your schedule."

"Patient? He's nowhere close. He's madder than a wet hen."

She grabbed a napkin and blew her nose. "He left declaring he won't be home when I leave or when I get back, because he's tired of having to spend his evenings with our families."

She was trembling. "I don't know what to do. I love my husband and I love my job, but I'm not sure I can have both."

Henry glanced at Thelma. "You two need to talk. I'll take care of these three. Go on."

Thelma reached for her daughter's hand. "Come. We'll go back to your place."

Once they settled in the apartment, Thelma asked, "When did the troubles start, Madison?"

"The day I started work."

Thelma studied her tired daughter's face. "Sweetheart, what is more important to you? Your job or your husband?"

An offended look darkened Madison's face. "My husband, of course."

"Your actions contradict that statement. What if the shoe was on the other foot? You two are still newlyweds, Honey. Jake wants and needs to be with you, not alone or with us or his folks. You had better do some serious thinking and praying and even more listening.

"For starters, I'm going to suggest that you call in and refuse the double shift. Sixteen more hours on the floor and you'll be a patient."

Searching her weepy and tired eyes, Thelma asked, "Why do you think you have to say yes to everyone who asks you to work an extra shift?"

"I thought that was part of being a good Christian, Mom."

"Your top priority is your husband, Madison. If that means saying no to others, then learn to say it. Being a good Christian worker does not take precedence over your husband or marriage … or you own health."

Madison nodded. "I have a hard time telling folks *no*, Mom."

Thelma put an arm around her shoulder. "Honey, you have some decisions to make and some fences to mend. I'll leave you to figure out what that involves." She kissed her on the cheek and went out the exterior entrance.

Madison was crying when she dialed the supervisor of nursing to say she wasn't physically able to work the double shift tonight.

When she dialed the Roberts' residence, Virginia answered.

"Is Jake there?"

"As a matter of fact, he is. Want me to get him for you?"

"No, don't tell him I called and don't let him leave before I get there." She hung up and dressed quickly.

When she showed up, Virginia met her at the door. "I'm glad you came."

"Would you send him into the sunroom?" Tears were non-stop at this point.

Virginia patted her shoulder and smiled knowingly.

Madison was looking out the windows at the gathering storm clouds when Jake walked in.

"What are you doing here? I thought you had to sleep so you can work." There was no kindness in his voice.

She turned and fell apart. "Jake ... I've been wrong ... and I'm sorry."

Before she could say anything else, he swept her up in his arms.

He kissed any part of her face he could reach while carrying her home. She was almost asleep by the time he laid her on the bed. When he started to pull away, she held on. "Don't go."

As he edged beside her, she snuggled close. "I've had a few things out of order, Jake."

"Shhh." And he held her close until she fell asleep.

She slept soundly until Jake gently alerted her she needed to get ready for work. She dressed quickly, grabbed the sack lunch he had prepared and waved a slip of paper in the air as she headed for the door. "I'm turning in my notice tonight."

The relieved look on his face made her regret she had waited so long.

He intercepted her. "Maddie, we need to find a place of our own."

She tiptoed to kiss him. "I know."

"See you tonight, Mrs. Roberts. Think I'll try to find some honey wine while you're gone." He winked.

Madison made it through her shift and was grateful she was off the next two days. She and Jake renewed their commitment to each other that weekend.

And the young nurse did not accept any more double shifts the next two weeks. She would find another way to use her medical training to benefit others. Right now, she had a marriage to mend.

Thirty-Eight

It was the Sunday before their cancelled wedding, and Josie was sitting in her spot with Madison and Jake. Every week, something Pastor Worthington shared caught her attention and spawned conversations or prompted questions with her mom or Jake and Madison.

Today's lesson intrigued her.

"Who are you? A doctor? A painter? An accountant? A machinist? A loser? A reject? An addict? A Methodist or a Catholic?" Pastor Worthington asked his parishioners.

"Why do we not have a definitive answer to that question? I hope we can help answer that question for you this morning.

"First, I need your help with a word association exercise. I'll start it and then in an orderly manner I'm asking you to continue until I stop you.

"Here we go … *Scam*."

"Swindler."

"Scheme."

"Trickster."

"Dupe."

"Shaft."

"Finagle."

"Con-artist."

"Bamboozle."

"Double cross."

"Pull a fast one."

"Hoodwink."

"Flimflam."

"Hustler."

"Bilk."
"Cheater."
"Deceiver."
"Liar."
"Satan."

Pastor smiled. "Interesting, isn't it? A con-artist is a thief and a liar, but there are no conventional armaments for this guy. His weapon of choice is deception and his battlefield is the mind. Why? Because his prize cannot be taken by force. It must be willingly forfeited.

"Ever thought about the first scam in history and the mastermind behind it?"

Pastor then read about Eve's encounter with the serpent as recorded in Genesis 3. "Satan insinuated that God's life-protecting boundary was depriving Eve of both pleasure and equality with God. Though both were lies, she took the bait and swallowed the hook.

"Now we understand why Jesus called Satan the father of lies in John 8:44. Listen to his further explanation about his enemy in John 10:10. *The thief (Satan) comes only to steal and kill and destroy; I have come that they may have LIFE and have it to the full.*"

There was a stirring inside Josie.

"By convincing Eve to act independently of God and rebel against the only boundary He had placed in their lives, the con-artist won.

"But why the scam? What was God's enemy after that he couldn't take by force?"

Pastor took a few seconds and scanned the faces of his congregation. "Satan's goal was God's children. In order to achieve that he had to convince then to trust him instead of God.

"Without awareness they forfeited their identity as God's children and became prisoners of God's enemy. They were now homeless and servants of a cruel master whose goal was their total destruction.

"The good news is that God in his foreknowledge knew this would happen. That's why Paul could write in Ephesians 1, *For He chose us in Him before the foundation of the world to be holy and blameless in His sight. In love, He predestined us to be adopted as His sons through Jesus Christ ... in Him we have redemption ...*

"Let's make the best known verse in the Bible personal this morning. *For God so loved me that He gave His Son, that if I choose to believe in Him, I shall not perish but have everlasting LIFE.*"

"Notice *Life* is now offered in God's Son. Choosing Him restores our lost identity."

"Galatians 3:26 confirms this truth. *You are all sons of God, through faith in Jesus Christ …*"

Pastor closed his Bible, descended the steps and scanned the crowd of about a hundred and fifty people.

"The trees of choice stand in the middle of each life. One will hold us prisoner to a world of lies and deception and keep us disconnected from the God whose image we bear. The other will restore our lost identity and put us back into relationship with the God who made us.

"So I ask you. Who are you? God created you to be His and through his Son made a way for that to be possible.

"And as His child He says that you are forgiven and redeemed. Who do you say you are?

"To disagree is to call Him a liar and validate Satan's lies.

"As His child He declared you are a new creation. He affirms that the old has gone. Who can you trust? The con artist or the God who died to prove His love?

"Truth and Life are now found in the person of Jesus, God's Son. And that is why Satan fights so hard to keep us ignorant of and blind to that wonderful news."

He closed in prayer and then invited anyone who was interested in talking more about the lesson to contact him.

Throughout lunch, Josie peppered Jake and Madison about their own journeys of faith and how one gets from life without God to life with Him. The truths presented were beginning to make sense.

When they got home, Jake called the pastor and set up an appointment for Josie and Madison to meet with him and his wife Monday evening.

And that was the night Josie said, "I do" to God. Their union was emotional.

Tears were flowing. "God doesn't see any of my sins anymore?"

Mrs. Worthington reached for her hand. "No, you slate has been wiped clean, Josie."

Pastor added, "Not only that, but you are a child of God. And, Josie, He adores and treasures you."

"Me? Loved and treasured by God?"

The girl couldn't quit crying. Mrs. Worthington put an arm around her shoulder and shared the story of the prostitute who washed Jesus' feet with her tears. "I believe your tears are washing his feet tonight, Josie.

"Do you realize, Honey, that in God's sight, you are as clean as a young virgin getting ready to wed her husband?"

"Me? A virgin?" Memories of the first night George came into her bedroom surfaced.

That image released her from the shame she had known since she was seven years old. She fell into the elderly woman's arms and wept like a little girl who had been lost for fifteen years and had finally found her way back home.

"For years I've felt like I was trapped in a bottomless abyss. Tonight God has rescued me and I'm safe in His arms."

Her heart was full and yet so light ... it was unexplainable. Joy unspeakable rose from inside her. Now she understood Jake and Ethan.

Madison had watched and wept. On the trip home she convinced Josie to save this secret for Thanksgiving when the families would be together. "This will be great for Dad's blessing basket."

Josie wrote Ethan as soon as she got home and mailed it early the next morning. She knew he would be excited. She came so close to telling her mom several times before Thursday, but resisted.

Thanksgiving arrived and there was a new bounce in her step as she exited her house around noon. As she unlatched the gate joining the properties, Nick and his sisters pulled into the Diamond driveway. She knew they had been visiting baby Mary from time to time, but why were they here today?

A voice she had not heard in over two months greeted her.

"Hi, Josie." His captivating blue eyes were riveted on her.

"Hi, Nicolas." She was back on the roller coaster except this time she hit the big drop. She broke eye contact immediately and turned her attention to his sisters.

As Gina and Bella began filling her in on what had been happening, Nick interrupted. "I'll let you three catch up. Talk to you later, Josie." And away he went.

Gina grabbed her hand. "Hey, what is going on with you and Nicolas? The man is driving us crazy."

"Are you aware that I've not seen or talked to him in weeks?"

Gina nodded. "Yeah, he said something about both of you needing some time before you married. I personally think that would be hard, but I bet it will make the honeymoon pretty exciting."

Bella punched Gina.

"You two are off track. Whatever is going on with Nicolas has nothing to do with me," Josie assured them.

Gina chimed in. "Well, he's up to something. He bought a house here in Charlottesville and has been working on it every weekend. And I heard him make plans to be off work two weeks after Thanksgiving."

Jake was standing at the door. "You three better get in here if you want any turkey."

Mandy was stationed inside the door with Henry's blessing basket. Josie filled out a card and folded it before dropping it in the basket. Gina and Bella did likewise.

The girls had stirred Josie's curiosity. She began to sneak peeks at Nicolas. Every time he caught her looking, his smile enlarged. She was back on the roller coaster and that wasn't good for digesting turkey and dressing.

After the turkeys had been carved and the trays of dressing consumed, Henry asked everyone to meet in the great room. Folks found a spot or made a nest. Josie settled with Bella and Gina. Madison was snuggling with baby Mary.

Henry pulled out the blessing basket and asked Molly to be the card reader. "Morgan, will you be the card chooser?"

With his blue eyes dancing, he pulled his first card out of the basket and handed it to Molly. *A new mommy and daddy and lots of brothers and sisters.*

Everyone shouted "Morgan."

He showed off his hallmark grin. "Molly helped me write it."

The next card was read. *Two new sons and a new daughter!*

Jake and Josie's Discovery

The crowd pointed to Henry and Thelma. Henry raised his hand.

Daniel spoke up. "Gee, Dad, most families are content with a new kid every few years. Are you going for some kind of record?"

"Just taking them as God gives them." He looked at Thelma and grinned.

Card three caused Molly to blush. *A positive pregnancy test?*

Mouths dropped and eyes enlarged as folks began scanning the crowd for Madison. Jake leaped over a few folks to kneel in front of her. "Is that yours?"

She nodded and bedlam broke loose. Jake handed Mary to Gina. He pulled Madison to her feet with every intention of kissing her. "Enough of that stuff, Son," William teased. The grandfathers congratulated Jake while the grandmothers hugged Madison and cried. When the others returned to their seats, Jake pulled Madison away from the crowd into the adjoining hall.

He was smothering her with kisses. "Jake, behave!"

"We've made a baby, Madison. Do you have any idea when this happened?"

She tried to squelch the teasing laughter that was rising. "Jake, I refuse to name this child *Making Up*" He let out a Tarzan yell that disturbed the entire gathering.

Madison grabbed his hand and hauled him further down the hall. "This is not the jungle, Tarzan, and under-aged children are present."

"Sorry, Jane. I just had a feeling something special happened that weekend. When did you find out?"

"Yesterday. You're not upset with me for waiting, are you?"

"It was perfect. Did you see our folks?" He walked her back up the hall. "Look at them. They are still talking about it."

"No, they are trying to figure out who invited Tarzan to this party." She punched his chest.

Molly was waving another card in the air. *A son brought back from the dead.*

Heads turned towards Thelma. She raised her hand and pointed heavenward.

"The next card says *Making up.*"

That one puzzled everyone except Madison who was still standing in the hallway entrance with Jake. She blushed and waved her hand. "That would be Jake's."

William caught Henry's eyes and both heads turned to Jake. Subdued smiles said it all.

"Ready?" Molly asked as Morgan handed her another card. *"A special boyfriend."*

The crowd grew quiet as folks started looking between Maria, Mandy, Gina and Bella. Henry spoke up. "Will the guilty party please stand?" Shyly, Maria rose to her feet.

"Confess, my daughter. Who has found favor in your eyes?" Henry asked in a courtly manner.

"You know him well, Dad. Grayson will be dropping in this evening." Maria quietly sat back down.

Henry cast a questioning glance at Thelma. "Did you know anything about this?"

"I've been suspicious, Dear." She patted his hand.

Morgan thrust another card in Molly's hand. *"Breaking a school swimming record."*

"Daniel," several of the Diamond siblings shouted.

Folks applauded and congratulated. Daniel bowed.

Molly waited until she had everyone's attention again. *"New guitar."*

"Mandy," the Diamond gang called out.

Morgan pulled another card out. *"My wife and a new business partner."*

"William," suggested some. "Mr. Roberts," echoed others.

Jake gave him a thumbs up.

Melinda was getting restless. "You haven't read mine, Molly. Read mine."

Thelma calmly assured her that all cards would be read.

"A new sister."

The Diamond clan had a new sister, but whose name hadn't been called?

Bella raised her hand and hugged Josie. *Yep, the girls are delusional.*

"A family for Mary."

Everyone stilled.

Remembering the two she had aborted, Josie looked at Gina. "She will thank you one day."

"I hope so."

Molly's voice broke the seriousness of moment. *"Morgan and Mary."*

Melinda started jumping up and down. "That's mine. That's mine."

Molly shyly read the next card. *"My family."*

"That has to be Molly's," suggested Dennis.

She agreed and quickly read the next card. *"Hamburgers."*

A dozen voices identified its owner. "Dennis!"

Molly puzzled over the next card. *"A new identity?"*

Folks were searching faces for the likely person and no one had an answer.

Josie raised her hand.

Jake eyed Madison and then zeroed in on Josie. "Would this have anything to do with Monday's visit with the Worthingtons?"

Josie nodded as a tear escaped. "Yes."

She kept her eyes on Virginia while she was talking. "Madison and I went to see Pastor Worthington and his wife Monday evening. Another one of your prayers has been answered, Mom."

Virginia bolted out of her chair and wept as she embraced her daughter. Thelma joined them. Jake wasn't far behind. Madison sat back and smiled.

Some of the younger ones had questioning expressions on their faces. When things settled down some, Henry asked Josie if she would mind sharing.

She didn't mind, though she did have some concern about Nick's reaction. His eyes never left hers as she related her story. A slight smile was the only response she could read.

Molly started waving a card in the air. "Hey, Dad, there are still two cards in the basket."

The noise level subsided and Molly proceeded. *"Free to be me."*

Folks were mentally going around the room trying to figure out who hadn't been named.

William reached for his wife's hand. "That would be Virginia."

Everyone remained silent waiting for the explanation to such an interesting statement. William told their story and managed a weak laugh. "It seems the joke is on me. I'm now the only non-believer in the family."

Henry chuckled. "God has a neat sense of humor, William. Why don't you just wave the white flag and surrender?"

"We'll talk on the green, Friend."

Molly had secured the last card and waited patiently. "*Choosing to love again.*"

Without a word, Henry rose and stood facing the first son of his loins. He reached for his hand and pulled the giant of a man into a bear hug. "When do we get to meet her?"

"This evening. Her name is April."

Josie wondered if anyone else had noticed that Nicolas obviously didn't place a card in the basket. Before she could comment to his sisters, Henry asked for everyone's attention.

"There is one more card to be read. I personally made the decision to save this one for last."

He reached in his pocket. "I'm going to ask the owner to read it and explain."

Nicolas stood and took the card from Henry. Silence reigned. "A new creation and hopefully a bride."

He made his way to Josie whose hands flew to her mouth as she tried to stifle the emotions that were rising as understanding was dawning.

Tears began cascading down her cheeks as Nicolas relayed how his visits to Mary usually concluded in the Diamond family chapel most days and how three weeks ago, he had his own God encounter.

"Jake alerted me that you were also on a spiritual pilgrimage, Josie."

He knelt in front of her. Opening a ring box, he reached for her left hand. "Josie, I have two questions to ask you. Will you marry me? Is Saturday too soon?"

"Marry? S-S-Saturday?"

"Yeah, you wouldn't believe how hard my sisters, your folks and the Diamonds have worked the last three weeks. All I need is a bride."

She was sobbing as she nodded. Nicolas slipped the ring on her finger and pulled her to her feet. "I have no reservations, Josie. Jake helped me understand many things about your past and Ethan's part in your life. I'm grateful for the friendship you and he share."

"And I have no reservations, Nicolas. The weeks we have been apart have helped me understand that I love Ethan like I love Jake. It's a strong bond, but it is not what I feel for you. And my past is just that—past! With yours and God's help, I won't be returning to the pig pens again."

"That's all I needed to hear." He kissed her rather passionately for the crowd that was surrounding them.

"Enough of that," Henry teased. "We'll see everyone here tomorrow at 6 p.m. for the rehearsal and rehearsal dinner will follow at the Roberts. The wedding will be here, 1 p.m., Saturday. Think you two can make it?"

Josie's head was swimming with all that had happened the last thirty minutes. Both nodded.

Thirty-Nine

Thelma and Virginia had the great room decorated in soft ivory with accents of autumn gold and cranberry added for contrast and color.

Madison's old room was being used by the bridal party. Gina and Bella had Josie arrayed in curlers and a facial mask when someone knocked on the door.

Virginia stuck her head in. "Josie, Thelma wants you in Henry's oval office in thirty minutes."

She panicked. "Hurry, girls. Get this gook off my face and these curlers out of my hair. I'll grab my robe and see what secret mischief Thelma has up her sleeve."

Thirty minutes brought the needed transformation. Josie was ready, except for donning her dress. She threw on her robe and headed for the Henry's office.

When she walked in, Thelma had the phone to her ear. "She's here, Ethan. Love you."

Her wedding butterflies metamorphosed into a herd of wild elephants. She hadn't talked to him since her engagement and he had written only once. She waited for Thelma to leave, sat down in Henry's swivel chair and faced the wall while nervously tangling her fingers in the phone cord.

"Hi."

"Hi, Josie." She could hear layers of emotion in his voice. "I won't keep you long. But I wanted to talk to you one last time before you marry."

She did love this guy. She always would. She sensed his struggles and tears formed.

"I guess you've figured out that I've wrestled with your engagement. I wanted you for myself and had hoped that somehow what I could offer you would be enough. It didn't take God long to show me how selfish that was, but still I hung on. I convinced myself that you'd be better off loving God's man in prison than you would be loving a man who didn't know Him."

Tears were wearing multiple paths through her makeup.

"When Mom told me about Nick's openness to God, I knew he was God's choice for you, but still I hung on. Being your friend has been one of the best things that ever happened to me. I don't like losing you, but I accept it."

She knew he was being strong for her and the tear flow increased.

"I'm glad you have someone to love—not just with letters, calls and scattered visits inside prison walls."

She heard his sharp intake of breath and knew she wasn't the only one shedding tears. "I know we can't talk or write anymore. I just wanted to thank you for being the best friend I've ever had. I'm going to miss you. No matter what, Josie, I'll always love you. God bless you and that fortunate husband of yours."

"Ethan, don't hang up. You need to know that I do love you. I love you because you were my safe place when I had nowhere else to turn. I love you because you taught me how to be open and honest. I love you because you helped me climb out of the deepest pit of my life. I love you because you taught me how to be a friend and have a friend. I love you because you taught me that my value wasn't based on my body.

"I love you most because you constantly and continually pointed me to the One who is perfect love, the only One who could change me from the inside out. I love you, because without you, I would never have known how to love Nick. And today I love you for releasing me to love this amazing man who will become my husband within the hour. You have been a precious gift to me."

She could hear his sniffles in the phone and they mixed with her own. He spoke up. "Hey, this is your wedding day. These tears need to stop. You have a groom to meet in a few minutes."

Unknown to Josie, Thelma had alerted Nicolas about the phone call. He had been standing just inside the door the entire time. He turned her chair around and reached for the phone.

"Ethan, this is Nick."

He pulled Josie close with his free arm and waited for the impact of hearing his voice to settle. "I wanted to thank you for the powerful influence you've had on Josie's life ... and through her ... mine.

"Thank you for being there for her when I wasn't. Thank you for loving her when others, including me, only used her. Thank you for unselfishly loving her even now. When our story is told, you will always be part of it. If we never meet this side of eternity, let's plan on spending an eon or two on the other side just catching up."

"You are a blessed man, Nick. Take good care of her." Ethan's voice broke.

"Yes, I am and I will."

He handed the phone back to Josie. "Bye, Ethan."

"Bye, Josie," he whispered and she heard the dial tone.

As Nick untangled her and the phone cord, she crumbled in his arms. He held her close.

"Come on you two. It's time." Thelma was wiping her own tears.

The irony of the last five minutes filled the couple with a holy awe that few could understand. The love and freedom they knew and shared had much to do with a man behind bars who had learned what it means to be free on the inside.

Thelma smiled through her tears. "Thank you for loving my son."

"He's a big part of this day and our lives, Ms. Thelma," Nicolas offered.

Thelma was shooing them away from each other. Nick stole a kiss and winked. "I hope you brought another change of clothes."

"Oh, I have something with you in mind, Mr. Amato."

He abruptly stopped and faced her. "I almost forgot. I have something for you." He reached into his pocket and pulled out a small square box. "Turn around and lift your hair."

He reached his hands around her neck and clasped a lovely silver necklace with a Mobius pendant. She lifted it to examine. There were strange markings all around it. She twirled around ... holding it out for him to see. "What does it say?"

"It is Hebrew for *I am my Beloved's and He is mine.*" His eyes pierced hers. "You are my beloved, Josie, and I want to be yours, but more importantly—we are His and He is ours."

He kissed her with the promise of more to come. "I think I hear music. Let's have ourselves a wedding."

Epilogue

Four years later, Nicolas was rushing Josie to the hospital with labor pains five minutes apart. She had insisted they not act rash or panic. While that seemed to be working fine for her, he was confident he had failed on both accounts.

She finally called her folks just before they left to inform them the baby was on the way. He had no idea where they were. He did manage to alert Jake and Madison. They had their hands full with three-year-old Nathan Henderson and two-month-old Grace Elizabeth. He had not been able to reach his sisters or mother. That left Nicolas on his own.

He breathed a sigh of relief when they wheeled her through the ER and wasted no time checking her into the maternity ward. He collapsed in a chair that some nurse pointed to when he asked how long it was going to take.

He took another deep breath. Maybe that had been his problem. He had forgotten to breathe the last five hours.

Another man about his age was sitting calmly in the corner reading the newspaper. Nick had the strangest urge to rip it out of his hands. Instead, he cleared his throat and politely asked, "Been here long?"

His peer laid aside the newspaper and smiled. "Since yesterday, but it won't be long now."

"Yesterday? It takes that long to have a baby? Mamma Mia! I'll never make it." And with that he started pacing.

The other gentleman chuckled. "Oh, it was just precautionary. She's only been in labor for the last four hours. Our local doctor wanted her here in case there were any complications."

"But you seem calm."

The nice looking gentleman smiled. "This is not our first and the wife assured me she can handle it. Your first, huh?"

That statement touched a tender spot and Nick eased his body into the chair across from the stranger. "Well, yes ... and no."

"Want to talk about it? I think we have time."

Nick considered the man for a moment. "Is it possible that you are an *in-the-beginning-God* believer?"

The man's eyes grew large. "As a matter of fact, I am."

Without understanding the urge or need, Nick briefly shared the story of their two aborted babies. He was not ashamed of the stray tears that broke through his masculine walls from time to time. Whether the man cared or understood wasn't the point. Nick needed to get it out and this felt like the right time. But oddly enough, his story seemed to touch the other waiting father.

About the time the story ended, a middle aged couple and a man who could be Tom Selleck's brother came rushing into the room. "How is she? Have you heard anything?"

Before his friend could answer, a nurse stuck her head in and motioned for him. Nicolas heard her tell him that his wife was fine. "She wants you to meet your sons."

The grandparents and Tom's look-alike started peppering the nurse with all kinds of questions. His new friend turned and offered his hand. "Nick, it was nice to meet you. Maybe we'll get a chance to talk again before we leave. Have to go see my wife and check out my new sons." And the foursome disappeared.

Twins? That possibility had never entered his mind. Panic and pacing took over again. By the time William and Virginia arrived he had drained the big bottled water tank dry and worn a path to the restroom.

Four hours after entering the hospital, a nurse came for Nicolas. "Mr. Amato, you are the father of a robust, nine pound son."

"A Son? Nine pounds?" He brought the palm of his hand to his forehead. "Jumping Jehoshaphat, I didn't know they came that big."

The nurse laughed. "Well, looking at you, I understand. Come with me. Your wife has some words for you regarding that fact."

He followed her down the hall wondering if this was all a dream. The sight that greeted him quickly confirmed it was not. His bedraggled, but gorgeous wife was nuzzling a good size baby on her chest. Love for both soared. With tears dripping off his cheeks, he merged with the scene.

Three days later, he had come to take his family home. As Josie was dressing the baby, Nicolas pulled a gift out of one of two bags. "Let me hold him when you finish. I have something for you."

She carefully transferred their son to his father. Love filled his arms and heart. He watched as Josie tore into the package.

"Oh, Nicolas, where did you find this?"

"I made it. Pastor Joe has a wonderful woodworking shop. That's where I've been spending my time when I wasn't here with you two."

She was tracing the letters with her fingers. "Ethan means strong?"

"Yes," he laughed. "I was tempted to make it *big and strong*."

"It's beautiful."

His gaze moved between his wife and his son. "Remember my story about the waiting room and sharing about our other babies with the father of twins?"

"Yes," she offered while reaching for baby Ethan.

"While making Ethan's plaque it occurred to me that we have two children in heaven. I wanted … no, I needed something to make that real inside me. So I cut out two more. He pulled out another plaque.

"At first I thought I'd leave them blank, since we didn't know if they were boys or girls. But that was too impersonal."

He smiled. "So I figured a girl for you and a boy for me would be okay. I wanted to ask you about the names, but that would have spoiled the surprise. So I prayed and thought … and thought and prayed for two days. Late last night they came.

A tear escaped his own eyes at this point. "The girl's name came first." When he held up the second plaque, Josie broke. "You named her after the grandmother who moaned her loss. Virginia means *maiden*." She reached for his hand. "A baby Virginia in heaven."

He pulled a third plaque out of the bag and turned it so she could see the name. "I decided our first son's name should honor the young man who could have been and offered to be his father."

She touched the name. "David means *beloved*."

As they fingered the plaques representing their children who were with Jesus, they grieved and rejoiced. "I know we are forgiven, Josie, but having Ethan has helped me understand the loss. I wept for our babies last night."

"Nicolas Amato, I didn't think it was possible to love you more than I do, but you just keep proving me wrong."

He straightened slowly with a playful grin she had learned to love. "Well, now. I was going to save the last surprise for later, but I think this is the perfect time."

He reached into another bag and pulled out a fourth plaque that was not only larger, but horizontal. Josie studied him. "Have you slept at all since I've been here?"

He gave her a fake yawn. "Not much. I've been too excited."

He flipped the plaque so she could read it. Josie's hand flew to her mouth and her eyes searched his. "Are you serious?"

"Yes. It's a well-known fact that Amato is Italian for *beloved*."

"Beloved? That's our name?"

"Yes, Josie. We are the *Beloved* family."

She gazed at the gift of love in her arms as tears of joy and gratitude dropped onto his blanket. "We are God's beloveds."

Nicolas' touched the Mobius hanging from the chain around her neck. "That would be us and any others God gives." With a silly grin taking over his face, he added, "Out of curiosity I looked up the meaning of your name and guess what."

Her eyes lit up. "What?"

"It means *God will add*. I guess I need to go house shopping again." He winked and kissed her and then baby Ethan.

"Yes, well, we are going to have to talk about the size of these babies we are making."

He headed for the door.

"You wait right there. What does Nicolas mean?"

He stepped back in the room. "Victory of the people."

She mulled that over in her mind. "Hmm. Didn't I read somewhere that he was credited for saving the daughters of a poor man from prostitution? Wasn't he the patron saint of children? Wasn't he the man behind the legend of St. Nicholas who became our Santa Claus?"

He walked back to her side. "I started researching the names innocently, but by the time I finished, I was amazed and am still pondering."

He gently rubbed his son's cheeks. "I'll let you decide where the family plaques should go, but I definitely want them up."

He headed back out the door. "Mrs. Beloved, I am going to bring the car to the side entrance so I can take my family home. Meet you there."

Josie's heart and mind were overflowing with the goodness of God. Between the hormonal and joyful tears, she was a soggy saint.

When Nicolas reached the pick-up spot, he found himself second in line. Looking closer he realized the first car belonged to his new friend. Josie was nowhere in sight, so he jumped out and approached the father who was loading a lovely wife and a baby into his vehicle.

"Hey, I'd given up hope of seeing you before we left." He helped the kind stranger get their belongings in the trunk and back seat.

The father of twins put a hand on his shoulder while shaking the other one vigorously. "It's good to see you survived. So what did you have?"

"A fine son and the wife is doing great. How about yours?"

A sadness swept over the man and tears gathered in his eyes. "The Lord called Andrew home last night. Benjamin is healthy."

His son died? "Man! That has to be tough. How's your wife doing?"

"Grieving, but remembering to be grateful for the three healthy ones we do have."

The man looked at Nicolas. "We both have babies in heaven now. I can identify with your loss and pain."

Tears formed in Nick's eyes. "But you wanted yours. It's been hard for the wife and me to forgive ourselves in our case."

About that moment, Nicolas caught sight of Josie and Ethan being wheeled out, but Josie's eyes were not on him. She was staring at the mother in the vehicle. The men began looking back and forth between their wives who were obviously making some kind of connection. Almost simultaneously they both began weeping.

"Nick, would you mind holding Ethan for a minute?" Josie asked as she was wheeled closer.

The moment her hands were free, she moved out of her chair and approached the car. "Callie?"

Reaching for Nicolas' arm, Josie drew him close. "God sent me someone who loves me like David loved you."

Looking at Callie's husband, she added as the tears raced down her cheeks, "I see God brought another love into your life. I'm so happy for you."

The man extended his hand. "I'm Jesse and evidently you know my wife."

She accepted his hand. "I'm Josie and this is my husband, Nicolas."

Understanding dawned on both young men about the same time. They looked at each other and then their wives. Jesse moved quickly to rescue his son.

A grieving Callie slowly opened her door,
her heart
and her arms.
And she who is loved and treasured,
embraced God's Beloved.
★★★★★★★

Can a mother forget the baby at her breast
and have no compassion on the child she has borne?
Though she may forget,
I will not forget you!
See,
I have engraved you on the palms of my hands ...
Isaiah 49:15–16a
Love never comes to an end.

Dear Reader,

Hearing the stories of men and women who have lived with the silent pain, secret shame and detrimental fallout that results from sexual abuse and addiction has been a challenging part of my life for thirty plus years. Walking with them through the healing processes that God's love brings and watching them learn to replace lies with His truth that sets them free from their past and live in the reality of their identity as God's children continues to be one of the greatest joys of my life.

Their voices and my own experience inspired this book. Their hope and mine is that this story encourages other victims to speak up and seek help.

I pray that Jake's and Josie's stories become part of that process for many readers.

Our challenge is two-fold. Stop the crime by identifying the abusers and their victims. Where legal intervention is needed, don't hesitate. Get help for both.

If you are hesitant to reach out to those around you, send me a note. Hope and help are available.

Pricejb490@gmail.com
facebook.com/JBPrice

What readers are saying about JB Price's first book, *Callie's Treasures*.

Laurie H.

I read *Callie's Treasures* in one night because with each turn of event in the story, I was discontent until I knew the outcome. While reading the book, I became invested in the relationships between Callie, David and Jesse because I could relate to their emotional struggles and their spiritual journeys. I hurt with them when the complexity of the relationships were difficult to sort out. I felt anger when they made the wrong decisions. I cried bitter tears when all felt lost. There are so many layers within this story that no matter where you are in your personal discovery about real love, true forgiveness or your deepest loss, you will be challenged to dissect what you believe and to accept your unfathomable value to our Creator.

Joyce R

Mesmerizing! I was totally captivated by *Callie's Treasures*. The unexpected twists and turns of the plot, the joys and heartaches, surprising delights and the gut wrenching losses these characters experienced left me begging for more. How do you describe the unconditional, unending, unexplainable love God the Father has for us? By telling a great story – and this certainly is one of the greatest I've read. Don't miss this opportunity to see how God's ultimate plan for humanity plays out in the lives of people who first receive and then give, abundant, extravagant, redeeming love, mercy and forgiveness. You won't regret it!

Angela S

Awesome book. I started it one morning and could not quit until it was finished. I laughed. I cried and filled a waste can with Kleenex. It is a must read for anyone who is searching for a beautiful definition of the Father God's love for each of his children. Thanks JB Price for a treasure to the coming generations.

Barbara H.

What a compelling story! What deep truth revealed! I'm not sure readers even realize it until they step back and ponder. Looking forward to the sequel.

Jennifer H

More than just a story, this is a guidebook for life. Wish I had had it as a younger person to read. The story line became so exciting and was so unexpected that I began feeling as though I knew the characters and cared deeply for them. I couldn't put it down until I had finished. Cannot wait for more from JB Price.

Lokelani T

This story is told with beautiful detail and relatable to my life and current situations. I loved the wisdom in the characters. I could relate to the author's heart in being treasured.

Linda S

A truly beautifully written book of learning how to love, how much we are loved and how to live loved. The story of total forgiveness is one that anyone can relate to and learn from. Though a novel, the book shows how real life situations affect our lives and those around us. I could visualize the characters and locations. If you miss reading *Callie's Treasures*, you will miss a blessing.

Connie B

I really enjoyed this book. It caught my attention from the first chapter. Though an easy read, it is also thought provoking. There are spiritual lessons within the story line. It flows easily and makes you want to know what happens next. It has some unexpected endings and new beginnings. A must read.

Pat K

It gave me a greater understanding of love and intimacy. I shared it with a couple of friends and they both said they loved it and couldn't put it down.

Janice S

This is an excellent first novel by this author. I would highly recommend it to anyone seeking truth about God's love.

Doris T

This is a wonderful book. I kept wanting to read it even when I didn't have time.

Mary V

This book has many twists and turns. I loved it, because God' grace was found at every corner. What a great example of God's unconditional love.

Lisa B

Callie's Treasures is an amazing story about relationships and our need for a loving relationship with Jesus Christ. It shows how such a relationship will overflow into the lives of those around us with His unselfish love, instead of our selfish human love. It is a must read.

Acknowledgements

To the God who loves us too much to leave us like we are: Thank You for ignoring my reasons for not writing and pushing me out of my comfort zone. Ultimately, all my stories are about You. Thank You for love that heals our wounds and truth that exposes our lies so we can live free from our past.

To my earthly family: Thank you for graciously allowing me the time needed to write this story and the many ways you continue to make me proud that I'm part of your lives.

To my prayer partners: I wouldn't attempt writing without you.

To the wounded who shared their stories of abuse … and healing and freedom: This story is for you and because of you.

To my book buddies: Thank you for giving of your time and sharing your wisdom. I smile when I read a passage you inspired or questioned.

To the 2014 retreat ladies: Thank you for believing that God could use a seventy-two-year-old woman to write a story that would hold your interest for a weekend and impact your lives for eternity.

To my special inmate friends: Thank you for allowing me to blend threads of your stories into this one.

To Navigation Advertising: Thank you for another attractive cover.

To Westbow Publishers: Thank you for giving me the opportunity to share this story with others.

About The Author

JB Price's novels are the overflow of seventy-two years of life on planet Earth, which includes thirty-plus years of walking with women through life's good times and those that challenge.

Her books deal with life issues women find difficult to share due to the pain and shame involved.

It is her prayer that the stories reveal the power of God's love to heal those wounds and set the captives free.

She and her hubby of fifty years live on a small farm in Rutherford County, Tennessee.

Printed in the United States
By Bookmasters